"Close your eyes and relax."

His voice in her ear was low and husky, his breath warm against her skin, raising the fine hairs on her nape and sending a tingle of excitement down her spine.

This was not what she had expected or planned. She had thought to be the proverbial femme fatale, to have complete control over the situation, not to find it inexplicably sliding from her own grasp.

"Feels good, does it?" Hawk inquired, his lips brushing her hair.

"It feels heavenly," she replied truthfully.

His mouth continued on down the strands of her hair to the incredibly sensitive place where her nape joined her shoulder. Softly, he pressed his lips to the highly responsive spot.

An unwitting moan escaped from her throat.

Although she had intentionally set into motion the events that would bring about precisely this occurence, she had badly misjudged her own reactions to it. Having stoutly assured herself that submitting to Hawk's advances was only the necessary means to a vital end, she had believed she would have better control over her emotions. She had counted on that, in fact.

Quite wrongly, it appeared.

REBECCA BRANDEWYNE

HIGH STAKES

MIRA

ISBN 1-55166-430-5

HIGH STAKES

Copyright © 1999 by Rebecca Brandewyne.

Printed in U.S.A.

For my friend and pen pal,
Wesley.
For thought-provoking correspondence.

CONTENTS

High Stakes

This is the day which down the void abysm
Power is lost and yawns for Heaven's despotism,
And Conquest is dragged captive through the deep;
Love, from its awful throne of patient abode
In the wise heart, from the last giddy road
Of dread endurance, from the slippery, steep,
And narrow verge of crag-like agony, springs
And folds over the world its healing wings.

Learning the Game, Corporate Politics,
    and Endurance—
These are the seals of that most firm assurance
Which bars the pit over Destruction's strength;
And if, with infirm hand, Eternity,
Mother of many acts and hours, should free
The serpent that would clasp her with his length,
These are the spells by which to reassume
An empire o'er the disentangled doom.

To suffer woes which Hope thinks infinite;
To forgive wrongs darker than death or night;
To defy Power, which seems omnipotent;

To love, and bear; to risk all for High Stakes
That from their own wreck, salvation makes
Triumph and change; neither falter, nor repent;
This, like glorious Power Regained, is to be
Good, great and joyous, beautiful and free;
This is alone Life; Joy, Empire, and Victory!*

---

*Poem adapted from *Prometheus Unbound,* by Percy Bysshe Shelley.

Prologue

Power Lost

Power tends to corrupt
and absolute power corrupts absolutely.

> *Letter to Bishop Mandell Creighton*
> —Lord Acton

Flight into the Storm

Poor naked wretches, wheresoe'er you are,
That bide the pelting of this pitiless storm,
How shall your houseless heads and unfed
  sides,
Your loop'd and window'd raggedness,
  defend you
From seasons such as these?

King Lear
—William Shakespeare

A Mansion, The Southwest, Thirty Years Ago

"They're going to kill us, aren't they?" Natalie Marlowe's voice trembled with fear, and her turquoise eyes were wide in her pale, beautiful face as she gazed up anxiously at her tall, dark husband standing by her side.

"Not if I can help it." Roland Marlowe's own

voice was low, reassuring. Still, his handsome visage was grim with foreboding as he hurriedly ush-
ered his wife down the long, curving flight of stairs
that led from the second-story landing of their multi-
million-dollar mansion to the expansive, Italian-
marble-floored foyer below.

"I don't understand why you just don't call the
police," Natalie declared anxiously for the umpteenth time that evening as she tried without success
to hush the tiny mewls of distress of the baby she
clutched in her arms. Angelina, their newborn
daughter and only child, was hungry and fussy, her
usual schedule unavoidably disrupted by the furtive,
nerve-racking events of this wild, terrible night.

"And tell them what, exactly, Nat?" Roland
asked, a sharp note of anger and impatience born of
his deep worry now creeping into his tone. "We've
been over all this before. We have no proof of anything whatsoever. All we have are our own suspicions—which may be entirely without foundation,
despite however much we may think otherwise. And
without any evidence to back up our accusations,
we would look like fools or, worse, lunatics to the
police, our own behavior open to question—and you
know we daren't risk that. No. You've simply got
to trust me, darling. The course I've chosen is best.
If we can get away from here, totally disappear for
a while, then I can use our own considerable resources to gather the information we need to fight

our enemies. But now is not the time to take a stand, Nat. We don't know for certain who's on our side and who isn't, and we're grossly outnumbered and outgunned, besides. Damn my father!'' This last was a snarl lost in the howling wind outside as the front doors to the mansion were abruptly flung open.

A panicked scream erupted from Natalie's throat, and for a moment she stood frozen with terror at the sight of the man who seemed to loom menacingly on the threshold, his towering, brawny figure silhouetted against the lightning-shattered horizon beyond. Then he advanced into the foyer, where the soft-glowing lamplight illuminated the craggy but kindly copper countenance of their trusted Native American chauffeur and bodyguard.

Natalie heaved an enormous sigh of relief, which, at the thought of what they faced, turned into a small, ragged sob of despair she was unable to choke back.

"I'm so sorry, Mrs. Marlowe. I didn't mean to startle you," Jim Tallcloud apologized gruffly, his eyes both pitying and shadowed with concern, for he, just like his employers, knew the dangers they were up against. He turned to Roland. "I've brought the Mercedes around front, sir, and stowed the last of the luggage in the trunk. So if there's nothing else, then we're ready to leave."

"No, there's nothing more."

"We really should be going, then, Mr. Roland,"

the chauffeur urged when his employers appeared to hesitate, glancing around lingeringly, painfully, at the home where they had been so happy together and which they must now abandon.

Finally, realizing Jim was right, the Marlowes stepped out into the savage night, not knowing whether, despite all their secrecy and precautions, they were even now observed by those who had caused them to embark upon this clandestine journey.

Jim's wife, Faith, who worked as the Marlowes' housekeeper, was already perched apprehensively in the plush leather back seat of the sleek black automobile. She was holding her own baby daughter, Leah, who had been born just a few days before Natalie's child.

Shivering in the wind that snaked through the trees and the rain that was changing to drizzle, Natalie slid in beside Faith, thinking in that instant that the other woman had been aptly named. Because despite the fact that Faith, too, was afraid, she possessed a quiet courage and stoicism that had sustained them all throughout their ordeal. Natalie didn't know what they would have done without her.

"Here, Ms. Natalie," Faith said gently now, beginning to unbutton her plain white cotton blouse as she observed how Angelina fretted in Natalie's arms. "Give me Miss Angelina, and I'll feed her.

That ought to hush her, and maybe then she'll go back to sleep.''

Not for the first time Natalie was grateful that the two infants had been born so close together. After she had left the hospital following her daughter's birth, her own milk had unexpectedly dried up, so she was unable to nurse Angelina. Fortunately, however, Faith had milk enough for two and was as fiercely devoted to one child as the other.

"Yes…yes, I know my Angel's hungry and upset, the poor little dear." Natalie glanced down lovingly at the small, fragile, black-haired baby she embraced tightly before at last handing her to Faith and taking Leah, who somehow managed to slumber on peacefully, blissfully unaware of this night's tumultuous events.

Up front, the two men had settled into the vehicle's bucket seats, and now, his pulse racing, Jim gingerly started the Mercedes. Despite how many times he had carefully gone over the car, he was uneasy by the thought that there could be something he had missed, some newfangled, technologically sophisticated, miniature device invented by Roland's eremitical, idiosyncratic, but utterly brilliant father, and employed by the cutthroats and madmen at Marlowe Micronics, Incorporated, to blow them all to kingdom come. But much to his relief, the automobile instead purred like a mountain cat, offering no signs of deadly disruption. The chauffeur depressed the accelerator, guiding the vehicle around the circular drive and taking the fork that would lead to the rear of the expansive estate.

No sense in tempting fate by brazenly exiting through the front gates.

Covertly, the Mercedes crept along the little-used back drive through the darkness and the showering rain, Jim afraid to turn on the headlights until they were well clear of the mansion.

The minutes ticked by interminably, excruciatingly. The trepidation and tension in the car were almost palpable. Natalie could hear the pounding of her own heart, feel the perspiration beading her upper lip and trickling down between her full breasts, despite the low hum of the air conditioner. She almost leaped out of her skin when, without warning, Roland ignited his gold lighter, holding the flame to a cigarette he'd drawn from the matching case in his jacket, inhaling deeply to steady his nerves.

"I'll get the gate," the chauffeur announced in the taut stillness inside the Mercedes.

"No, I'll do it." Before the tersely spoken words were even out of his mouth, Roland was already opening his door, slipping into the night to haul wide the wrought-iron gate that guarded the far end of the property and barred their escape.

The gate was so seldom employed by the mansion's inhabitants that over the years its latch had halfway rusted shut. To Natalie's dismay, it was some moments before Roland managed to free it. But finally, it gave way, and the gate swung free, creaking loudly in protest on its unoiled hinges.

Jim eased the car through, pausing just beyond, while Roland resecured the gate, then got back inside. As the automobile rolled out onto the isolated dirt road that wound away from the estate, the tires crunched on the wet sand.

The rain had started to come harder again, spattering the windshield, obscuring the chauffeur's view and compelling him to turn on the wipers. But still he left the headlights off, cautiously inching the vehicle along, not wanting to attract the attention of anybody who might be holed up in the mountains or bluffs somewhere, watching the mansion for signs of activity. It seemed unlikely that anyone would be out on such a night as this, but gambling on that supposition was a risk those in the Mercedes could not afford to take.

Still, despite everything, they all managed to relax slightly as, once they were more than a mile from the mansion, Jim at last flicked on the car's headlights, casting the road into blurred relief before them. The powerful automobile swept forward as fast as the chauffeur dared to push it in the storm that had smoldered and seethed all day and that now chose to release the full force of its fury upon them. Jim reflected grimly that the violent downpour was both a curse and a blessing—a curse because it impeded rapid progress of the vehicle on the sandy road awash with churning puddles that had formed in ruts and potholes baked hard by the desert sun, a blessing because it would make pursuit of the Mercedes more difficult, if not impossible.

For the first time, the big Native American dared to hope they would actually make good their escape from the ruthless, monomaniacal cadre that had seized control of MMI and that had, at the very least, somehow managed to turn its chairman of the board, Merritt Marlowe, against his own son, Roland.

Merritt Marlowe was, by anybody's account, a genius. He was also wildly reclusive and eccentric, to the point that there were those who labeled him a complete nutcase. Still, the fact that there was without a doubt more than a grain of truth to this last assertion was generally dismissed by everyone who knew him—or who wanted to know him—because, at age fifty, Merritt was a much-sought-after individual, a billionaire, and therefore one of the richest men in the country.

At one time, he had been one of the country's most handsome, most eligible bachelors, as well. That was before he had wed Roland's mother, Isabel Standish, one of the brightest, most beautiful luminaries of stage and screen.

Merritt had been only twenty-four years old when he had spied her on film and been immediately captivated by her. But already he was president of his own burgeoning technological empire—then called Marlowe Manufacturing—having received a number of lucrative government contracts during World War II for designing and developing cutting-edge equipment that had been put to efficient use in everything from airplanes to submarines. While others had been working on producing the atom bomb, Merritt had been laying the groundwork for the computer age—not to mention investing his considerable earnings in fledgling but innovative, visionary corporations whose stock would, in the coming decades, be worth a fortune.

He had wooed Isabel so persistently with exotic flowers, expensive jewelry, and extravagant outings that all of Tinsel Town had agreed she would be the world's biggest fool not to abandon her stellar acting career and say yes to his marriage proposal. A year after their fairy-tale wedding, their only child, Roland, had been born. A year after that, Isabel had met a tragic and untimely death when the airplane she had boarded to fly home to the United States from a French Riviera vacation had crashed en route, exploding on impact with the Atlantic Ocean.

That moment had proved pivotal, changing Merritt's life forever. Because it was then, the media's tabloids would decades later proclaim, that he had gone totally off his rocker.

Overnight, he developed an incurable phobia about flying, purchasing a railroad company and a cruise line so he would never have to travel by air again. He had his own private railroad car fitted out like an armored tank, in case of a railway accident; and he had also acquired a small submarine, which accompanied him on every ocean voyage, in case the cruise ship sank.

He had ordered a screening room constructed in one wing of the Marlowe mansion he had earlier built for Isabel on scenic desert land overlooked by mountains and bluffs, but which was otherwise undeveloped and located in the middle of nowhere. When the screening room was finished, Merritt spent endless hours alone in it, watching Isabel's movies over and over, until he could recite large blocks of dialogue by heart. During the screenings, he consumed nothing but Coca-Cola and Poppin' Hot popcorn.

When it was rumored that Poppin' Hot was in dire financial straits and would soon go out of business, Merritt had promptly bought up the company so he would always have a supply. Only a few weeks afterward, for no apparent reason, he had abruptly decided that the Poppin' Hot popcorn kernels were laced with pesticides. He had switched to Jewel-Box jelly beans, strenuously insisting, however, that all the white ones be removed from the opened cartons, since they were, in reality, poisonous mistletoe berries in disguise.

He had begun washing his hands with disinfectant

every hour on the hour, convinced that germs were invading his body through the lines that crisscrossed his palms, the same way that cracks in the surface of the dry, sun-baked desert soaked up rainwater during the infrequent but violent storms that descended upon the land. Eventually, not even the constant washings and the disinfectant had passed muster, and first thing upon rising each morning, Merritt had taken to donning a fresh, clean pair of surgical gloves, as well as a surgical mask, to protect himself from contaminants.

One couldn't be too careful, he had been overheard muttering darkly to himself on numerous occasions. Only look what had befallen Isabel because she hadn't known that treacherous corrosive agents had swarmed over and eaten away at the metal of the jet she had boarded on the last day of her young life, creating hairline fractures in the structure of the plane, which, thus unable to stand the strain of flight, had broken apart in midair, plummeting to its fiery demise.

That there had been no actual, concrete proof of this theory was immaterial. He, Merritt Marlowe, *knew* and understood the mysterious forces of the universe, which unceasingly wreaked havoc on the world and all its pathetic inhabitants.

If not for those insidious, destructive energies, a man could live forever.

He, Merritt Marlowe, would be that immortal.

And now, perhaps, he was dead instead.

Certainly, Roland had neither seen nor spoken to his father for the past few years—not from choice, but because he had been informed time and again that Merritt was unforgivably angry with him and wanted nothing more to do with him, ever.

"Sorry, old boy." Winston Pryce, one of the undisputed golden boys of MMI, had shaken his head regretfully every time Roland had tried some new avenue of approach to his genius father, who had gradually over the years become a virtual hermit and, perhaps by now, a genuine lunatic, too. "But Merritt's real hacked off at the way you've been voting your shares lately. He says you've obviously forgotten whose son you are, that you're no doubt even now just biding your time, waiting eagerly for him to die so you can take over the whole of his global enterprise."

"You know that's not true, Winston," Roland had strenuously and truthfully insisted, to no avail. He had been unable to achieve admittance to his father, who had some years before deeded over his desert mansion to his son as a wedding present and moved into a penthouse atop the skyscraper that housed the headquarters of MMI.

Both within and without the corporation, Merritt's luxurious rooftop apartment was frequently referred to as the Pentagon because its security was just as strict. In keeping with his instructions, the two floors directly beneath his own were completely empty and sealed off to prevent anyone from gaining access to them, and the two private elevators that led to his penthouse required both electronic keys and codes to operate, the latter of which were changed weekly.

If not for that, Roland would have just taken one of the cars up to his father's apartment and demanded admittance. But once Roland had been effectively cut out of the company's power structure, he had ceased to have the necessary elevator codes revealed to him, and the number for Merritt's private telephone line had been changed, too. Even the letters Roland had written to his father had been returned to him, unopened and unread.

At first, hurt, angry, and confused about why Merritt should have turned against him, Roland had not considered that anyone but he himself might be to blame. It was only gradually that, after thinking the matter through, he had realized there was, in reality, something badly wrong at MMI.

No one, he had eventually discovered, except for a mere handful of men who held powerful positions on the international corporation's board of directors, had actually seen his father in ages. It was upon learning this information that Roland had begun to suspect Merritt had finally gone wholly insane, or else was otherwise totally incapacitated—perhaps even dead.

Initially, Roland had told himself sternly that

these suppositions were absolutely ludicrous, that there was no way a small group of men could have seized control of MMI from its founder and chairman of the board without everybody in the company learning about it. But then, the more Roland dwelled on the matter, the more he had recognized that because of his father's bizarre behavior over the years, such a thing actually *could* be possible.

In his childhood, he hadn't truly grasped the fact that Merritt really wasn't all there in the head. It was only as Roland grew older that he had at last realized that, if not for an overriding combination of extraordinary genius and wealth, his father would have been locked up in a sanatorium someplace.

But because of Merritt's brilliance and riches, people were more than willing to overlook his strange, erratic behavior, to dismiss it as being merely the eccentricity invariably attributed to creative thinkers, artists, and inventors alike. Such people were always somewhere else mentally and emotionally, absorbed by their work, and often given to obsessions, compulsions, and phobias. That such things did not, however, normally dominate their lives was something Roland had not understood until he had reached adulthood.

As a child, he had known only that his father was different, a man who belonged to the ranks of the world's preeminent scientists and industrialists rather than its blue-collar workers. Roland had loved trailing along hand in hand with Merritt, striding through the winding, dimly lighted, echoing corridors of the corporate offices long after everyone else had gone home for the evening. Or else sitting with his father in the darkened screening room of their mansion, watching Roland's mother in a hundred different movie scenes, so he had come to know her even though she no longer lived.

Merritt had always been especially kind to him at those times, carefully checking their shared carton of Jewel-Box jelly beans to be certain all the white ones had been removed and making sure his Coca-Cola had plenty of ice.

It had not seemed possible to Roland that the cuckoo but caring father he remembered from childhood had so firmly and utterly turned against him. Nor, when he had thought about it, did it appear likely that Merritt would have made the various business decisions that had been reached at MMI in the last several years.

At the time, Roland had wondered at his father's judgments, and disagreeing with them, he had voted against them. But later, once he had become convinced that, despite how impossible it seemed, control of MMI had indeed been wrested from Merritt's grasp, Roland had recognized that his father had never been behind those decisions, had, in fact, been effectively removed from the picture, maybe even murdered.

Still, Roland had not known what to do, where to turn, or whom to trust. Anyone in the upper echelons of MMI might be involved in the conspiracy—including the entire board of directors, because it would have taken at least some of them to have covered up a crime of this magnitude. Clearly, someone was acting in Merritt's stead, making decisions that affected the whole corporation worldwide and forging his signature on official documents and interoffice memos.

Forced out of the inner circle of power and authority, Roland had done his best to investigate the affair as quietly and unobtrusively as possible. He had known that without any evidence to back up his speculations, no one—including the police—would believe his incredible story. He would most likely even be thought to have gone off the deep end, just like his father.

But it was not until some weeks ago, when the first attempt had been made on his own life, that Roland had comprehended the fact that as Merritt Marlowe's only child and principal heir, he himself was in danger.

Somehow, despite the furtiveness of his probing, he had aroused someone's suspicions, and whoever was behind the conspiracy couldn't afford to leave him alive to step into his father's shoes and possibly expose what had taken place. So his unknown foes had tried to run him down with an automobile, and it was only the quick action of Jim Tallcloud, tackling him and knocking him out of the way of the oncoming vehicle, that had saved his life.

"Are you all right, sir?" the chauffeur had asked anxiously as he had assisted Roland to his feet and helped to brush off his suit jacket and trousers.

"Yes…yes, I think so. My God! That crazy fool! It's a wonder he didn't hit me! If it hadn't been for you, Jim, he would have! He must've had an old-fashioned three-martini lunch and been driving drunk!"

"If you'll forgive me for saying so, Mr. Roland…I don't think so." Jim's face had been perplexed and deeply troubled. "I noticed him earlier, sitting in his car at the curb, a ways down the street. It seemed to me, sir, that he was waiting for someone, and then when he saw you come out of the MMI building, he started his engine and barreled right toward you. I believe he deliberately intended to run you over, Mr. Roland."

At that news, Roland's blood had run cold. It wasn't just his father who was a target, he had understood then. It was himself—and probably Natalie and their baby, too. After all, what was the point in eliminating him when his wife and daughter stood in the line of inheritance, also?

Roland had seen no choice then but to take Natalie and the Tallclouds into his confidence, thinking that Jim could hardly be part of the conspiracy, acting as he had to save his employer's life. At first, they had been as skeptical of Roland's conclusions with regard to Merritt and MMI as he himself had once been. Still, there was no denying the fact that somebody had tried to murder Roland, since Jim had been certain the attempt to run his employer down had been deliberate.

After a second—but, fortunately, also botched—attempt to kill Roland, Natalie and the Tallclouds had realized his suspicions must be right, and they had decided that they could no longer go on residing at the Marlowe mansion. The conspirators could not be certain if Roland might have shared his misgivings or with whom, but obviously, his wife and their two closest employees would be considered prime candidates for his confidences. As a result, they were all in jeopardy.

They decided to flee across the border into Mexico, where they planned to go into hiding until they could unearth solid proof to support their belief that a consortium of powerful and unscrupulous men had grabbed control of MMI, either killed or otherwise incapacitated Merritt, and tried twice to murder Roland. He was not without his own personal financial assets, and the cadre wouldn't be able to cut him off from those. Besides which, now that the conspirators knew he was on to them, he could afford to make some moves against them openly, buying up MMI stock, for example, to increase his own power base within the corporation.

Roland had left behind a letter to the board of directors, in which, citing personal reasons, he had officially resigned as president of the company. By the time it was received, he and the rest would be safely out of the country—by car, because they had felt that offered their best chance of escape. The airport and train and bus stations would surely be closely watched. But, as any illegal alien knew, there were any number of ways to slip undetected across the U.S.–Mexico border, especially if you had a lot of money.

Now, after lighting another cigarette, Roland turned to glance back and smile gently, encouragingly, at his wife in the back seat. To his relief, she looked less frightened than she had earlier, although her piquant face was still pale. She held the sleeping Leah close against her breast, while Faith nursed Angelina.

"It'll be all right, Nat. You'll see," Roland told her softly as he gazed at her lovingly. "We'll get through this somehow, I promise. Once the board of directors receives my letter of resignation, they may not even bother with us anymore."

Natalie wanted desperately to believe him, and so she prayed he was right. But deep down inside, she experienced a sinking feeling at the pit of her stomach, knowing the conspirators would never stop looking for them. There was too much power and money at stake, a global enterprise poised to become one of the major players in the technological revolution that many in business and industry felt was right around the corner.

"I love you, Roland," Natalie whispered, smiling bravely and blinking back the tears that stung her eyes.

"I love you, too, Nat."

Those were the last words either of them ever spoke. Without warning, something exploded beneath the Mercedes, abruptly causing the car to careen wildly out of control.

For what seemed an eternity, the automobile lifted from the road, flying through the air. Then it struck the ground violently, shifting and sliding precariously on the wet sand, while Jim somehow fought to regain mastery of the intractable vehicle. But he could not stop its reckless motion, and it skidded and spun into a roll, tumbling over and over before finally righting itself and slamming brutally into a lone, stunted, twisted tree that grew alongside the road.

For some moments, stunned and hurting, the chauffeur slumped in his seat, his head resting against the steering wheel, causing the horn to blare unceasingly.

Beyond the Mercedes, the storm continued unabated, the rain pounding down in sheets illuminated brightly by the steady glare of the one headlight that still shone. The driving downpour beat upon the battered roof and pummeled the shattered windshield. Lightning ripped apart the sky. Thunder boomed in response, and the wind snaked through the mountains and bluffs to howl across the desert.

But it was the continued blasting of the automobile's horn that finally brought Jim dazedly to his senses. In the seat next to him, Roland sat motionlessly, his face a pulpy mass of cuts and blood from where it had impacted the windshield, his neck undoubtedly—given the way his head lolled—broken. Still shaking in the aftermath of the accident and from his own injuries, the chauffeur groped for a pulse, just to make sure. But there wasn't one, not even a flicker.

At age twenty-five, Roland Marlowe was dead.

Unbuckling his seat belt, Jim hauled himself with effort from the vehicle. The back door on Faith's side of the Mercedes was jammed shut, and he couldn't pry it open. So he staggered around the trunk to the other rear passenger door. It was flung wide, creaking on its hinges in the wind.

Beyond, Natalie lay sprawled on the soaked desert earth. She had obviously been thrown clear of the wreckage. Dropping to his knees, the chauffeur lifted her wrist and pressed his fingers against it. Unable to believe that she, too, was dead, he then felt for the pulse at her neck. Still there was nothing.

Jim was just fixing to turn away when he spied the tiny hand protruding from beneath Natalie's corpse. His breath caught in his throat as he realized her body was crushing one of the babies. Which one had she been holding when the car had veered so unexpectedly out of control? He didn't know. He had been too intent trying to get the automobile safely through the storm and away from the Marlowe mansion.

Now, as the chauffeur slowly turned Natalie over, he could not repress the cry of anguish that erupted from his throat as he spied his daughter, Leah, lying motionless beneath her. The infant wasn't breathing. He did not know whether she had died as a result of the crash or had been suffocated beneath Natalie's weight. He longed to take the child in his arms, to rock her and grieve and say a prayer over her little dead body. But there was no time; there was nothing he could do now for his newborn daughter.

He had to see to his wife—and Angelina.

Book One

Learning the Game

In battle or business, whatever the game,
In law or love, it is ever the same;
In the struggle for power, or the scramble for pelf,
Let this be your motto—Rely on yourself!
For whether the prize be a ribbon or throne,
The victor is he who can go it alone!

The Game of Life
—Eugène Pottier

One

The Crossroads

Desires and Adorations,
Wingèd Persuasions and veiled Destinies,
Splendours, and Glooms, and glimmering
    Incarnations
Of hopes and fears, and twilight Phantasies;
And Sorrow, with her family of Sighs,
And Pleasure, blind with tears, led by the gleam
Of her own dying smile instead of eyes,
Came in slow pomp.

    Adonais
    —Percy Bysshe Shelley

A Small Town, The Southwest, Sixteen Years Later

All her young life, Leah Tallcloud had known she was different.

For one thing, instead of her eyes being dark brown, like those of her parents and all her friends, they were a startling shade of turquoise. And for another thing, even though her skin was a warm, golden honey color from her being out in the desert sun all the time, it was still lighter than that of everybody else she knew. In winter, when her tan faded, she could have passed for white, despite her long black hair, which her mother, Faith, insisted she keep neatly plaited in two braids, Native American fashion.

Once, a long time ago, Leah had asked her parents why, unlike them, she had blue eyes and pale skin. They had informed her that it was because Faith was not a full-blooded Indian and that her half-white heritage had chosen to make its presence known in Leah. For several years, that answer had satisfied their daughter. But lately, at age sixteen, Leah had begun to be more than a little troubled by questions again.

There was the way her family moved all the time, for instance. The Tallclouds had lived all over the southwestern United States, never staying in one place for more than a year or two. They had even, a couple of times, resided across the border in Mexico. And, always, they rented small houses in out-of-the-way places, never in any of the cities or larger towns that dotted the Southwest.

As a result, Leah had grown to her teens in relative isolation, seldom making any close friends, since she had learned early on that she would only lose them whenever her parents decided to move again. Not that she had much time for friends, anyway. Between her studies and her chores, she invariably had more than enough to do to fill up her days.

Still, she had often longed wistfully to be a part of the groups at the various schools she had attended over the years. Instead, she had always been on the outside, looking in.

On those rare occasions when she had actually brought a friend home, Jim and Faith Tallcloud, while polite, had made it clear by their stiffness and reserve that they weren't interested in encouraging the relationship. Made instinctively uncomfortable by her parents' attitude, Leah's few friends had hardly ever returned.

These days, she had begun to feel more and more resentful about that. She was becoming a young woman—and starting, however shyly, to take an interest in boys. From the admiring glances that many of them cast her way, she knew they noticed her, too, and found her attractive.

That realization had gone far in bolstering her self-confidence because, even though deep down inside Leah understood that there was nothing wrong with her, that her parents' apparent restlessness and overprotectiveness were to blame for her lack of social life, she still suffered constant pangs of insecurity.

Every time she gazed into a mirror, she saw that she was different from all those who peopled her limited world—blue-eyed, lighter skinned. Even her long, shining black hair had a bluish rather than a brownish cast, and her features were more finely chiseled...more, well, *white*. She didn't look like either of her parents.

Because of that, she sometimes imagined wildly that Jim and Faith had kidnapped her. But if that were so, then her real parents had obviously not cared, had never paid the ransom demanded for her—and that thought was so unbearably painful that Leah always determinedly shoved it from her mind. It just wasn't true. If the Tallclouds had abducted her for nefarious purposes, they would certainly never have kept her alive and raised her as their own daughter.

And no matter what, she knew her father and mother loved her deeply.

They showed her in countless ways, Jim sitting at the kitchen table long after supper to help her with her homework, and Faith teaching her how to run a household, how to cook and clean and shop for groceries. There were many other lessons, as well,

Leah's parents having from the beginning of her education insisted that many of the public school systems these days were simply backward and inadequate, insufficient to prepare her for life in the real world.

So, since kindergarten, she'd had a strict schedule of home study, too, during which she had learned about film, theater, dance, music, art, and antiques, and to speak Spanish and French. When she was ten, she had started on what her parents had told her was the most important course of instruction of all: economics. They had given her an allowance of ten dollars a week as part of their program to instruct her in how to manage money.

It had seemed to Leah an extraordinary sum, for if asked, she would have said her family was poor, her father working as a jack-of-all-trades and her mother cleaning the houses of those who were financially able to afford a maid once or twice a week. But somehow, her parents had found the means to give her the handsome allowance.

Since then, every morning before breakfast, Jim sat down with his daughter at the kitchen table, newspaper in hand, and they analyzed the stock market together. Leah's ten dollars a week represented a hypothetical ten thousand dollars that she had to invest, her father keeping track of everything in a notebook. If, at the end of the week, she lost a thousand of her imaginary dollars in the stock market, she had to give back a real dollar from her allowance. But if she made a thousand conjectural dollars, then Jim would beam proudly, take out his wallet, and hand her an extra dollar to add to the rest of her allowance.

On Saturdays, the Tallclouds would pile into their battered old pickup truck and drive to the nearest town to do their grocery shopping, and there, Leah would be able to spend a portion of her profits. The remainder she had to bank for her college fund.

Today, she wanted to buy some cosmetics, having finally persuaded her mother to allow her to wear makeup—although Leah had been applying it secretly, at school, for the past two years. So now, as she stared at her reflection in the dresser mirror in her tiny bedroom, Leah was even more excited than usual about going into town. Not that town was much to speak of, being so small that it wasn't even located on most maps. Still, though hardly more than a crossroads, it did boast a diner, a bank, and an old-fashioned corner grocery with gas pumps out front.

This last was undeniably the hub of town, drawing people from miles around. So Leah had made an effort to look her best, brushing her long black hair until it gleamed and donning her prettiest sundress. Of white cotton trimmed with eyelet lace, it set off her hair and skin beautifully and really made her eyes stand out in her face, she thought.

Now she wondered uncertainly if she should pin up her hair, whether that would make her look older and more sophisticated. At last, deciding that it would, she gathered her mass of hair up, sweeping it into a French twist and securing it in place with a big, gold plastic clip.

Yes, that was much better. Surely she looked twenty, at least.

With the cache of cosmetics hidden in her purse, Leah carefully made up her face, thinking that since she now had permission, her mother couldn't possibly object. As a final touch, she added a pair of gold hoop earrings, turning her head this way and that to get the full effect.

"Leah, are you ready?" The sound of her mother's voice from the kitchen reached her ears.

"Yes, Mom, I'm coming," Leah called back. With a last glance in the mirror to reassure herself that she looked fine, she picked up her handbag, slung the strap over her shoulder, and hurried from her bedroom to join her parents.

"My God, Leah!" Faith cried as she turned from a cabinet and spied her daughter standing in the doorway of the kitchen. "What have you done to yourself? You look...you look..."

"Like a young woman for a change?" Leah inquired, a note of tartness and exasperation creeping into her voice. "Well, good! Oh, Mom, when are you going to realize I'm not a child anymore? That

I want to be like other teenagers and have a good time once in a while? And I think I'm entitled to that, besides. I work hard, Mom, you know I do. Between my studies and my chores, I hardly ever have any time to myself, to make friends or to do anything else that even smacks of having fun—'' At the expression on her mother's face, Leah broke off abruptly, biting her lower lip contritely. Then she continued more quietly. ''I'm sorry, Mom. I didn't mean to hurt your feelings. Really, I didn't. It's just that I...well, I get tired of working all the time, of not having any friends, of being...different, that's all.''

Despite herself, Faith Tallcloud's face softened at the admission. She knew better than anyone that the life they lived hadn't been easy for the daughter they had claimed as their own, the daughter who should have been entitled to so much more than they had ever been able to give her over the years. But since the night of that fatal accident in the Marlowes' Mercedes sixteen years ago, Jim and Faith had lived in constant fear.

It was Jim's opinion that despite all his precautions, the unknown consortium who had seized control of Marlowe Micronics, Incorporated, had somehow managed to insinuate a miniature explosive device into the automobile, causing the accident that had claimed the lives of Roland and Natalie Marlowe and the Tallclouds' own baby daughter, Leah.

That terrible night, knowing there was nothing they could do for their dead employers, the Tallclouds had rearranged the bodies in the car, making it appear as though Roland had been the one driving, and that Natalie had sat beside him, holding their newborn, Angelina.

Except that it hadn't been Angelina whom Jim and Faith had left behind in the vehicle, but their own dead infant, Leah. Angelina had survived, and they had taken her with them when they had fled the scene, believing it was highly unlikely that anyone would ever suspect that the baby in the Mercedes wasn't Angelina Marlowe.

And no one had.

As the Tallclouds had made their way from the site of the lethal accident, the automobile had exploded behind them, burning its occupants and destroying any evidence that would have made the police think anything other than that Roland had lost control of the car during the storm and that the gas tank had blown up as a result of the vehicle's crashing into the lone tree.

Jim and Faith had returned to their apartment over the garage at the Marlowe mansion, the former insisting that was the easiest way for them to avoid suspicion from all quarters. When questioned both by the police and by the executives who had come around from MMI afterward, the Tallclouds had never deviated from the cover story they had concocted: that they didn't know anything except that Roland had asked to have the Mercedes brought around front that night, then had told Jim to go on back to bed, that he would drive the automobile himself.

After the funeral, Jim and Faith had given notice and moved away. They had been fairly sure their story had been believed. Certainly, the police had never questioned it, and the car crash had been written off as an unfortunate accident.

But there was always the chance that the cadre that had taken over MMI would prove more suspicious and thorough in their own investigation than the police and the sensationalizing tabloids had. For that reason, the Tallclouds had ever since lived quietly, almost furtively, in an effort not to attract any undue attention to themselves.

After all, they had nothing except Jim's and Roland's suspicions to support their story that Merritt Marlowe was either dead or otherwise incapacitated and that his global enterprise had been commandeered by a group of powerful, unscrupulous men.

And suspicions didn't constitute proof.

Even the fact that Roland and his wife had been killed wasn't evidence of foul play, since their deaths had appeared to be accidental. Who would listen to a working-class, Native American couple, Jim had asked Faith, when even Roland himself had feared that he wouldn't be believed?

No, they couldn't take the risks that telling the truth about that horrible night of the car crash would entail, Jim had declared. And finally, Faith had concurred.

There was Angelina to consider. If it were ever learned that she was still alive, she would, as Merritt Marlowe's sole surviving heir, never be safe from whoever was behind the conspiracy at MMI. Yes, Jim was right, Faith had decided. They must keep silent about what they knew and what they suspected—for Angelina's sake, if nothing else.

So they had called her Leah, reared her as their own daughter, and kept the truth hidden from her. That had been simple enough when she was small.

But now, looking at the pretty teenager who stood before her, Faith knew the day of reckoning could not be postponed much longer. Leah—Angelina— needed to be told who she really was and why she was "different," why she could never be like other young women unless and until the real truth was learned about her family and MMI.

However, this was not yet the moment for those revelations. So instead, determinedly blinking back tears, Faith forced herself to smile gently.

"I'm sorry, Leah," she murmured. "I guess I'm just like every other mother—guilty of thinking of you as my baby and failing to see how you're growing up, becoming a young woman. Someday, when you're a mother yourself, you'll understand. Time just seems to fly by the older you get, and yet, perversely, in other ways it's as though it stands still. It seems to me it was only yesterday that you were cutting your first tooth, learning how to walk and talk. So it was a shock to me, I suppose, to see you standing there looking as though you're expecting some young man to call for you at any moment. I don't know where all the time's gone. I feel old all of a sudden, as though I've turned into my own mother.''

''Oh, Mom, you're not old,'' Leah insisted, all her earlier petulance dissipating and her heart lurching in a queer, frightened way at her mother's words. She didn't want anything to happen to her mother. Tears abruptly stinging her own eyes, too, Leah dashed across the kitchen to hug Faith tightly. ''I didn't mean to upset you,'' she reiterated fiercely. ''You and Dad are the best parents in the whole wide world! I know you've both done your very best for me.''

''We've tried. But you're right, Leah,'' Faith acknowledged reluctantly. ''You *do* need to work less, to make friends your own age, and to get out more so you can see what the world's like. Your dad and I are just overprotective, I guess. The world can be a terrible, treacherous place, and we've never wanted anything bad to happen to you. So we've tried to keep you from suffering any of its cruelties and injustices—and in doing so, we've subjected you to others no less painful. I see that now. But we'll try to do better in the future, I promise."

"You've done just fine, Mom."

The screen door leading to the back porch opened, and Jim stepped inside. "Are you two ready to go into town?" he asked, then did a double take as he got a good look at his daughter. He started to say something, then, at the warning glance from his wife, he changed his mind. After a moment, he continued gruffly, "Well, my goodness. Don't you look pretty and all grown up, Leah? I don't know that I want to be taking you into town, after all. I might have to get me a big stick to beat all the boys into keeping their distance."

Leah blushed and grinned at her father's teasing. "I doubt it."

"I don't." Jim winked at her. "But I have to confess that even if all your other beaux prefer this new hairstyle, I, at least, will miss tugging on your braids every now and then."

"I don't have any beaux, Dad," Leah replied as the three of them headed outside to the pickup truck parked by the back porch. "You don't count."

"I don't count?" Jim feigned dismay as he opened the passenger door to the truck and assisted first Faith and then Leah inside. "Now I *know* it won't be long before I'll be walking you down some church aisle and giving you away to some young fool who won't appreciate you even one-tenth as much as your mother and I do.''

Grumbling under his breath at the very idea, Jim stamped around to the driver's side of the cab and climbed inside. Reaching for the set of keys dangling from the ignition, he started the engine and depressed the accelerator, guiding the pickup around the sandy patch of desert that served as a yard and then onto the harder track that led to the dusty road beyond.

"Did you remember the cooler?" Faith inquired, just as she had for more Saturdays than Leah could recollect.

Jim nodded. He hadn't ever forgotten, but Faith always asked, just to be sure. They would need the cooler to keep the refrigerated and frozen foods cold on the long drive home in the desert heat. That was just one of the many things Leah had learned over the years from her parents.

Now, at the realization, she felt ashamed of her earlier behavior. Logically, she knew that Jim and Faith loved her, that there must be some good explanation for how furtively they lived, why they were so protective of her. That the world was a dangerous place wasn't reason enough. There just had to be more to it than that.

Still, Leah didn't want to upset her mother any more than she already had this morning. There would be a better time for the questions that plagued her. She felt certain of that. So she said nothing else that might conceivably agitate either of her parents.

Instead, she gazed out her open window at the passing scenery, relishing the feel of the breeze that swept down from the mountains and bluffs to bring a breath of coolness to the desert below. The air conditioner in the truck hadn't worked for some days now. In order to fix it, her father had had to wait for a part to come in. It was one of the things they would pick up in town today.

Overhead, the yellow sun shone brightly in the turquoise sky that arced over a relatively desolate scene: purple-blue mountains covered with scrub and the occasional twisted tree; red-gold bluffs and canyons through which wound arroyos with trickling streams that could become gushing torrents in the spring when the snow at the higher altitudes melted, and that could dry up to nothing in the blistering summers; and wide expanses of honey-colored desert terrain dotted with green cacti and other native plants. Yet, for all its barrenness, there was a strange, wild beauty to the vista that had always appealed to Leah.

She couldn't imagine living anywhere but the Southwest. She was glad that no matter how many times her parents had moved over the years, they had, with the exceptions of their brief forays into Mexico, at least always stayed in this part of the United States. Of course, their roots were here, in the Indian reservations that sprawled over the region, all that remained of the lands the Native Americans had once called their own, places often as bleak as the landscape itself.

The Indians there were in some respects a world away from the one her parents lived in, a different breed, clinging to the old ways, not wanting to be assimilated into the mainstream culture. Leah had from time to time seen some of them, the young men, mostly, who came into town on weekends to blow their hard-earned cash, to get rip-roaring drunk, and to wind up fighting with one another. They were, she always imagined, not far removed from the proud, savage warriors of yesterday. Still, she always got a peculiar little shiver whenever she saw them. No matter how wild they were, there was something exciting about them.

She envied them their freedom to come and go as they pleased. But perhaps now that she had spoken up to her mother, her own life would prove less restrictive. She would hope for that, Leah told herself.

The town, such as it was, came into view at last, shimmering in the waves of summer heat that rose from the hard-baked earth. Small and not much to look, it huddled at the crossroads, a motley collection of adobe buildings that appeared as though they had stood there for over three hundred years. And for all Leah knew, they had. The town's antecedents lay in days long gone by, when it had held the only trading post for miles around. There was still one of these located across from the corner grocery, a souvenir shop that sold turquoise-and-silver jewelry, Indian dolls, blankets, pottery, and postcards, among other trinkets.

Jim pulled the pickup off the road and into the grocery store's sandy parking lot, already filled with an assortment of other vehicles—rusted clunkers and beat-up old trucks like their own, mostly, although there were a couple of thirdhand motorcycles, too. Hardly anybody who lived around these parts had a lot of money. The pickup eased to a halt alongside a modern gas pump, one of the few indications that time hadn't totally passed the town by. Opening the passenger door, Leah stepped down from the cab, then helped her mother out. As Jim began to gas up the truck, the two women walked toward the store together.

An old-fashioned wooden porch with hitching rails and an overhanging roof ran the length of the front of the building. To one side of the sturdy oak door propped open with a small, upended old wine cask stood a Coke machine and some Mission chairs. In these last, two weather-beaten, copper-skinned men sat, playing a game of checkers they had erected on a big, empty beer barrel between them, while an elderly Indian woman looked on, occasionally smacking buzzing flies with the plastic swatter she held in one gnarled hand. On the other side of the door, a group of young males lounged, smoking cigarettes and drinking cold beer from long-necked amber bottles that dripped in the summer heat.

The young men eyed Leah both appreciatively and speculatively as she approached, giving low wolf whistles and calling out admiring, slightly risqué remarks. Embarrassed, she flushed at their teasing, which gradually died away at her mother's stern, quelling stare.

"Hey, *mamacita,* we didn't mean no harm or disrespect," one of them declared, grinning sassily at the two women.

Faith only harrumphed frostily and, taking Leah firmly by the elbow, propelled her inside the store. Leah didn't dare glance at her mother. She knew she had no one but herself to blame for having attracted the attention and remarks of the rowdy males outside. They might have ignored her if she'd been dressed more conservatively and worn her hair in its usual braids.

"You might as well go on and pick out your makeup, Leah." Faith sighed resignedly as she bent to retrieve a shopping basket from the stack by the door. "I reckon you can't stuff a genie back into its bottle after it's already escaped, and I suppose that if the truth were known, you've been hiding cosmetics in your purse and applying them at school for quite some time now, thinking that what your dad and I didn't know wouldn't hurt us. But I guess all teenage girls do that, that it's just a stage they go through. As much as it pains me to admit it, I confess I did the same thing when I was your age.''

"Thanks for being so understanding, Mom.'' Leah smiled ruefully, realizing then that she had never fooled her mother one bit about the cosmetics. "I'm sorry about what happened out front.''

"Don't worry about it. That's just the way young men—and even older ones who ought to know better—behave, and you shouldn't have to be ashamed of the fact that you're a pretty girl who's going to be an even more beautiful woman, Leah. And the truth is that when all is said and done, I'm real proud of you.'' Smiling tenderly, Faith stretched out one hand to pat her daughter's cheek gently. "You're everything that a mother could hope for in a child. So go on now. Get your makeup.''

Her heart welling with love for her mother, Leah turned to make her way to where the cosmetics were displayed.

The grocery store, being so old, had dark wooden floors and cramped aisles. Still, despite the limited space, there seemed to be an overwhelming selection from which to choose. Always before, Leah had felt so pressured by guilt and the need for secrecy that she had grabbed from the cosmetic racks whatever had looked good, and paid for it before she could be observed by anyone who might mention her purchases to her parents. So today was really the first time that she felt comfortable enough to make a leisurely examination of all that caught her eye.

L'Oréal, Revlon, Cover Girl, and Maybelline products dominated the racks, each offering testers that Leah took full advantage of, trying shades of foundation, eye shadow, and lipstick. Her own innate good taste caused her to steer clear of the more flamboyant hues. Instinctively, she preferred the softer colors and a more natural look.

At last, Leah settled on her choices. Mentally, to be certain she had enough money, she added up the prices of the items she had selected. Makeup was expensive, and she wanted a proper cosmetics bag to keep it all in, too. In preparation for this day, she had saved almost every penny of her allowance for the last few months. Just a compact of creamy powder base cost more than ten dollars. Still, she was sure what she had hoarded would cover the total amount.

She tucked all the items into her shopping basket, then carried it to the checkout counter. There, a laconic clerk rang up all her purchases and put them in a small sack for her. Her parents, she observed, were still doing the weekly grocery shopping. But since they didn't really need her help, and it was hot and she had enough money left over for a cola, Leah wandered out to the wooden front porch, where the Coke machine stood.

Reaching into her handbag for her change purse, she slotted quarters into the machine, pretending not to notice the group of young males who still loitered around the storefront. A couple of them cast appraising glances in her direction. But most of them now had their attention riveted on a brewing fight. As she popped the top on the aluminum can that rolled with a *clunk* from the machine, then took a sip of the ice-cold cola, Leah's own eyes were drawn to the tense scene unfolding before her.

Amid a circle of onlookers, two of the young men stood toe-to-toe in the parking lot, exchanging harsh, heated words. From what Leah could hear, the argument was over a woman. One of the men was shorter and stocky, with a pockmarked face and a nasty sneer. It was obvious that he had been drinking, and it was he who appeared to have instigated the quarrel.

But it was the other man who made her breath catch in her throat.

He was tall. That was the first thing she noticed about him. At least six foot two or three, she judged, and built like a mountain cat, all muscle and sinew, emanating power and grace. Maybe four or five years older than she was, he had not yet achieved his full growth. Still, the promise of formidability and virility was in every hard plane and long bone of his body.

His skin was the dark, rich copper of a full-blooded Indian. The short-sleeved, blue chambray work shirt he wore was unbuttoned and its tails were loose, baring sleek, corded arms and a broad, rippling chest gleaming with sweat in the hot yellow blaze of the sun, now directly overhead. A thong with some kind of Indian amulet suspended from it hung around his neck. His firm, washboard stomach tapered to narrow hips and buttocks, supple thighs and calves, all enticingly revealed by a pair of tight, old, faded button-fly jeans cinched at his lean waist with a worn leather belt that sported a turquoise-and-silver buckle. Scuffed black boots were upon his feet.

His elegantly chiseled, hawkish features bespoke the same proud Native American heritage as his skin. Adding to the effect was the fact that he wore his glossy black hair long and unrestrained, so it tumbled down past his shoulder blades, like the mane of a wild mustang running free. On one side, he had woven a slender warrior's braid, plaited with a thong and adorned with two eagle feathers, in the fashion of his ancestors.

Beneath thick, unruly brows that swooped like the wings of a raven, his heavily lashed eyes glittered like shards of obsidian. His aquiline nose was set above a sensuous, full-lipped mouth that exposed white, even teeth when he flashed a hard, derisive smile at his opponent.

All in all, the young man looked, Leah thought, like some ancient Indian god come to life there in the sandy parking lot.

Staring at him, unable to tear her eyes away, she felt something strange and inexplicably exciting stir to life inside her, something she had never experienced before. It was as though a fire had been ignited at the very core of her womanhood, to smolder painfully for a long, unbearable moment before erupting into a flame that spread through her entire body, leaving her feeling as though she were actually melting beneath the scorching rays of the sun. There was a sudden warm rush of moisture between her thighs, dampening the inset of her panties. She pressed her thighs together hard, feeling their stickiness in the summer heat.

Her breasts ached and tingled, their nipples tautening into stiff little peaks that strained against the white cotton of her sundress.

For an instant, as though sensing her reaction to him, the young man glanced in her direction, his eyes locking with hers, seeming to pierce to her very soul. Leah inhaled sharply, her nostrils flaring. His own response was much the same, as though they recognized in each other a kindred spirit. Then someone called his name, ''Hawk,'' and his attention was once more drawn to the fierce disagreement between him and the pock-faced male.

The spell was broken. Startled, Leah realized she was actually trembling from the force of her emotions, gripping her can of cola so tightly that she had even dented it slightly. To wet her dry mouth, she raised the can to her lips and took another long, thirsty swallow. When she finally lowered the can, it was to discover that the shouting match had progressed to shoving.

Then, before she knew it, the battle was on.

Two

The Fistfight

And drunk delight of battle with my peers,
Far on the ringing plains of windy Troy.
I am a part of all that I have met;
Yet all experience is an arch wherethro'
Gleams that untravell'd world, whose margin fades
For ever and for ever when I move.
How dull it is to pause, to make an end,
To rust unburnish'd, not to shine in use!
As tho' to breathe were life.

Ulysses
—Alfred, Lord Tennyson

The sun continued to beat down with unrelenting fury upon the small town at the crossroads, burning so brightly in the cloudless turquoise sky that it seemed like a great, white-hot ball of fire hovering above, blinding Hawk Bladehunter as he and Skeeter Greywolf circled each other warily. The rough shoves and then the quick, initial blows they had exchanged had been only a prelude to test each other's deftness and courage, to see if the other man would back down from the confrontation. The guarded circling now was part of the same ritual.

It happened that way in nature, too, when male animals vied with each other for supremacy. Hawk had witnessed such battles on numerous occasions. Man was not so very different from beast, after all. Both fought over the exact same things: sex, territory, and dominance.

He and Skeeter were going at it over the first of these—in the form of Skeeter's wife. Her name was Phoebe, and she had come to Hawk's trailer last night after Skeeter had beaten her up again. Hawk hadn't done anything more than tend her cuts and bruises, give her a safe place to sleep, and advise her to divorce her worthless, drunken, abusive husband. But Skeeter, of course, didn't believe that was all that had happened—because had their roles been reversed, he would have done his damnedest to cuckold Hawk.

Not that Hawk had a wife. Still, he knew the thoughts in Skeeter's pea brain, the way his warped mind worked, the fact that he couldn't understand that everybody didn't think and act the way he did. Skeeter would have screwed Hawk's wife; ergo, Hawk must have screwed his. In reality, Hawk felt nothing for Phoebe but pity and a certain amount of contempt that she kept on going back to Skeeter, no matter how badly he treated her.

Since arriving at the grocery store, Hawk had done his best to avoid the argument that had been forced on him, but Skeeter had been spoiling for a fight. Now, they were beyond the point where Hawk could walk away with his pride and ego intact. Like it or not, he was going to have to flatten Skeeter.

Still, despite how the idea annoyed him, Hawk knew deep down inside that if he were honest with himself, some treacherously vain, arrogant part of himself was also taking a perverse pleasure in displaying his prowess to *her*—the girl who stood watching from the old-fashioned wooden porch of the grocery store.

He had noticed her the moment she drove up with her folks in their battered old truck—mainly because she seemed so out of place in it. There was something uptown about her that wasn't seen much around these parts, like she belonged in one of those expensive, long, sleek black vehicles in mobster movies, not in a pickup that hadn't seen better days for at least ten years.

Hawk was twenty-one, and the girl was surely four or five years younger, he judged…too young

for him—jailbait, in fact. So he knew he would be
a fool to mess with her. But that hadn't stopped him
from giving her the once-over, and the way she had
looked back at him had fairly taken his breath away.

There had been something in her turquoise eyes,
something that had wakened not just a sexual response in him, but a spiritual one, as though he had
glanced into a mirror and seen the other half of his
soul staring back at him. His grandfather, an Apache
shaman, would have called it destiny. Hawk knew
only that it had made him shiver of a sudden, as
though a goose had just walked over his grave. It
was with difficulty that he had compelled his attention back to the matter at hand.

But from the corners of his eyes, he could still
see the girl, her gaze fastened on the unfolding fracas between him and Skeeter. Hawk wondered what
she was thinking as she watched them circling each
other, whether, as some women would have, she was
experiencing a thrill at seeing two men come to
blows, or whether she was instead shocked and ap-
palled at the sight. Some instinct told him it was the
latter.

Her beautiful young face was pale beneath her
tan, as though she was unused to violence, and she
gripped her can of cola like a lifeline. Her countenance was beaded with a dewy sheen of perspiration
that made Hawk think of how she would look after
being made love to, and he longed to walk away

from Skeeter, to go and grab the girl, to take her away someplace private, and to show her what it was to have a man—because somehow, he sensed she was as yet sexually inexperienced, and the idea of being her first appealed to him.

But his desires were impossible, he knew. Even if Skeeter hadn't been closing in on him, there were the girl's parents to consider—and they hadn't looked like a couple who would take the deflowering of their daughter lightly. They might even set the law on him.

So, reluctantly, Hawk forced himself to concentrate on his adversary instead, knowing that no matter how much he might want her, the girl was a distraction he simply couldn't afford at the moment, one who might even get him killed. Skeeter was a mean, surly drunk and had been swilling beer since before breakfast.

He had come around earlier to beat on Hawk's door and pound on the sides of the trailer, swearing and yelling. Through one of the windows, Hawk had shouted at him to get lost, and at last, after kicking the door viciously several times, denting it badly, Skeeter had stormed off. Even so, Hawk had realized it was not the end of the matter, and he had heartily wished that Phoebe had chosen some other place besides his own in which to seek refuge.

He had known the repercussions that would follow her spending the night in his trailer. Still, he had not had the heart to turn her away when, crying, she had knocked on his door, sporting among other injuries a puffy black eye and a swollen, split lip. He couldn't imagine why Skeeter believed every man for miles around wanted his wife—and that she encouraged their advances. That was his lame excuse for knocking her around.

But Phoebe wasn't even attractive, Hawk thought now. She didn't come close to the girl who stood on the wide-planked porch of the grocery store. Now, *there* were a face and body worth fighting for! Were *she* Skeeter's wife, he might indeed have just cause for suspicion. But poor Phoebe was, as far as Hawk knew, so downtrodden that she hardly ever even glanced at another man—and if she did, that still wasn't any reason for Skeeter to misuse her.

"I know you fucked my wife, Hawk," Skeeter now spat drunkenly, slurring his words as he continued to circle, lurching a little on the sandy ground. "She didn't come home last night. She was at your place—*all night.* So what the hell else am I supposed to think?"

"That she ran away from you because you beat her up, and that she came to me because she needed someplace safe to stay?" Hawk suggested scornfully. "Does it make you feel like a big man, Skeeter, a mighty Apache warrior, using your poor wife as a punching bag? Because in my book, you're nothing but scum, lower than dirt! A *real* man doesn't have to hit women in order to bolster his self-esteem. That's not the way of a warrior, but of a snake that crawls on its belly, hissing and striking like a frightened fool at anything that crosses its path!''

"Damn you, Hawk!" Skeeter reddened at the sarcastic insults, which had hit home. "You think you're such a big deal, better than any of the rest of us—college boy! But you ain't. You're out for whatever you can get, just like everybody else. But you're not taking my Phoebe!''

"I don't want your Phoebe. She's not even my type, and if you knew anything at all about me, you'd know that," Hawk insisted coolly, his black eyes narrowed, glinting like shards of jet in the sunlight. "I'm just sorry for her, is all. I don't know why she doesn't leave you for good, the way you mistreat her. But I'll tell you what, Skeeter. You'd better think twice about tangling with me, because I'm not Phoebe. I hit back—hard.''

Skeeter didn't heed the warning, however. Instead, he suddenly charged like an enraged bull at Hawk, so intent on gaining his revenge that he couldn't halt his impetus when Hawk stepped lightly aside. His fist came up in the process to smash with an audible crack against Skeeter's jaw, breaking open his bottom lip and staggering him so that he spun about, then sank heavily to his knees.

For a long moment, Skeeter just knelt upon the

earth, dazed. Then he shook his head to clear it, and his own dark eyes narrowed as he determinedly compelled them to focus. Gingerly, he lifted his hand to the corner of his mouth, his lip curling angrily when his fingers came away smeared with blood.

"You bastard, Hawk! I'll kill you for that!"

"Oh, I'm just quaking in my boots at the very idea." Hawk's own mouth curved into a jeering smile that did not quite reach his hard eyes as he stared contemptuously at his fallen foe. "So why don't you get up from there and go on home, Skeeter. You're drunk—and hardly even worth my time sober, besides."

"Not so frigging drunk that I can't pound you into the ground, Hawk!" Skeeter was only further infuriated by his rival's insolent gibes.

Stumbling to his feet, he barreled toward Hawk again, only to receive another powerful punch to his jaw for his pains. This time the blow sent him sprawling backward, so he landed smack on his posterior amid a chorus of hoots and laughter from the onlookers present. Gritting his teeth at the open mockery of his cohorts, Skeeter once more resolutely struggled upright, silently cursing Hawk and beginning the circling ritual again, searching for an opening in his opponent's defense.

Neither young man was a novice at bare-knuckle brawling. Since childhood both had been involved in numerous fistfights, which had left each experienced in the rough, proverbially Western style of settling a difference of opinion. But whereas Skeeter was a hothead, Hawk was cool and collected, having learned early on that recklessness was seldom an advantage in a fray. He could stand here all day and sidestep his adversary, if necessary.

However, it seemed that despite his inebriated condition, Skeeter had finally realized his rash tactics required alteration. Instead of lunging forward again, he now homed in slowly, and at last he and Hawk got down to the nitty-gritty, standing toe-to-toe and pummeling each other unmercifully.

From where she stood watching the melee, Leah could hear the fierce sound of the vicious blows, and involuntarily, she cringed as she stared at the two young men, horrified. Except in the movies and on television, she had never actually witnessed a real, live fight before. She had led too sheltered a life for that. So to her, the violence of the males was distressing. Yet even so, she found herself morbidly enthralled by it, unable to tear her eyes away—although it was the taller of the two men who actually kept her gaze riveted on the conflict.

Darkly handsome and muscular, he appeared to her the ultimate warrior, narcissistic, imperious, determined to reign supreme, no matter the cost. There wasn't a doubt in Leah's mind that he would prevail; it was simply inconceivable to her that he would lose. In her mind, he was not a man fashioned for defeat, but, rather, for victory—unconquerable.

Without difficulty, she could imagine him in an earlier era, mounted upon a pinto stallion, weapon in hand, shouting an Apache war cry as he galloped into battle. That was the kind of blood that ran in his veins, she thought.

He was nothing at all like the other, shorter man, whom she instinctively recognized as a trouble-maker. The pock-faced male made her skin crawl. She felt sure he was indeed guilty of beating his poor wife, as the taller man had claimed.

Leah had not been so protected by her parents that she didn't know such things happened in the world. Still, until this moment, they had never seemed quite real to her. No matter how often her parents moved, how furtively they lived, whatever they might be hiding, she was unshakably certain of one thing: Jim and Faith Tallcloud had a loving marriage. Leah had never seen her father raise a hand to her mother, never witnessed him be anything but kind. That other men were not so caring and considerate of their wives was a deeply unsettling notion.

Obviously, the young man called Hawk found it so, too. For an instant, Leah wondered what it would be like to be wed to him, to lie in a bed with his beautiful, gleaming copper body pressed close against her own. At the images that thought evoked in her mind, she felt the sensation she had experienced earlier begin anew, a slow-burning heat that seeped throughout her whole body, setting her atremble. She knew little more than the rudiments of what happened between a man and a woman, and had no firsthand knowledge at all. But that did not stop her from thinking now about losing her virginity to a man like Hawk.

He probably knew everything about making love, she reflected, sighing. Maybe, despite his denials, he really *had* slept with the pock-faced male's wife. From the taunts the two young men had exchanged, Leah gathered this was not the first time the woman had been a bone of contention between them.

Even so, it was shocking to her that they should have come to this savage confrontation—which the stockier man, called Skeeter, ought to have known he stood little chance of winning. Hawk's lithe maneuvers and lightning reflexes were those of somebody accustomed to such battles and more than capable of defending himself, especially against an obviously drunken foe.

He bashed and battered Skeeter ruthlessly, blackening Skeeter's eye and bloodying his nose, neatly sidestepping again to avoid like retaliation as both combatants continued to whale away at each other without surcease. Like animals, they shoved and grappled their way around the parking lot, all their previously pent-up emotions now unleashed. Their faces were cut and bruised, covered with blood.

Their hard, virile bodies strained with effort, sinewy arms bulging, rippling, as each man stood and slugged the other, grunting and groaning, wincing with pain.

Poised on the balls of their booted feet, they moved lightly, a macabre imitation of the Indian rain dances Leah had seen now and then over the years— or of predatory animals, wary and stealthy in their stalking, wild and brutal, knowing no law but that of the land. Another sharp whack attested to a damaged rib. Skeeter doubled over with pain, panting hard, grimacing and positioning one arm to protect the now-vulnerable spot as he prudently backed away. Hawk's smile was chilling as he advanced in equal measure, his knuckles as bruising as those of a prizefighter as he hammered Skeeter's face and abdomen before once more knocking him down.

Without hesitation, Hawk flung himself upon his fallen adversary. But Skeeter was angry and a scrapper, fast enough to swing his legs up in a defensive gesture, kicking Hawk squarely in the groin and heaving him back, making him stumble and fall. Then, tiredly, the two young males staggered to their feet, Skeeter bringing his tight fist up under Hawk's chin, snapping his head back and sending him reeling from the impetus.

Both men were sweating, bleeding, gasping for breath, their limbs aching, grown leaden from the unrelenting tussle. Yet even now they did not desist, bodies slamming into each other, arms locking, legs kicking and hooking as each man dragged the other down again.

Dully, Leah wondered why nobody had stepped in to put a halt to the terrible fight. But as she glanced around expectantly, she realized that far from being made uneasy by the conflict, the rest of the onlookers were actually shouting hoarsely with glee, egging the combatants on and placing bets on the outcome.

She thought that maybe she should go inside the grocery store and fetch her father, that he would surely make some attempt to stop the battle. But then it occurred to her that Hawk and Skeeter might be enraged by her interference and turn on Jim Tall-cloud, and she didn't want her father to be hurt. So instead, she stood where she was, her heart leaping without warning to her throat as she observed Skeeter suddenly yank the knife from the sheath at his belted waist.

He means to kill Hawk! The thought came, unbidden, to Leah's mind, horrifying her as she saw the blade flash brightly, lethally, in the searing sunlight.

But even as she watched, half starting toward the two young males, some idea forming dimly in her brain of doing something, anything, to save Hawk's life, he reached down and pulled an equally deadly knife from where it had been concealed in his boot.

Leah was sure, then, that she was about to see murder done, although as she looked around wildly, panicked, nobody else present appeared too concerned.

Instead, money seemed to be changing hands even faster than before, and the elated yelling had reached a feverish pitch. She had never witnessed anything like this before. It was as though everyone at the corner grocery store had run mad. Even the elderly woman previously engrossed in watching the checker game, which had ground to a halt midway, was smacking her flyswatter enthusiastically against the hitching rail, chuckling and croaking encouragement.

"Sure is something, ain't it?" one of the old men who had been playing checkers announced, shaking his head and smiling ruefully. "Better 'n Saturday-night wrestling, almost. My money's on Hawk. How 'bout yours, George?" he asked his cohort.

"Oh, I don't mind backing Skeeter, Willie. He may be an ugly runt, but he's sure as hell damned mean," George replied laconically. "Shall we say a dollar, then?"

"Done."

Leah couldn't believe her eyes and ears. She thought they must be playing tricks on her. Two young men were going at it with lethal blades—and all that those present could think about was wagering on the outcome. But then, in some dark corner of her mind, she realized that a brawl was probably considered major entertainment in a town so small. And maybe those watching knew that, despite the fact that weapons were now involved, neither of the males would be seriously injured.

She would pray for that, Leah told herself as, with a flick of his wrist, Hawk deftly twirled his knife in his fingers before tossing it from side to side, catching hold of it securely with his left hand, even though he was right-handed. Leah didn't know it, but this was a technique known as border shifting, designed to warn a foe about just how savage and dangerous a man he had dared to cross.

But Skeeter did not heed the threat. Instead, he just smiled, a wide, deceptive grin that did not lighten his flat black eyes. Then, lunging forward, he struck out with his blade at Hawk.

Leah was certain the weapon would at least draw blood. But much to her relief, Hawk twisted nimbly away. And until she saw the thin weal of blood, she didn't even realize that in the process, in a maneuver so fleet and subtle that it seemed in retrospect like some ancient Native American magic, he had sliced open Skeeter's arm.

The pock-faced man was infuriated by the red stripe that welled on his skin, and he renewed his attack with a frenzy. Now, the knives arced through the air, making sharp, whooshing noises that even the hollering of the watching throng didn't muffle.

Again and again, the blades darted outward in quick, sweeping movements, so fast that Leah could hardly take the scene in. She didn't need to hear the crowd's shouts of approval to know she was witnessing real expertise at work.

Skeeter's homely visage was filmed with sweat. Hawk resembled a devil as, with an intimidating rapidity, he flicked and spun his glittering knife, switching it back and forth between his hands, keeping his opponent guessing about whether he would strike with the left or the right. Leah half expected the blade to go sailing from Hawk's fingers, so swiftly did he manipulate it. But it did not, and even Skeeter grunted in grudging admiration. From the look on his face, Leah thought that maybe he had begun to wish he had walked away from the quarrel instead of causing it to escalate.

The cat-and-mouse game he and Hawk played was now clearly starting to unnerve him. Licking his dry lips to moisten them, Skeeter sprang forward again, his knife slashing out toward Hawk's belly. As lithely as a mountain cat, Hawk dodged the intended strike, bouncing lightly on the balls of his feet; and as Skeeter rushed past him, Hawk sliced a second long gash into him, wondering all the while if he were actually going to have to kill Skeeter.

Blood dripped from the thin wound in Skeeter's side and from the blade of Hawk's knife, making Leah feel sick to her stomach as she spied it. She yearned to turn away from the sight, but was somehow unable to do so, and she took another long swallow of cola in the hope of quelling her rising nausea.

Skeeter's hand dropped once more to his injured side. His breath came in labored rasps. It was obvious that both his broken rib and this most recent bloody wound were taking their toll on him. Despite his drunkenness, he now appeared to recognize that he was getting the worst of the fracas and was not likely to prevail. His mouth was tight with anger at the realization. But despite the effects of all the liquor he had consumed and his raging emotions, Skeeter was clearly not foolish enough to persist in fighting a losing battle.

After a long, taut moment in which he faced Hawk irately, he finally turned and strode away, climbing into a nearby pickup truck and starting the engine with a roar. As he tore off, spewing gravel in his wake, Leah saw him grab from the dashboard a bottle of what looked to be tequila and begin to swig it thirstily while he screeched out onto the main road. She thought it would be a miracle if he didn't wind up killing someone, driving drunk. Still, she was so relieved to see him go that she hardly even registered the mixture of gleeful whoops and pshaws of disgust that emanated from the crowd as the bets made earlier were now paid off.

No one except her seemed to be paying any attention to Hawk. He stood there motionless in the parking lot, breathing hard, the knife still poised in his hand, his eyes narrowed as he watched Skeeter take off. Then, realizing that blood was congealing on the blade of his weapon, Hawk abruptly wiped it on his jeans, then bent to slip it back into his boot. Rising, he glanced over at Leah again, and such was the way his eyes traveled the length of her once more that an involuntary shudder of excitement chased up her spine.

She wondered what would have happened had they been alone together at the corner grocery store. Unbidden, images of him kissing her savagely, running his hands over her body feverishly, and pressing her down to cover her possessively with his own weight filled her mind. She thought that at this moment, he did not look like a man who would take no for an answer, and she shivered again, suddenly afraid of the unknown and feeling not quite so sophisticated and grown up, after all.

Three

On the Road Home

Like two doomed ships that pass in storm
    We had crossed each other's way:
But we made no sign, we said no word,
    We had no word to say.

The Ballad of Reading Gaol
—Oscar Wilde

"Leah, it's time to go now," Faith announced as she and Jim exited the grocery store, paper bags in hand.

Startled from her reverie by the sound of her mother's voice behind her, Leah flinched almost violently. Her attention had been focused so intently on Hawk and the brutal fight that she had actually forgotten all about her parents and the groceries.

"I'm—I'm sorry, Mom. I—I was daydreaming, I guess." She explained her lack of assistance lamely, blushing guiltily.

Faith didn't know whether to laugh or cry as her gaze followed the tall, handsome young man who had so obviously captured her daughter's eye. She had hoped she and Jim still had some years yet before they would be forced to relinquish Leah to the world and all its dangers. But if nothing else, today had made Faith vividly aware of how vain that hope had been. Sighing, she contented herself with a wry smile.

"Yes, so I see. There are still a couple more sacks inside, on the counter."

"I'll get them right away," Leah offered hastily, glad to escape from her mother's all-too-perceptive glance.

It was embarrassing, she thought, having your mother know you had been fantasizing about a man. She shouldn't have been standing there, staring at him so openly. Mortified now, she wondered if everyone else had observed her attraction to him. Then she decided that they had all been riveted by the brawl, just as she had been, and so had probably not noticed anything else.

It was cool and relatively dark within the grocery store after the heat and glare of the bright sunlight outside, and it took Leah's eyes an instant to readjust as she stepped back inside. Then she spotted the paper bags just where her mother had said they were, and she hefted one in each arm. Turning toward the open doorway, she stopped dead in her tracks, her heart pounding as she spied Hawk silhouetted there.

For a long moment, they just looked at each other, as they had before the fracas had started outside. Then, realizing she was staring again, Leah abruptly lowered her eyes, feeling a surge of crimson heat rush to her cheeks. Not daring to glance at Hawk once more, she moved toward the doorway, wondering anxiously if he intended to go on standing there, blocking her path, forcing some kind of a confrontation between them.

Even though the sacks weren't all that heavy, maybe he would offer to carry her groceries for her. She half relished, half dreaded the idea. Her parents didn't like her talking to strangers. Her mother would be deeply agitated, and her father would give her a stern lecture later.

So it was with mixed feelings that she saw Hawk step aside to allow her to pass. Still, the cramped quarters of the grocery store were such that Leah barely had room to get by, and as she turned sideways in order to slip past, she found herself face-to-face with his broad, naked chest.

She had never been so close to a young man before, especially one with his shirt hanging wide-open. His dark, copper flesh was smooth and muscular, filmed with a thin sheen of perspiration that made his chest glisten. From his neck hung the Indian amulet she had observed earlier. Up close, Leah could see that it was composed of thong, feathers, beads, and a big, sleekly polished chunk of turquoise. Native Americans called the stones "pieces of sky," because their color was that of the firmament that stretched above the Southwestern mountains, bluffs, and deserts.

The amulet gleamed against Hawk's chest, and Leah had a strange, compelling urge to reach out and touch it, to run her palms over his skin, to press her lips to his bare torso. He smelled of sandalwood, musk, sweat, and smoke, masculine aromas that were unfamiliar and therefore intoxicating to her senses.

Her mouth was dry from nerves and her unbidden longing to taste him. She wanted to go on standing there, inhaling the scents of him, drinking him in. But the paper bags she held had begun to grow unwieldy in her arms, and as a result, she was forced to move on by.

Outside, Leah slowly made her way to her parents' pickup, which her father now had backed up to the grocery store. The tailgate was down, and Jim and Faith were loading the groceries into the bed, Faith tucking the cold and frozen foods into the ice chest. Leah handed her father the remaining sacks.

Then the Tallclouds climbed into the truck and

Jim started the engine. As they drove away from the crossroads, Leah could not help glancing back through her open window. Her heart lurched in her breast with a peculiar sensation that was at once a thrill and an ache as she saw Hawk standing on the porch of the grocery store, watching her departure.

He had stood so close to the girl that he could have reached out and touched her. Even now, Hawk could still smell the sweet, enticing fragrance of her in his nostrils.

Desert roses, he thought. She had smelled of desert roses, sunlight, fresh soap, and a clean female-ness quite unlike anything he had ever previously associated with a woman, as though she had bathed in a pure, clear-running mountain stream before coming into town.

She had been tall and slender, as graceful as a deer.

Her eyes had been like clear summer pools reflecting the sky, the color of the turquoise stone he wore around his neck. Hawk didn't think he had ever seen eyes exactly that color before. Their image lingered in his mind, haunting him. They weren't Native American eyes.

The girl had at least some white blood in her, then, a realization confirmed for him by the memory of her gold-dusted skin, paler than what he was accustomed to seeing on the Indian reservation where he lived.

He didn't recall ever seeing the girl around before, which meant she didn't live in town or on the reservation. Maybe she and her folks had just been passing through. And now she was gone, and Hawk would probably never see her again. He felt an odd pang of regret at that, as though he had been given a glimpse of something he had searched for all his life—and had had it snatched away before he had a chance to try to grasp it.

Still, there was nothing he could do about it. He didn't know the girl, or even her name. He might have learned this last by introducing himself, offering to carry her groceries for her. But in the end, pride had kept him silent.

What did he have to give somebody like her? His good looks, his athletic body? That hardly compensated for a rundown trailer on an Indian reservation and a weekly paycheck that barely covered his expenses. Most evenings, he wasn't even home, but enrolled in night classes at the local state university, so he could get his degree and grab hold of the bottom rung of some corporate ladder. He intended to make something of himself. He didn't plan on spending his whole life on the reservation, either living in the past or drinking himself into a stupor every night, the way most of his friends did.

A girl like the one who had just left the crossroads

deserved better and undoubtedly expected it, too. She might have been attracted to him, but she hadn't been the sort of wild, rebellious teen looking to get drunk and laid—and for no better reason than to spite her parents. No matter how much she had interested him, there hadn't seemed any real point in making her acquaintance. So why in the hell did he feel as though he ought to have his ass kicked for letting her get away?

Cursing silently, Hawk turned from the doorway of the grocery store, heading for the coolers in the rear. Between Skeeter and the unknown girl, he felt as though nothing had gone right all day. It had put him in an even worse mood than the one that had descended upon him last night, when Phoebe Greywolf had come rapping on his door, beaten black-and-blue, scared, all teary-eyed and breathlessly pleading. He vowed irritably that if she ever showed up again, he was going to pretend not to be home, even though he knew he wouldn't, in good conscience, really be able to turn her away.

Opening the lid of one of the battered, old-fashioned coolers, Hawk withdrew a six-pack of bottled beer. The heat and the fight with Skeeter had made him thirsty, and he felt as though after all he had been through today, he deserved to wet his whistle with something stronger than the cola, iced tea, or lemonade he would usually have chosen.

After paying for the beer and a pack of cigarettes,

he meandered back outside, acknowledging the occasional congratulations of those who had witnessed his conflict with Skeeter and won money off his victory—such as it had been.

Hawk supposed he ought to be glad his opponent had finally backed down and that he hadn't had to wound him too seriously. But as he reflected on the matter, he still scowled to himself, knowing Skeeter was the kind to come sneaking around his trailer some moonless night to slash all the tires on his thirdhand convertible for revenge.

Now, Hawk thought he should probably have at least stuck his rival badly enough to have landed him in the nearest clinic for a while. That way, Hawk wouldn't have had to be constantly on his guard, looking out his trailer windows at every little unfamiliar sound in the wee hours of the morning.

Still, if he had stabbed Skeeter hard and deep enough to hurt him, there would have been trouble with the law over it, and despite the fact that the two of them had come to blows, neither he nor Skeeter wanted that. Indians never prospered in the white man's jail, and the one night Hawk had spent there, for fighting in some bar, had convinced him to attempt to avoid a return engagement. He had felt like a caged animal, gleaning an inkling of understanding that was as close as he ever wanted to come to knowing what his ancestors had experienced when they had been rounded up and locked in stockades during the days when they had represented a threat to the white man's way of life.

Sliding into the driver's seat of his battered old 1966 Thunderbird, Hawk unscrewed the top from one of the long-necked bottles of beer from the six-pack, taking more than one long swallow before tucking the bottle securely between his legs. Then he tore the wrapper from the pack of Marlboros he had bought, shook out a cigarette, and lit it, inhaling deeply. Finally, turning the key in the ignition, he wheeled the convertible from the parking lot and out onto the road. He had already had enough excitement to last him the weekend.

The reservation lay ahead—and his trailer could use a good cleaning.

The Tallclouds had stopped briefly once before leaving town, to pick up the part Leah's father needed to repair the broken air conditioner in their truck. Now, they were headed toward home, where Leah, suddenly dispirited, knew little awaited her but chores and studies. She groaned inwardly at the thought.

So much for all her new makeup. What good was it when she didn't have anybody to put it on for? she wondered a trifle resentfully. Seeing the young male called Hawk and witnessing his fight at the crossroads was about the most exciting thing that had ever happened in her entire young life. And now it was over, and she had nothing to look forward to but a return to her humdrum existence. Surely there had to be more to life than this!

But then, as from beneath her thick black lashes Leah glanced surreptitiously at her parents, she felt another surge of guilt. They loved her and were doing the best they could for her. It was wrong of her to be so embittered and ungrateful. She was lucky to have such a caring family, parents who worked hard and didn't drink or abuse her, a full-time father instead of a divorced daddy who came around only on weekends.

Many kids her age were a lot worse off than she was, from broken homes and already hooked on alcohol or drugs. Some girls her age, Leah acknowledged, were little better than prostitutes, trading their bodies for cigarettes, beer, and marijuana. She had seen them at school and elsewhere, coming on to all the older boys.

Still, if she were honest with herself, Leah knew that deep down inside she envied those girls their popularity, even if she didn't admire how they got it. She was willing to bet that if she had smiled seductively at Hawk and "accidentally" brushed up against him suggestively, he *would* have offered to carry her groceries for her instead of just letting her pass by without a single word!

Maybe she ought to have been more brazen. But then, he would only have got the wrong idea about her—and nothing would have come of it, anyway. What had she been expecting? That a man she didn't even know was going to be so overcome with desire for her that he would actually out of the blue ask her for a date?

That was just silly and unrealistic, the kind of romantic foolishness that only happened in novels. If Hawk had been interested in her, it was for one reason only. And while Leah was curious, becoming increasingly aware of her own sexuality and attraction to boys, she realized she wasn't yet ready to surrender herself—especially to someone she didn't even know!

But that was what Hawk had wanted from her. She had known it instinctively, and now, as she remembered the way his eyes had slowly assessed her, she shivered again, perversely excited and yet frightened, too.

She had been given the once-over before, but no man had ever really looked at her the way Hawk had, as though he were not only mentally stripping her naked, but also staring down into the very depths of her soul, ferreting out her innermost thoughts. Despite herself, she couldn't help but wonder once more what it would have been like to sleep with him.

Leah was so lost in her musings that it was some minutes before her father's worried voice penetrated her consciousness, dragging her from her reverie.

"That truck's coming up behind us awful fast...must be doing over seventy," Jim observed, his brow knitted in an anxious frown as he glanced in the big mirrors on the sides of the pickup. "Faith, Leah, have the two of you got your seat belts fastened?"

"Yes, Dad." Gazing into the mirror on the passenger side of their truck, Leah saw that her father was right. The vehicle that had appeared behind them was barreling along at such a high rate of velocity that it almost looked like a dust devil, such was the cloud of dirt it was stirring up on the sandy road. As it got closer, she could see that the speeding pickup was weaving all over the place, too. "I think the driver must be drunk, Dad. He's all over the road."

"I'm afraid you may be right, Leah." There was a grim edge to her father's voice as he eased their own vehicle to the right, almost onto the verge, so the charging truck would have more than enough room to pass them. "It's all right, Faith." Jim patted his wife's arm reassuringly.

It was only then that Leah realized her mother's face was ashen with fear. Her eyes were staring ahead blankly; her fists were clenched so tightly that the knuckles showed white. In that moment, Leah, too, grew abruptly afraid. She had never seen her mother look that way before. Faith was always the stoical one, cool and collected in a crisis. It ought to have been her comforting Jim, not the other way around.

"Don't worry, Mom. Dad's slowed down and given him plenty of road to get around us." But Leah's words had no more effect upon her mother than Jim's own had had. Faith continued to sit pale and frozen on the seat, little incoherent whimpers now issuing from her mouth. Leah thought her mother might have been praying, but the only words she could make out were "my baby," and she supposed she must not have heard correctly.

Then her mother's voice was drowned out by the incessant blare of the horn of the madly accelerating pickup as it careened up behind them, slinging gravel every which way and almost ramming into their tailgate. As she gazed back apprehensively out the rear window, Leah observed to her shock that the ugly, pockmarked face hunched over the steering wheel was that of Skeeter.

Leah's trepidation escalated at the sight, for she knew Skeeter had already been drunk at the crossroads and had left town not only in a rage, but also with a bottle glued to his lips. Even as she watched, he upended that same bottle to his mouth, swigging down the last of its contents before tossing it out his open window to shatter on the road.

He blasted his horn again rudely, then veered left to come lurching up alongside them. He had his radio cranked up so loud that Leah didn't just hear it, she felt the air pulsate with the driving beat of the heavy-metal music that was playing.

Leering, Skeeter hollered something at them; Leah didn't know what. Then he stamped on his accelerator, making his truck jerk forward erratically. To Leah's horror, as it did so, it fishtailed in the road, smashing into the side of their own vehicle.

The blow jolted her fiercely, slamming her into the passenger door. Her father slowed down even more, trying to keep their pickup on the road. But Skeeter's truck bashed into them again before he sped on, once more jostling them violently and leaving them enveloped in a cloud of choking dust.

Leah heard something that sounded like a bomb bursting beneath the pickup. Faith screamed. Then the vehicle skidded half off the road and bumped to a halt with an impetus that nearly flung Leah into the windshield, despite the seat belt that restrained her. Her father had borne the worst of it, but even so, he had his arm stretched out across Faith to protect her, and his hand was clutching Leah's shoulder.

"All right? Are you both all right?" Jim asked anxiously.

"Yes...I think so, Dad," Leah said shakily. "Mom...Mom, are you okay?" Faith only nodded, her breathing ragged, her face still white. "What happened? What was it that sounded like an explosion, Dad? Did Skeeter throw a bottle or something at us?"

"Skeeter? Leah, do you know that wild young man?" her father inquired sharply.

"No." She shook her head firmly. "It's just that he was at the grocery store earlier, drinking and fighting in the parking lot. I heard some of the others there call him Skeeter. I'm pretty sure he's one of the young toughs from the reservation."

"I wouldn't be at all surprised," Jim replied dryly, a note of anger beginning to creep into his tone now that the danger was past and he knew his wife and daughter were not seriously injured. "Well, I'd better get out and see what the damage to the truck amounts to. A flat tire, at least. That was the explosive sound you heard, Leah. We had a blowout. We're lucky we were going so slowly. Otherwise, the pickup might have flipped over. Faith…Faith, sweetheart, are you going to be all right?" He took his wife's hand comfortingly in his.

Faith nodded again, her breath still coming in short, hard rasps, although a little color was starting to return to her face.

"Leah, look after your mother for me, please. Why don't you get her a cola or something else cold to drink from the cooler?"

"Of course, Dad." Opening her door, Leah climbed down from the truck, casting a wary glance around the ground as she did so.

Even though it was unlikely that any rattlesnakes would be lurking about, baking in the hot sun, she still worried. Hurrying to the back of the pickup, she grabbed a cola from the cooler, then returned to the cab.

Popping the top on the can, she handed the Coke to her mother. "Here, Mom, drink this. It's so hot, and all that bouncing around has probably upset your stomach. To tell you the truth, I'm feeling a little queasy myself."

Faith managed a tremulous smile. "Yes, I *did* believe I was going to be sick for a moment. That horrible young man! What *could* he have been thinking? It was—it was like some dreadful nightmare...." Her voice trailed away. Her hands, wrapped around the cola can, still shook in the aftermath of the accident.

Reaching out, Leah steadied the can. "Mom, I've never seen you so upset before. But it's going to be okay, really. One side of the truck's scraped and dented pretty badly, and we've got a flat tire. But none of us was hurt, and Dad can probably repair most of the damage himself. He's fixing to change the tire right now, and when we get home, we'll call the sheriff and file a report about Skeeter running us off the road. I feel certain he'll be arrested, that he's been in trouble with the law before."

"Undoubtedly. Still, I don't think we need to drag the sheriff into this," Faith insisted shakily after a minute. "We'd have to press charges against that terrible young man and testify at his trial if he didn't

plead guilty. There could be…publicity…an article
in the paper, maybe even a news report on TV. No,
I believe it's probably for the best if we just forget
what happened, Leah. As you said, none of us was
injured, and your dad can repair the pickup.''

"But, Mom, that's not right, that's not fair! Skeeter ought to pay for what he did!'' Leah stared at her
mother, aghast. It wasn't like Faith not to want to
see justice done, and Leah was confused by her
mother's words. Then, stricken, she suddenly realized Faith's reluctance to get in touch with the sheriff stemmed not from any lack of desire to see Skeeter duly punished, but from fear of any publicity that
might result. ''Mom, what're you so afraid of?
What're you and Dad hiding from, running from?
Did—did Dad commit some kind of crime in the
past…get into a fight and—and kill somebody,
maybe? Is he—is he wanted by the law? Is that why
we live so quietly and furtively, why we move
around all the time, and why you don't encourage
me to make any friends?''

"Oh, no, Leah, of course not!'' Faith declared
firmly, deliberately taking a deep breath and forcing
herself to marshal her wits. ''I don't know how you
could even think such awful things about your father! He's a good man…the best!''

"I know that. I didn't say he wasn't, Mom.
But…well, he *was* young once, and he *did* grow up
on a reservation, just like Skeeter and those other

toughs hanging around the grocery store today. And while you and Dad were inside, there was a brawl out in the parking lot, and Skeeter pulled a knife on another guy named Hawk. I thought...I really thought that maybe I was going to see murder done, Mom. So that's why I could understand it if Dad...well, you know, if something like that had happened in his past and he hadn't waited around for the law to show up afterward.''

"No, it's nothing like that," Faith reiterated, sighing. "Look, Leah, I know there're things about the way we live that bother you, and that you've reached an age where your curiosity's no longer going to be satisfied by evasive answers, either. Frankly, I had hoped to put off this conversation until you turned twenty-one, but I guess that was like crying for the moon. Still, now's not the time to discuss all this. We'll talk about it when we get home, okay?''

"All right, Mom," Leah said slowly, her heart pounding as she realized she was right, that there *was* some mystery concerning her parents, that they *were* hiding something from her.

"Faith, Leah, I'm all set now. Do you two want to get out of the truck so I can jack it up and change the flat tire?" Jim's face appeared at the open window of the driver's door.

"Sure, Dad. You want some help?"

"That'd be nice."

Presently, the Tallclouds were under way again, Leah quiet, lost in thought as she wondered what revelations her parents would impart to her after they arrived back home.

And as she sat in silence, staring unseeingly out her window and pondering what Jim and Faith would tell her, she did not know that, afterward, her life would be irrevocably and forever changed.

Four

Opening Pandora's Box

And long we try in vain to speak and act
Our hidden self, and what we say and do
Is eloquent, is well—but 'tis not true!

> *The Buried Life*
> —Matthew Arnold

Leah was not who she had always believed herself
to be.

That was the one fact that stood out clearly in her
mind, which was otherwise a mass of chaos. She
was stunned and incredulous at the news her parents—who were not really her parents at all—had
imparted to her. She felt as though the very foundation of her entire life had been violently shaken,
smashed into a million pieces.

Her name was not really Leah Tallcloud.

It was Angelina Marlowe.

The real Leah Tallcloud had died sixteen years ago, before she had ever truly had a chance to live—died in the same automobile accident that had also killed Angelina's parents, Roland and Natalie Marlowe. Angelina's father had been president of a global enterprise called Marlowe Micronics, Incorporated, a company on the technological cutting edge since World War II. It had been started as Marlowe Manufacturing, by Angelina's grandfather, Merritt Marlowe, a self-made billionaire and eccentric recluse.

Despite her sheltered upbringing, even Leah—no matter what, she could not yet think of herself as Angelina—had heard of Merritt Marlowe. He was the kind of man who had become a legend in his own time.

But his riches had not brought him happiness. Instead, he had lost his wife, Angelina's movie-star grandmother, Isabel Standish, at an early age. Apparently, that was when he had begun to grow increasingly more irrational and reclusive—until it had become possible for a consortium of power-hungry, greedy, unscrupulous men to seize control of MMI.

Angelina's father was the only one who had ever suspected what had happened, and to silence him the cadre had murdered him and her mother. The Tallclouds were certain of that, quite sure that despite all of Jim's precautions that fateful night sixteen years ago, it had been some sophisticated, miniature device manufactured by MMI that had exploded beneath the Mercedes, causing it to veer so wildly out of control and leading to the lethal crash that had left her an orphan.

Fearing that Angelina's own life would be in danger were it learned that she had survived, the Tallclouds had taken her in and reared her as their own daughter, giving her the name of the baby they had lost forever that night. This was why they had always lived so quietly and furtively. They had no legal claim on the Angelina who had become Leah; for obvious reasons, they had never formally adopted her.

Thus they were afraid that if the consortium who had killed her parents ever discovered her true identity and whereabouts, they would take legal measures to wrest her from the Tallclouds and ensure that she, too, eventually suffered a fatal "accident."

Leah shivered uncontrollably at the chilling thought that all these years, somewhere out there, unbeknown to her, some men had wished her dead. Men who believed that they had destroyed her along with her real parents. Men who would, even now, if they ever unearthed her, take steps to eliminate her, to wipe her from the face of the earth as though she had never existed.

She had never in her wildest dreams imagined

anything like this. It was like something out of a James Bond movie, and she simply couldn't take it all in, couldn't credit the fact that it was real. Indeed, she would have thought Jim and Faith had made it all up had they not given her proof of their words.

The night of the automobile accident, before the gasoline tank had caught fire and blown up the Mercedes, Jim had managed to open the trunk and remove Roland Marlowe's black leather attaché case. Into it, Roland had carefully placed every single document he had believed would be of value in building a case against his enemies: his private journal, in which he had recorded all of his suspicions; the dates of business transactions he had considered uncharacteristic of his father; details of the two failed attempts on his own life; a list of the steps he was taking to try to gather evidence supporting his belief that a consortium of men, including members of MMI's board of directors, had either killed or else somehow incapacitated his father and grabbed control of MMI.

Also in the briefcase were Roland and Natalie's marriage certificate, Angelina's own birth certificate, her hospital records and bracelet, and an affidavit prepared by the law firm that had handled her father's affairs. The affidavit was signed by her parents, and duly witnessed, containing her fingerprints and stating that they belonged to her, Angelina Noelle Marlowe.

It was clear that Roland had worried about what would become of his infant daughter should anything happen to him and Natalie, and that he had wanted Angelina to be able to prove her identity beyond a shadow of a doubt, should the need for that ever arise. Not knowing the future of medicine, where DNA research would lead, he had taken what precautions he could to safeguard his daughter.

"He and Natalie loved you very much," Faith had told her daughter earlier, and now, as Leah stared at all the documents in the attaché case, a lump rose in her throat, choking her, as she realized her mother—she could not yet think of Faith as anyone else, either—had spoken the truth. Her parents had never abandoned her to kidnappers, as she had sometimes wildly imagined in the past. They had loved her dearly, had done everything they could to protect her.

As Leah slowly leafed through the photographs and newspaper clippings also contained in the briefcase, she recognized that her real parents had been very young when they had died, not even ten years older than she was now. Roland had been a handsome man who had bequeathed to her his blue-black hair, his raven-wing eyebrows, and his full, generous mouth. From her beautiful mother, Natalie, she had received her striking turquoise eyes, her high cheekbones, and her delicately chiseled nose.

Wonderingly, she gazed into the mirror over her

dressing table, and for the first time in her life, Leah knew where her face had come from, whose blood ran in her veins. That, she thought, meant a great deal more to her than the knowledge that she was Merritt Marlowe's only grandchild, the sole, surviving heiress to his vast fortune.

No matter how hard she tried to grasp this last, it was simply unreal to her.

The chasm separating dirt-poor Leah Tallcloud from billionairess Angelina Marlowe was just too wide for her to bridge. There was no way of knowing whether or not her grandfather was even still alive, and even if he were, he would believe her long dead. He would years ago have changed his last will and testament if he had been able, disposing of his wealth however billionaires without any living relatives they wished to enrich did so.

She could not count on receiving even a share of Merritt Marlowe's riches, despite the fact that Jim and Faith had insisted she was entitled to her inheritance and must do everything possible to claim it. This was what they had lived for, what they had trained her for as best as they were able since her childhood—to someday take back her true identity and her rightful place at MMI.

In addition to everything else in Roland Marlowe's attaché case, there had once been fifty thousand dollars in cash, Leah's father had informed her earlier. It was from his former employer that Jim had learned enough about investments and the stock market that he had, over the years, been able to double that sum of money.

"It was Mr. Roland's cash," Jim had explained to his daughter, "so of course, your mother and I didn't feel as though we had any right to it. Naturally, we've used some of it from time to time for your upkeep, things you've required and to which, under the circumstances, we felt you were rightly entitled. But the rest is for you— No, before you protest, let me tell you that your mother and I are *not* as poor as you might, until today, have believed. We were well paid when we worked for Mr. Roland and Ms. Natalie, so we've got a tidy little nest egg of our own put away, too. We've lived quietly and below our means only in order to avoid attracting attention to ourselves and to you, suspicions that could be dangerous to us all. And you're going to need that money in the future, Leah—not only for college, but also to begin to try to expose the truth about your real parents' deaths and Marlowe Micronics, Incorporated."

To Leah, at sixteen, this goal seemed an impossible dream. How was she, a lone girl with relatively limited financial means and other resources compared to the powerful men at MMI, to accomplish this monumental task, to fight the ruthless cadre in charge of the firm, when even her father had failed in the attempt?

"You have a good deal going for you that Mr. Roland lacked, Leah," Jim had pointed out to her quietly. "The first of which is that these men don't know you're still alive. After sixteen years, they've got to feel pretty confident about the fact that they got away with murder. And nobody expects you to tackle them any time soon, besides. You have many years ahead of you in which to prepare, to decide how best to go about reclaiming your identity and inheritance. In the meanwhile, you'll go on being Leah Tallcloud, just as you've been for the past sixteen years, so you'll be safe. You simply *must,* Leah. Until you're ready, you can never breathe a word to anyone about the fact that you're really Angelina Marlowe. It's just too dangerous. These men are not only thieves, they're cold-blooded killers. Don't ever make the mistake of forgetting that—or of underestimating them, either. They will stop at nothing to get what they want."

Now, as Leah recalled her father's words, she shuddered violently.

He was right, of course. The fact that she was truly Angelina Marlowe must be a secret she kept locked away in the darkest, most-guarded portion of her heart—not only for herself, but also for the Tallclouds. Because even at sixteen, Leah was astute enough to realize it was not only her the consortium would come for if they ever learned of her existence, but also for the caring Native American couple she had until today believed to be her parents.

Jim and Faith knew too much. They, also, were a threat to all that the group of men had so mercilessly achieved.

Who *were* these men who, at least twenty years ago, had set their sights so high that they had dared to commit murder and heaven only knew what other mayhem to carry out their bold, unsavory scheme?

Over the years, the Tallclouds had kept a close watch on MMI and its doings. In Roland's briefcase, they, too, had stored everything they could think of that might someday be of use to the girl they had taken in that fatal night so long ago. The girl they loved and reared as their own daughter.

There were copies of MMI's annual stock reports, clippings from the business pages of newspapers, magazines, and trade journals recording assets acquired, new technologies developed, and so forth, as well as the hirings, firings, retirings, and promotions within MMI's upper echelons of management. Plainly, anyone who had sat on the worldwide corporation's board of directors for the past twenty years was to be considered a prime suspect.

As Leah studied the faces in the pictures that accompanied the articles, she could not help but wonder which of the men, if any, had killed Roland and Natalie Marlowe—had attempted to kill her, too, and would try again if ever the need arose.

Of course, several of the men were dead now—of old age, diseases, and accidents. But it was only natural to assume that over the years, younger conspirators had moved up within the ranks and that new ones had come on board. So even with all the information at her disposal, it would be difficult for Leah to ferret out her enemies at MMI.

Her enemies.

She shivered again at that thought.

Until today, she hadn't known she had an adversary in the world, much less a whole group of them who represented a mortal danger to her. It was a terrifying realization, especially for a girl just sixteen years old, whose major concerns had previously been whether or not she was going to be allowed to start wearing makeup and going out with boys.

Desperately, Leah wished she had never badgered her mother for explanations about why they lived the way they did. If only she hadn't been so rebellious and persistent! Then she wouldn't have known about any of this until she was twenty-one.

But it was too late now to turn back the clock, to lock up Roland's attaché case and pretend she had never seen its contents, had never been informed of her real identity and family history, of the goal Jim and Faith hoped she would someday achieve.

Deeply depressed, Leah felt old of a sudden, as though the weight of the entire world had settled upon her slender shoulders. She wanted to be young and innocent again, to have no cares or worries beyond whether or not she had aced her exams at school and had enough money saved for a new dress or pair of shoes.

But that was not possible now. Like the mythological Pandora, she had opened a box of horrors, and there was no shutting it up again.

Her only consolation was that at least she understood now why she was different, especially physically, from just about everybody else she knew. Any Native American blood she possessed came via her father and was considerably diluted. It wasn't just that she could have passed for white. She *was* white—and that, too, was a jolt. It was as though her whole cultural heritage had been stripped away in an instant, leaving her floundering.

Marlowe. What kind of a name was that? English? French? Whatever, it was a far cry from Tallcloud. It put her in places she had never been before—and not just culturally, but socially, as well.

At last, after what seemed like hours, Leah slowly gathered up all the documents, photographs, and clippings now spread in disarray upon her bed. After reorganizing them neatly, she tucked them back into Roland's briefcase. Then she closed the lid and snapped the locks on either side of the handle firmly shut. Picking up the attaché case, she made her way from her bedroom to the kitchen, where her parents sat at the table, eating cherry pie and drinking coffee. She set the briefcase down on the table.

"It all still seems...so incredible, so hard to believe," she said softly.

"Leah, we know this has been quite a—a shock to you." Rising, Faith wrapped her arms comfortingly around her daughter, hugging her close. "That's why we didn't want to tell you until you were older and more able to understand, to cope. But I'm afraid your curiosity was such that you weren't going to be satisfied with anything less than the truth—and really, you *did* deserve that, no matter how much we wanted to hide the past from you as long as we could."

"Oh, Mom— I can still call you that, can't I? I mean, I know now that Roland and Natalie Marlowe were my—my real parents, but you and Dad are all the parents I've ever known, and I just can't stop thinking of you as that."

"No, of course you can't. And we don't want you to, Leah," Faith insisted, deeply touched. "You're our daughter, as much as if you'd been born to us, and we love you dearly—just as we loved Mr. Roland and Ms. Natalie, and our own baby who was lost. But they've lain in their graves for close to sixteen years now, and you're all we have left. For that alone, we would have protected you however we could. Now you understand why you haven't had what one would consider a normal life, Leah, don't you? Not that you would have had one, anyway, as Merritt Marlowe's only granddaughter. But at least this way you've been able to grow up relatively peacefully—and not as the focus of the media and all those dreadful tabloids."

"Yes, I don't think I would have liked that very much," Leah admitted. She sat down at the table while Faith moved to cut another piece of the cherry pie she had baked earlier, sliding the slice onto a plate for her daughter.

"Are you grown up and sophisticated enough today to want a cup of coffee, Leah?" Faith inquired, her dark eyes twinkling as she fetched a fork from the silverware drawer and handed it to her daughter. "Or would you still prefer a glass of milk?"

"Milk will do just fine, Mom." Leah managed a wan smile in return. "In fact, I don't feel nearly as grown up and sophisticated now as I did this morning. Instead, I—I feel just like a schoolgirl who's uncovered a terrible secret and fervently wishes she hadn't."

"That feeling will pass in time, Leah," Jim assured her, laying his hand upon hers and giving it a gentle, reassuring squeeze. "And maybe it's better this way, after all. Because now you know who you are and what you have to do, why you've had to study so hard all these years and learn as much as you can about finances and the stock market."

"There's a part of me that still wishes I didn't," Leah confessed as she cut into her piece of pie, savoring the taste of the sweet, rich cherries and flaky crust. "But now, there's also a part that—despite how frightened I am—is angry, too. A group of horrible, evil men murdered my parents and your baby, and maybe even my grandfather. *And they got away with it!* That's just not right, Dad! I know life's not fair. But if there's even the slightest chance that I might someday be able to expose those men, to make them pay for their crimes, then I want to do it. The only thing is, I just don't see how I can manage it."

"Well, there's plenty of time yet for you to worry about that." Jim sipped his coffee from the cup that Faith had just refilled. "Plenty of time for us to make plans so that if and when the opportunity arises for you to reclaim your true identity and inheritance, you'll be able to take advantage of it. Meanwhile, we'll continue all your lessons just as we've been doing, so that one of these days, you'll be more than qualified to walk right into Marlowe Micronics, Incorporated, and get a good-paying job. Because if you want to know the truth, I think that'd be the ideal place to start."

"You're probably right, Dad," Leah agreed thoughtfully, her eyes narrowing as she licked the thick, sticky cherry syrup from her fork. "I could do that. I'll just bet I could."

And from that moment on, that became not just her goal in life, but an all-consuming obsession.

Five

Moonlight and Madness

There is a pleasure sure
In being mad which none but madmen know.

The Spanish Friar
—John Dryden

The Desert, The Southwest, Four Years Later

Since graduating from college, Hawk Bladehunter had had one obsession in life, and that was to get hired on at Marlowe Micronics, Incorporated, the crème de la crème of companies within the technological industry worldwide. He thought his lengthy interview today with the corporation's personnel manager had gone very well, so he was hopeful he would get the job he had applied for—an entry-level position in the company's research-and-development department.

That was where the real action was, Hawk thought with satisfaction as he drove his 1966 Thunderbird down the two-lane highway that stretched across the desert, toward the glittering neon city that rose in the distance, in the middle of nowhere.

R and D was the place where the ideas that eventually became MMI products were generated, evolving into designs that were then built, tested, and refined before being put into actual production. More than anything in the world, Hawk wanted to be a part of that, to be on the cutting edge of the technological industry that was growing in leaps and bounds.

It had taken hundreds of thousands of years for Man to reach the point where, finally, in the twentieth century, he could journey to the moon. But less than a decade after that had seen an unmanned landing on Mars, and other satellites speeding past Jupiter and the outer planets, toward the edge of the solar system. From Wilbur and Orville Wright's aviation pioneering at Kitty Hawk, Man had quickly progressed to the stealth bomber and the space shuttle, while Jacques Cousteau and his invention of the Aqua-Lung had opened up the dark, unknown depths of the earth's oceans. Microchips had revolutionized the entire world, putting computers not just in offices, but also in homes.

These were indeed exciting times in which to live, Hawk mused as he cranked up the volume on the convertible's radio. He slapped one hand on the steering wheel in time to the hypnotic drumbeat of Paul Revere and the Raiders' haunting remake of "Cherokee Nation," currently playing on the golden-oldies station to which the radio was tuned, while lead singer Mark Lindsay's sensuous, versatile voice echoed on the night wind.

Hawk's long, glossy black hair streamed back wildly from his handsomely chiseled copper visage. Sparks flew from the glowing orange tip of the cigarette he dragged on as he drove, inhaling the last of it deeply, then blowing a stream of smoke from his nostrils before flicking the butt over the side of the open automobile. The butt whirled away in the wind, trailing burning embers like a Catherine wheel.

He took a long swallow from the cold, long-necked bottle of beer he held between his legs as he sped down the blacktop, only to choke on the liquid as, without warning, a tall, amorphous white form suddenly materialized in the middle of the highway before him, illuminated by the bright yellow beams of his headlights. Quickly jamming the bottle down alongside the bucket seat to secure it, Hawk slammed on the brakes, tires screeching and burning, laying rubber for several yards before the Thunderbird came to a bone-jarring halt, nearly pitching him through the windshield.

"Good God!" he spat, utterly stricken as he realized that what he had almost run over was not the ghost he had at first superstitiously supposed, but a real, live, breathing human being.

Hawk was so stunned and rattled that for a moment he couldn't even think, could only sit there shaking in his seat, relieved that he had been able to stop in time. Then, abruptly throwing the gearshift into Park, wrenching open the driver's door and flinging it wide, he leaped from the convertible, swearing up a storm.

"You goddamned crazy old coot!" he shouted angrily as he strode toward the tall but slightly stooped figure who continued to stand in the middle of the road, unmoving and seemingly oblivious of his narrow escape from death. "What in the hell do you think you're doing? Trying to get yourself killed?"

"I'm free." The words were croaked out in a low, raspy voice that was both astonished and jubilant. "I'm free! I got away!"

Much to Hawk's amazement, the elderly man laughed then, a wild, raucous sound, and danced a sort of jig that was surprisingly nimble, given his apparent age and obviously poor condition. Despite his height, he was painfully gaunt, as though he had been long ill or undernourished—a circumstance only accentuated by the loose, shapeless white hospital gown he wore, which was what had made him appear so ghostlike in the glare of Hawk's headlights. The old-timer was clearly naked beneath the garment, his bare backside showing as he chortled and danced, and he was unkempt, as well, with straggling gray hair and scraggly beard stubble.

Gradually, as the adrenaline racing through Hawk's body began to slow, he realized that his initial impression of the elderly man must be correct: he simply *had* to be a lunatic escaped from one of the local sanatoriums or nursing homes—or at least seriously senile. No doubt, medical attendants were even now searching for him.

Plainly, he needed to be returned to wherever he had come from. Unfortunately, Hawk didn't know where that was. Still, he couldn't just leave the old-timer out here in the boondocks. Somebody else speeding along the blacktop might not be as quick on the brakes as Hawk had been. Besides which, the elderly man might wander off the main road into the desert, where he could be bitten by a rattlesnake or else become lost and die of exposure.

"What's your name, old-timer?" Hawk inquired, his tone gentle now.

The elderly man quit whooping and dancing then, his merriment fading and a sly, wary expression coming upon his thin, haggard face, which, despite his age and infirmity, still bore traces of the hand-someness he must have enjoyed in his younger days.

"Who's asking—and what's it to you, anyway?" he demanded imperiously, drawing himself up to his full height and suddenly seeming to possess an authority and dignity he had previously lacked.

"I'm Hawk Bladehunter." Not knowing what else to do, Hawk stretched out his hand politely, just as though he and the old-timer were introducing themselves at a business meeting rather than standing out in the middle of the highway, with the Thunderbird's headlights trained on them and its engine still running. "And in case you haven't noticed, you're on foot and not exactly dressed for a midnight stroll. I just thought you might need a ride, is all."

For a long moment, the elderly man appraised Hawk with a sharpness that was surprising in the face of his apparent mental infirmity. "You'll forgive me, but I don't ever shake hands with people," he then announced firmly. "That's the way germs spread, get into your system, and kill you. I usually wear surgical gloves to protect myself, but I must have mislaid them somewhere…don't seem to have them with me."

He patted his hospital gown searchingly, as though assuming it would have pockets in which he might locate his missing gloves. But the gown lacked pockets, and there were no gloves to be found—despite the fact that Hawk made a display of looking around for them, too, more to humor the old-timer than because he expected to see a pair of surgical gloves lying on the road.

"That's okay. I'm not planning on taking offense just because you don't want to shake hands with me." Hawk withdrew his own outstretched hand. "I can understand your concern about germs. There are a lot of those floating around everywhere these days. In fact, this night air is probably rife with them, and you shouldn't be out here in it, especially wearing only a—a nightshirt. Why don't you let me give you a lift home—or wherever it is you're headed to?"

"I live out here, somewhere…in a mansion I built for my beautiful wife. I've been gone for quite a while now, and she'll be worried about me. So that's where I was going…home." The previously acute focus of the elderly man's eyes when he had assessed Hawk now blurred again into uncertainty and confusion. "Only, to tell you the truth, I can't remember where my mansion is. I seem to have misplaced it, just like my surgical gloves."

"Well, why don't you get into my car, then, and I'll drive you around so you can look for it?" Hawk suggested, in a way that he hoped would not rouse the old-timer's suspicions.

The eyes now clouded with a lost expression had revealed that the elderly man had at least some moments of lucidity, when his mind was as sharp and clear as the proverbial tack, capable of reason and competent inquiry. Hawk didn't want to frighten him, cause him to set up a howl and to struggle against getting into the convertible.

Although Hawk felt confident that he could constrain the old-timer and bundle him bodily into the vehicle if need be, he would rather not be compelled to do that. He knew from experience that even apparently slight, bony, aged people could nevertheless be surprisingly strong—wiry rather than weak. Witness his own grandfather, who could still beat him at arm wrestling, despite the fact that his grandfather was in his sixties and Hawk was a prime, muscular twenty-five-year-old.

"You don't look like one of *them*," the elderly man declared at last. "And the truth is that I *have* walked a very long way. I'm tired and I want to go home. All right. I accept your offer of a ride to my mansion. But, mind. Don't try any tricks with me, young man! I may be old, but I'm not dead—at least, not yet—and I know how to take care of myself better than you might think!"

"I'm sure you do," Hawk insisted smoothly, motioning toward the Thunderbird. "Come on, then, and we'll see if we can find out where you live."

After a moment, to Hawk's relief, the old-timer started toward the convertible. Hawk opened the passenger door for him, and the elderly man settled himself into the seat. Walking around the hood of the vehicle, Hawk got into his own seat, then slid the gearshift into Drive. The car sped once more down the two-lane blacktop, Hawk reaching out with one hand to turn down the volume on the radio.

"You know, you never did tell me your name," he said to his passenger.

"That's because I thought you already knew it." The old-timer slouched in his seat, his eyes closing wearily. "Most people do. I'm famous...have been for years. It started with all that technological stuff I developed during World War Two, and just grew from there. I used to have millions of dollars...maybe even billions. I guess I probably still do, although I don't know for sure or not. My damned board of directors got greedy and turned against me. The next thing I knew, they had incapacitated me—drugs, you know—and were running my whole global enterprise. There's no telling what they've done. That's why I've got to get home to my wife, so I can get back on my feet. She's famous, too—the most beautiful actress in Tinsel Town, or at least she was until I married her and took her away from all that."

"What's her name?" Hawk was beginning to get an idea of just how crazy his passenger actually was, for the background the elderly man had described to him fitted only one man whom Hawk knew of, and that was Merritt Marlowe, the chairman of the board of Marlowe Micronics, Incorporated.

"Her name? Why, it's Isabel...Isabel Standish Marlowe. You been living under a rock or something, young man, that you don't know who my wife is?" His eyes abruptly flying open, the old-timer frowned fiercely at Hawk for a moment.

"No, sir." Hawk was now certain his passenger was a certifiable lunatic, thinking himself to be Merritt Marlowe. Still, it seemed best under the circumstances to humor the elderly man. "It's just that I...ah...don't watch too many movies. I work days, and until my recent graduation, I attended night classes at the university so I could get my degree. I'm afraid that kind of a schedule didn't leave me a whole lot of time for any extracurricular activities."

"No, I suppose not," the elderly man agreed, his ruffled feathers apparently soothed. "Still, you're young. You've got plenty of time ahead of you for all the things you've missed out the past few years...." Lapsing into silence, he closed his eyes once more; and after some minutes, Hawk realized the old-timer had fallen asleep, was snoring gently.

Good, Hawk thought. That made his job a whole lot easier. Stepping on the gas, he sent the Thunderbird flying down the highway, toward the neon city in the distance. If he was lucky, he would reach the emergency room of the nearest hospital before the elderly man awoke and started to put up a fuss about not having been driven to "his mansion in the desert."

Hawk knew the place the old-timer had been talking about. It still belonged to Merritt Marlowe, although it had sat empty for years, since the deaths of Marlowe's son, daughter-in-law, and infant granddaughter in an automobile accident. That had been a real tragedy, causing the eccentric, reclusive billionaire to become even more of a hermit than before.

As far as Hawk knew, except for the board of directors of MMI, nobody had actually seen Merritt Marlowe for ages. Imagine the Thunderbird's elderly passenger thinking himself to be the famous billionaire! Hawk would have laughed aloud at the very idea if it hadn't been so pathetic.

"I hope I never wind up in *your* shoes, old-timer," he told his sleeping passenger, "because the truth is that I'd rather be dead than nuts! And I for damned sure don't ever want to wind up in some old nursing home, either! I wonder how you managed to outwit the people who're supposed to be looking after you? I'll bet they're frantic, hunting for you and trying to figure out where you wandered off to."

At last, Hawk reached the neon city that, unlike his passenger, never slumbered. Carefully navigating the brightly lit streets crowded with traffic, he made his way to the nearest hospital. There, after fetching a couple of attendants from the emergency room, he deposited his passenger, hoping the old-timer would not be too angry with him upon awaking and finding himself ensconced in a hospital bed instead of Merritt Marlowe's deserted mansion.

In truth, it was doubtful if the elderly man would even remember him, Hawk reassured himself, knowing that no matter what, he had done the right thing.

Cranking the volume on the radio back up, he wheeled the Thunderbird from the parking lot, heading toward the apartment he had recently rented in town.

Merritt Marlowe, indeed! Hawk shook his head, laughing softly, ruefully, at the thought. He'd heard some crack-brained notions in his time, but that one surely had to take first prize!

Book Two

Corporate Politics

Where some people are very wealthy
and others have nothing,
the result will be either extreme democracy
or absolute oligarchy,
or despotism will come from either of those
   excesses.
> *Politics*
> —Aristotle

Six

Marlowe Micronics, Incorporated

This bud of love, by summer's ripening breath,
May prove a beauteous flower when next we meet.

> *Romeo and Juliet*
> —William Shakespeare

The Neon City, The Southwest, The Present

The building that housed the headquarters of Marlowe Micronics, Incorporated, was a towering glass-and-steel skyscraper that reflected the bright morning desert sun blindingly, so that Leah had to shade her eyes against the glare as she stared at the edifice for several long minutes.

Her heart hammered in her breast. It seemed that she had waited all her life for this moment. Yet now that it was actually here, she was utterly terrified.

It just didn't appear possible to her that, shortly, she was going to walk into that imposing structure as a brand-new, full-time employee. She was to be the assistant to one Mr. Hawk Bladehunter, vice president in charge of the research-and-development department of MMI.

An expanse of trees, flower beds, and lush green grass that cost a fortune to maintain in the desert heat fronted the MMI headquarters. In the center of the sand-colored, pebbled paving blocks that formed the large sidewalk leading up to the sweeping concrete steps was a huge stone fountain spraying water into a round pool that was used as a wishing well, as the many coins lying at its bottom attested. A small, discreet sign on the low wall of the pool informed passersby that all the money collected was donated to Change Children's Lives, a worthy local charity.

Opening her black leather handbag, Leah fished a quarter from her change purse and tossed it into the fountain. As she did so, she wished hard that she would be able to successfully carry out her mission here at MMI—although how she was going to do that was still a mystery to her.

Because, realistically speaking, how could she, a lone woman, possibly hope to prevail over the consortium of dominant, iniquitous men who had so many years ago seized control of her grandfather's vast empire and either murdered or somehow incapacitated him, and killed her birth parents? As she continued to gaze at the looming skyscraper, it seemed an insurmountable task, the dream of a madwoman.

In addition to MMI's headquarters, which consisted of the central structure and one large wing, the remainder of the block was taken up by the Sand Castle, a posh hotel and casino owned by MMI. Together, the two buildings formed a massive square complex with three swimming pools and a large, beautifully landscaped courtyard at their heart. On the ground floors of both wings were a seemingly endless array of upscale restaurants and shops, where MMI employees mingled during their lunch hours and after work with guests of the hotel and casino.

Leah knew it would take her days just to learn her way around the complex. During her three previous visits, for her interviews with MMI's personnel manager, it was only because of the assistance of the clear directional signs posted throughout the entire complex that she had not got lost.

Glancing at her wristwatch, she abruptly realized that if she didn't get moving, she was going to be late her very first day on the job—and that would never do. Although she had yet to meet her new boss, she had already been warned by the personnel manager that Hawk Bladehunter was a demanding taskmaster who had already run through several assistants because they couldn't live up to his high standards and expectations.

Forcing herself from her reverie, Leah deliberately took a couple of deep breaths, trying to compel her pounding heart to slow, her adrenaline to quit rushing through her body. But it didn't help. Her pulse still raced as she hurried up the steps and through one of the revolving doors of the MMI skyscraper.

Inside was the enormous lobby, actually a soaring atrium several stories high, filled with gorgeous tropical trees, plants, and flowers of all kinds, as well as exotic, squawking birds caged in an ornate aviary. One whole wall was fashioned of stone terraces that looked like a hanging garden, over which a waterfall cascaded into a large artificial pond at the bottom, in which koi swam. The heels of Leah's shoes clicked briskly on the highly polished marble floor as she made her way to the banks of elevators to one side and pressed the Up button.

Presently, she was whooshing skyward, hoping she wasn't going to be sick as the earth seemed suddenly to fall away beneath her feet, causing her stomach to lurch. She was glad she had been too nervous this morning to eat any breakfast and so had made do with only a couple of cups of strong black coffee—although the caffeine probably hadn't helped her jitters at all.

Once she reached the floor that housed the research-and-development department, she stepped from the car, relieved to see that she still had minutes enough remaining to make a quick stop in the ladies' room to use the facilities and check her appearance for the umpteenth time that morning. Her anxiety was such that she had felt as though she was going to pee in her underpants ever since she had left her town house earlier to drive to work.

When she had finished with the toilet, Leah washed her hands, using the air dryer to blow them damp, then smoothing back a couple of loose strands of her hair, which she had done up in a stylish, sophisticated French twist. Rummaging through her purse for her powder compact and lipstick, she freshened her makeup, even though it hardly needed it. Then, finally, she got out the pair of tortoiseshell glasses that she had bought before her interviews, and put them on.

She didn't actually need them to see, but felt they assisted her in presenting a very professional, businesslike image—not to mention providing her with some kind of camouflage for her true appearance.

From the comments her parents had made to her over the years, Leah was vividly aware that she had inherited her real mother's remarkable turquoise eyes, and she worried that someone at MMI with a

sharp glance and a long memory might recall that
Natalie Marlowe's eyes had been that startling shade
of blue-green. Leah thanked God that she didn't
have her birth mother's red hair, too. Otherwise, the
resemblance would have been even more striking.

She adjusted her well-tailored, black linen suit
and rearranged the colorful silk scarf at her throat.
Then, deciding that she had done all she could, she
sighed heavily and determinedly squared her shoulders.

"Quit stalling, Leah," she muttered impatiently
to herself. "Or you're surely going to be late, and
that will never do. You don't want to get off on the
wrong foot with Mr. Bladehunter, now, do you? No,
you don't, so you'd better get moving—*pronto*."

She reached her office with two minutes to spare,
only to draw up short at the sight of the tall, dark
man who stood within, gazing out the wide expanse
of windows behind her desk, apparently lost in reverie.

Leah was so wrought up that, for an instant, she
could only stare at him stupidly, wondering what he
was doing there and thinking he had somehow wandered in by mistake from the casino. What attracted
her initial attention was the jet-black ponytail that
hung down his back, falling just below his shoulder
blades and neatly constrained by an ornate but masculine silver clasp. It scarcely made him appear like
the typical corporate executive.

Then, at her entry, he turned toward her, and as he did so, she suddenly recognized him. Without warning, her breath caught in her throat, and she was transported back in time fourteen years, to the corner grocery store of a town where she had once lived, little more than a crossroads, too small to be located on most maps.

Hawk...

It was an unusual name. She ought to have realized, Leah thought dimly in some dark corner of her mind. She ought to have made the connection between her new boss and the young man embroiled in the knife fight in the grocery store's parking lot that hot summer day so long ago. That she hadn't she could only attribute to her fear that, by coming to work at MMI, she was somehow inevitably setting her feet upon a path from which there would be no turning back. That she was exposing herself to the real and threatening danger that had haunted her nightmares now for far more years than she liked to acknowledge.

Time had seen the promise of Hawk Bladehunter's youth fulfilled, she observed, once she had gathered her breath and composure. The young man Leah remembered had, in his prime, grown even more devastatingly attractive, his proud copper visage acquiring a provocatively brooding edge, his body maturing and filling out, emphasizing its innate strength and suppleness.

In his youth, he had been very much like the others of his ilk from the reservation—poor, rough, and ragged about the edges as a result of the circumstances in which he had been raised. But now, outwardly, there was nothing impoverished about him. In his exquisitely cut Armani suit and expensive turquoise-and-silver jewelry, he looked as though he could have stepped from the cover of *Gentleman's Quarterly.*

Still, no matter how high in life a man such as he ever climbed, he was never quite able to conceal the whiff of the mean streets that clung to him intangibly, giving him a hardness and wariness that those born to the proverbial silver spoon usually lacked. Beneath his deceptively lazy eyelids, his glittering obsidian glance was penetrating, missing nothing, and his stance was that of a man who was seldom, if ever, caught off guard.

He was, Leah recognized suddenly, the very first man she had ever thought about sleeping with, about surrendering her virginity to, the very first man who had ever truly made her aware of her own sexuality and desire.

He still had the ability to remind her of these last, she realized uncomfortably, feeling as though the temperature in the pleasantly cool room had shot up several degrees in just the few moments it had taken him to turn toward her. The sheer animal magnetism the man exuded was almost tangible, nearly overpowering her. So, surely, it would have affected any woman intoxicatingly, she reasoned—not just one as vulnerable and unsettled as she was.

"Ms. Tallcloud, I presume?" Hawk greeted her, his piercing black eyes coolly and deliberately assessing her from head to toe, although his handsomely sculpted face remained impassive, revealing nothing of his thoughts. At her brief nod of acknowledgment, he continued. "Good. You're punctual. I like that."

He walked toward her then, and something about the way he moved caused the image of a big jungle cat—a rare black tiger, sleek and massive with muscle and sinew—to come unbidden into Leah's mind. For a moment, she had the uncanny sensation that he was stalking her, and abruptly an icy shiver chased up her spine, prickling the fine hairs on her nape. Her heart seemed to leap to her throat, and it was only with difficulty that she mastered the panicked, almost uncontrollable urge to flee—to make good her escape before it was too late—that, without warning, wildly assailed her.

It's only your nerves jumping, Leah, she tried desperately to reassure herself. *Anyone in your position would feel the same.*

Still, as Hawk approached her, it was all she could do not to turn and run pell-mell from the office, but stay rooted where she was, force herself to hold out her hand politely. Swallowing hard, she spoke. "Mr.

Bladehunter? How do you do, sir? It's a pleasure to meet you. I hope we are going to work well together."

"As do I, Ms. Tallcloud." He took her outstretched hand in his own, shaking it firmly.

At the press of his warm palm against hers, Leah felt an unexpected electric shock jolt through her entire body, leaving her tingling and trembling. It was all she could do not to snatch her hand away rudely, and she was glad that he held it only briefly before releasing it of his own accord.

"Why don't you step this way into my office, Ms. Tallcloud?" Hawk indicated a door that stood open between the two rooms. "I thought we'd have a chat over coffee and sweet rolls, get to know each other a little before we begin work. I'm sure the personnel manager gave you a fairly detailed overview of what your job will entail. However, like everyone else, I have my own preferences and expectations as to how things should be done in my department, and I've found that it's always best in the long run to make those clear right up front so that, hopefully, we can avoid any misunderstandings at a later date."

"Yes, of course." Leah nodded as she accompanied him into the adjoining office.

Anxiously, she realized her palms were perspiring. Surreptitiously, she wiped them along the sides of her tight, narrow skirt, still feeling as though, despite the building's powerful air-conditioning system, she was too hot and in the process of melting.

She feared her crisp linen suit must be growing damp and wrinkled, but conversely, her mouth was dry, tasting like cotton. Hawk, however, appeared unaffected by whatever it was that held her in its disturbing grip. Almost impersonally, he motioned for her to be seated. Then he himself sat down in the big, forest green leather swivel chair behind his desk.

As she glanced around covertly, Leah noted that his was a large corner office, the kind of space reserved for the most powerful employees of any company, and that the furnishings were far more opulent than those in her own. From the plush, desert-colored carpet on the floor to the mixture of new and antique Santa Fe furniture throughout the room, to the original Native American paintings that hung on the walls, everything bespoke deliberately understated elegance and taste, just as the man himself did.

"Would you care to do the honors, Ms. Tallcloud, or shall I?" Hawk indicated the sterling-silver coffee service that sat on the occasional table beside her.

This was a test. That, Leah understood. Over the years, she had studied every form of corporate hierarchy and strategy that she could. So she had already learned several things about the man she was

to work for. The first of these was that he was no
amateur at corporate politics.

To begin with, he had waited for her in her own
office, thereby invading territory that was clearly de-
fined as hers, a tactic deliberately calculated to rattle
her. Then he had deftly maneuvered her into his own
office, so that she was now on his turf, where his
was naturally the dominant personality, a circumstance he had further amplified by choosing to sit
authoritatively behind his desk rather than in a more
friendly fashion beside her. Now he had—however
politely—essentially ordered her to pour their coffee.

Oh, he was good. He was very good, Leah
thought, not without a certain amount of admiration.
Even if she hadn't already been a bundle of nerves,
knowing that her true identity must be kept concealed at all costs, she would have been agitated by
her employer's actions.

"Please, allow me," she replied as smoothly as
she could manage, not wanting him to guess that
she was acutely aware of what kind of game he
played with her, much less that she knew all the
rules as well, if not even better, than he himself did.

In many respects, these opening moves of his
were like the gambits in a chess match. As a result,
he had already revealed a good deal about himself,
no doubt arrogantly assuming that he could best her
even so, or else that she would prove pathetically

ignorant of—and thus defenseless against—his stratagems.

Therefore, she made no haste to carry out his demand. Instead, Leah waited until she was sure her hands would not shake before she picked up the coffeepot and poured the hot black liquid into the two Sèvres china cups that also reposed on the serving tray.

"Do you take cream or sugar, Mr. Bladehunter?" she inquired, fancying that she had got just the right note of coolness in her tone—not enough to anger him, but enough to let him know that although she had acceded to his wishes, it was solely because he was her employer and for no other reason.

"No, thank you. Black will be fine."

She couldn't be certain, but she thought she detected a hint of humor in his voice, as though she had amused him in some way. And perhaps she had. A man such as he was would, in fact, derive a fair amount of entertainment and satisfaction at the idea of a challenge.

For a moment, it was all Leah could do not to smile. In a different situation, she would truly have enjoyed pitting her own razor-sharp wits against him, since he was so clearly a worthy opponent. As it was, however, she could only quail inwardly at the realization that Hawk Bladehunter was not going to prove an easy man to deceive. She would need to remain constantly on her toes to stay one step ahead of him, and that was an additional strain at MMI that she didn't look forward to.

After setting the coffee cup before him, she placed a cinnamon bun rich with white icing on a plate, then handed that to him, as well. Only then did she prepare her own coffee and roll, compelling herself to settle back in her chair and to cross her long, graceful legs in a manner that she knew showed them off to their best advantage.

All was fair not only in love and war, but also in corporate politics, and Leah had learned early on how to make full use of every weapon in her own arsenal. As she had intended, Hawk's gaze was inevitably drawn to sweep the length of her legs, sexily encased in off-black hose to coordinate with her suit. Much to her own satisfaction, a flash of desire flared momentarily in his dark eyes before he swiftly hooded them against her.

Good! she thought tersely. He was not as detached and in control as he might believe.

If he hadn't responded to her overture, she would have been worried that his self-possession was such that he had an iron grip on his emotions that nothing would shake. Now she knew differently. He was just like every other man—thinking of sex, on average, every ten minutes. Not that she wanted him to think of it in connection with *her,* of course, Leah told herself hastily. Still, it was worth remembering that

Hawk Bladehunter's libido was apparently as healthy as the next male's.

As he leaned back in his chair to survey her from beneath his half-closed lids, she thought she saw one corner of his mouth twitch ruefully at her seductive ploy, but as before, she couldn't be sure; he was so quick and adroit at hiding his emotions.

"I see from your résumé that you've held several different jobs with various companies over the years, Ms. Tallcloud, and that you appear to have used each one as a stepping-stone to increasingly more important and higher-paying positions," he said, in a neutral tone that did not reveal whether he approved of this, or actually found her disloyal and overly ambitious. "Your range of skills and experience should prove of enormous value to you here in the research-and-development department, since you will be dealing with a number of different aspects in your current job, everything from department management to its budget. As you're surely aware, our particular department represents one of the primary sources of income for MMI as a whole—although, of course, as the corporation has grown and diversified over the years, acquiring many other assets such as the hotel and casino, it has become less dependent upon our department than it once was. Still, we do continue to play a very important role here at MMI."

"Yes, I'm well aware of that fact," Leah re-

sponded truthfully, because in preparation for this
day, she had, of course, made it her business to learn
everything she possibly could about MMI.

Essentially, the research-and-development department was the heart and soul of her grandfather's
global enterprise, the cornerstone he had laid so
many years ago with his own inventiveness and
technological savvy. Today it was responsible for
the high-tech inner workings of any number of products on the market—everything from sophisticated
microchips for computers to elaborate guidance systems for missiles. MMI had its fingers in a lot of
pies, and not only in the private sector, but also in
governmental industries worldwide.

This was one of the reasons why the idea that a
cadre of ambitious, immoral men had years ago
grabbed control of her grandfather's empire was so
frightening. If they had not hesitated to do that, to
rid themselves of Merritt Marlowe however they
had, and to murder her real parents, what else might
they not scruple to do?

Many of the governments of Third World countries were especially vulnerable to outside influ-
ences, filled with bribery and corruption. A multi-
billion-dollar corporation that produced technology
particularly vital to weapons and defense systems
could put itself in the position of altering the face
of geopolitics if it chose to do so. As any worldwide
mover and shaker knew, there were any number of

both legal and illegal means of circumventing government restrictions on the sale of sensitive technology.

So who could even hazard a guess as to what the group of men in charge of MMI were really up to? For all Leah knew, they had over the years been responsible for instigating dictatorships, for staging coups and toppling regimes unfriendly to both their short- and long-term goals, and even for starting at least minor wars in Third World countries.

The idea was chilling. Still, it could not be dismissed. It would be extremely foolish of her to have rose-colored illusions about what she was up against. If Roland Marlowe's suspicions had been correct—and Leah had never uncovered any reason to assume they had not been—then the men who controlled MMI were highly dangerous and played for keeps.

Now, as she studied Hawk Bladehunter surreptitiously from beneath the fringe of her lashes, she wondered if he was one of those at MMI whom she must consider a mortal enemy.

He wouldn't, of course, have been one of the original consortium. He was not old enough for that. But he might be one of the men who had come on board to replace those who had eventually retired or died. Remembering the dangerous knife fight he had engaged in that day, Leah knew it would be the height of stupidity for her to imagine that Hawk was not capable of being a member of the cadre she hoped to expose and see punished for its crimes.

Looking at him, aware that he had grown up on a reservation where life was seldom easy, she felt that there was nothing soft or slack or sentimental about him. When last she had seen him, he had been nothing more than a dirt-poor young man struggling to make ends meet. That he had climbed so far so fast could only be a testament to his intelligence, skill, ambition, and drive. What else it might indicate, however, she had yet to discover.

At the very least, he had undoubtedly worked seventy-hour weeks minimum to get where he was today. That alone demonstrated that he could, if he so desired, bend himself to a single-mindedness that, particularly if employed for ill ends, would make him a ruthless adversary.

As Hawk shifted to a more comfortable position in his chair, Leah was again nervously reminded of a tiger. Unlike other jungle cats, when roused to fury, tigers were utterly merciless. Not content with just ripping out a victim's jugular vein, they would also savagely tear off its head and limbs. This was what made them so very dangerous if they turned into man-eaters, and why, in such a circumstance, they must be swiftly hunted down and killed.

Further, as Hawk himself had just moments ago pointed out, the research-and-development department of MMI was critical to its profit margin. Was it likely, then, that the man in charge of it would *not* be privy to the true state of affairs at the corporation?

Leah didn't know. Despite all that she had learned about MMI over the years, she had yet to form her own opinions about those who currently ran the company—primarily because she was well aware that the media frequently distorted the personalities of those it covered. She mustn't judge a man guilty, she had warned herself time and again, just because he had been portrayed by the media as a hard-nosed businessman. In reality, that could mean nothing more than that he didn't suffer fools gladly—something that could be said of herself or any other person who took a career seriously, determined to get ahead in life.

Certainly, it appeared applicable to Hawk Bladehunter.

"I'm glad to know you understand the importance of this department, Ms. Tallcloud," he said now, jolting her from her reverie. "As its head, I try to ensure that it runs both smoothly and exceedingly well—and I expect everyone under my direction to work diligently toward that end."

"Of course. I always endeavor to do no less than my best."

"Let us hope your best is good enough, then, for if not, you will soon find yourself in need of another position elsewhere."

"You're very blunt, Mr. Bladehunter," Leah observed dryly.

"So I've been told more than once. However, I have found that bluntness *does* have its advantages. It permits me to inform my employees in no uncertain terms precisely what I require from them. And in addition, it allows them to know exactly where they stand with me. I believe that way there are far fewer disruptions to the operations of this department. Therefore, if I'm displeased with your performance here at MMI, I will not hesitate to tell you so. On the other hand, I've never been accused of being stingy with praise where it is justly due, either. So although you will undoubtedly think me a hard taskmaster, I believe you will also find me a fair one. You were quite punctual this morning, and for the moment I'll assume this is your usual habit— which is a mark in your favor. Because of the nature of your job, there will be times when it will be necessary for you to come in early and to stay late. I trust that this will not be a problem, however, as I gather from your résumé that you are not married?" Hawk's voice rose just enough to turn this last remark into a question, and one thick black eyebrow quirked upward in a manner Leah was to come to know well over the passing weeks.

"No, I'm not," she answered shortly, hoping that would be the end of this particular line of inquiry. But to her dismay, it wasn't.

"You did not, however, check the Divorced box on MMI's employment application form." The crisp pages in the file that had already been started on her at the corporation rustled as he shuffled through them to find the one he sought. "May I assume, then, that you have chosen—at least for the past several years—to devote yourself exclusively to a career rather than to a family, and that you don't have any children?"

"Yes, that's right. Still, I fail to see what bearing any of that has on whether or not I am qualified to satisfactorily perform the work this position entails, Mr. Bladehunter." Despite herself, Leah found that her tone was more defensive than she would have liked.

"It has a great deal of bearing, actually, Ms. Tallcloud." Hawk paused, slowly sipping his steaming coffee as he scrutinized her speculatively. Then he continued. "You see, it has been my experience that women with children—especially small youngsters—are sometimes distracted on the job or even unable to show up for work, due to their offspring's problems and illnesses. Women without any kids, however, often reach a point in their lives where they start to hear their biological clocks ticking very loudly, and this, too, can interfere with their job performances. Either way, it's a headache I don't need in my department."

"Either way—with all due respect—my personal

life is really none of your business, Mr. Blade-hunter,'' Leah insisted firmly, relieved that his questions and observations had nothing to do, as she had just moments ago wildly imagined, with the fact that she was single and childless because all her time had been consumed with preparations for the day when she would take on the consortium at MMI. ''Further, I'm quite sure that it's against the law for you as my employer to be making inquiries in this area.''

Neither her accusation nor her implicit threat fazed him in the least. Instead, without warning, he smiled at her widely. Despite the fact that it was tinged with insolence, it was, Leah thought involuntarily, her heart doing an unexpected somersault, the most gorgeous smile she had ever seen, displaying white, even teeth and seeming to light up his entire saturnine face, as though the sun had suddenly come out on a cloudy day.

''Yes—but then, how do you know I'm asking as your employer, Ms. Tallcloud?'' he asked softly, mockingly.

She was caught off guard, taken aback by that. She didn't know how to reply, and much to her annoyance and embarrassment, she felt a rush of hot color abruptly stain her cheeks.

''You're blushing,'' Hawk noted, not without a certain amount of now-obvious triumph and amusement. ''Have I said something to offend?''

She was extraordinarily cool and collected, he

mused. Until now, he hadn't been quite sure that he could shake her composure, that she was actually wholly human. Almost, she had reminded him of some futuristic android, beautifully fashioned but totally devoid of emotion.

Except for her eyes.

Behind her modish tortoiseshell glasses, Leah Tallcloud had the most remarkable pair of eyes that Hawk could ever recollect seeing. Wide and expressive, the exact color of turquoise, they had nagged at him ceaselessly ever since he had turned from the windows of her office to observe her standing there in the doorway—looking like a graceful black swan with pieces of sky for eyes.

He had seen those eyes before somewhere; he was certain of it. But where? Then, suddenly, as he racked his brain yet again for the answer, he had it. She was the young woman who had stood on the wooden porch of the corner grocery store at the crossroads that summer day all those years ago, watching his knife fight with Skeeter Greywolf.

Yes, Hawk thought, he must be right. The eyes were the same, and the glossy blue-black hair swept up into an elegant French twist was just as he now remembered she had worn it that long-ago day, too.

He had wanted to sleep with her then, he recalled, to take her away to some private place and teach her what it was to have a man in her bed. If he were honest with himself—and Hawk was—he must admit he wanted to sleep with her now. The moment he had first laid eyes on her this morning, he had been highly attracted to her, had felt his groin tighten sharply with a hot rush of desire.

There were just some women a man never got over. It seemed that, for him, Leah Tallcloud was one of them. Not that he had dwelled on her at any great lengths over the years. Nevertheless, now and then she had crossed his mind, and he had wondered idly—and not without a certain amount of longing and regret—what had ever become of her.

Still, he had never thought to see her again. That she had so unexpectedly come back into his life was something he knew his shaman grandfather would have called fate.

Normally, Hawk made it a practice never to get personally involved with any of the women who worked in his department, it having been his experience that that led only to trouble. But he couldn't deny the prospect of taking Leah Tallcloud to his bed might prove tempting enough to cause him to break that rule.

He couldn't imagine that she was still a virgin, so he wouldn't be her first as he would have been all those years ago. Even so, he was willing to bet that she was very selective, that wooing and winning her would be a challenge—and it had been a long time since he had been offered one of those by a female.

Usually, women were so enamored of his good

looks, money, and position of power at MMI that he had no trouble at all in getting whatever he wanted from them. And of course, they all mistakenly thought that satisfying his desires was the way to get *him* to wed them. It wasn't, but even when Hawk played fair and let them know that, they never believed him, didn't understand that he didn't have to be in love with them to have sex with them, or even a long-term affair; that his single-mindedness was such that for years he had permitted nothing and no one to interfere with his career.

Which was why he could grasp better than most where Leah Tallcloud was coming from, why a female as beautiful and desirable as she was had never married. But now that he had achieved a good deal of what he had set out to accomplish, Hawk was beginning to think seriously about the fact that he had no wife or children; and he hadn't been able to resist probing to learn whether or not his new assistant's thoughts mirrored his own.

Leah herself was confused by Hawk's behavior. He had been so humorless, authoritative, and exacting throughout their interview that she had been thrown for a loop by his unexpected tactic of flirting with her. But of course, surely this was just another attempt on his part to unsettle her, to let her know he was definitely in charge of the research-and-development department at MMI—and damned well meant to stay so.

No doubt he tested all his female employees in this manner, to see if they rose to the bait. And if they did, he probably lost all respect for them, not to mention gave them the cold shoulder after he'd got what he wanted from them. That is, if he didn't fire them outright—which seemed to Leah like a very strong possibility, given how clear he had made it that he wanted no glitches or upheavals in the smooth operation of his department.

Well, she had not worked so long and hard to be made a fool of by a man—no matter how good-looking he was! Her sole aim at MMI was to see that the cadre of men who had destroyed her birth family paid for their crimes.

"Mr. Bladehunter, you are obviously cognizant of the fact that your observations about women and their children—or lack of them—are improper. And in my case, at least, they're also irrelevant. I assure you that I am not in the habit of allowing my personal life to interfere with my professional one." Leah spoke stiffly, uncomfortably aware that she sounded just like some prim spinster. "Therefore, I can only assume that you are teasing me for some unknown purpose of your own."

"Perhaps. But then again, perhaps not," Hawk rejoined lightly, grinning again, although he once more lazily hooded his eyes so she could not read his thoughts. "I will leave it for you to decide which. Now, if you're finished with your coffee and roll, I'd like for us to get started on business. There are several projects currently under way in the department, and you'll need to bring yourself up to speed on all of them. You'll also want to meet the other people you'll be working with, so the first thing I'd like to do this morning is give you a tour of the entire department and introduce you to everyone.''

"Of course." Setting aside her coffee cup and plate, Leah rose, unconsciously smoothing her skirt as she did so. Linen, while cool and comfortable, had a tendency to wrinkle. But there was no help for that. She picked up her clutch bag, which she had earlier tucked beside her on her chair. "Do you mind if I put away my purse first?"

"No, not at all." Hawk eyed her appreciatively as she preceded him from his office, her hips swaying lightly, seductively, in her clinging skirt, her long legs striding gracefully across the carpet. While he had succeeded in rattling her, she had recovered quickly. If she did everything else just as well, then she should prove a more than adequate assistant— and he would be a fool indeed to screw that up just because he was sexually attracted to her.

Still, her poise and intelligence piqued his interest as much as her face and body did. She reminded him in many respects of a Russian *matroshka* or a Chinese puzzle box. Opening either, one discovered only more wooden dolls or boxes inside, until one finally reached the heart of the object. It was rather like peeling away the layers of an onion, searching for the core.

After his interview with her this morning, Hawk thought there was a great deal to Leah Tallcloud that remained concealed beneath her beautiful but aloof exterior, that she was a highly complex woman whose essence would not be easily grasped—or conquered.

Again, he was tempted by the challenge she offered. It was going to be very interesting to see what, if anything, developed between them, he thought, smiling inwardly.

Seven

Getting to Know You

Give every man thy ear, but few thy voice;
Take each man's censure, but reserve thy
    judgment.
Costly thy habit as thy purse can buy,
But not express'd in fancy; rich, not gaudy;
For the apparel oft proclaims the man.

Hamlet
—William Shakespeare

She might be a woman with a mission, but she was definitely one without a plan, Leah acknowledged ruefully to herself as she gazed thoughtfully out the wide bank of windows in her office at Marlowe Micronics, Incorporated.

Her initial goal had been to obtain a job at her

grandfather's global enterprise. But now that she actually had one, she hadn't a clue as to what to do next, how to set about exposing the consortium.

She felt as though, for the past several weeks, she had been doing nothing but spinning her wheels—even though she was well aware that, in reality, she had been familiarizing herself with MMI, getting to know her fellow employees, and learning all the ins and outs of her new position.

As she had been warned by the personnel manager, Hawk Bladehunter was not the easiest man in the world to work for. However, as he himself had informed her on her first day on the job, although he was a demanding taskmaster, he was a fair one. He never failed to praise her when she excelled in her performance. But even if he hadn't, Leah knew she was good at what she did, that her boss had no cause for complaint where she was concerned.

Still, he had kept her so on her toes since her arrival that she had hardly had time to draw breath, much less to implement any kind of scheme to bring to justice the cadre of men she was after.

Today, however, thanks to diligently coming in early most mornings, staying late most evenings, and carrying work home with her just about every single night, she had finally managed to get ahead of schedule. Leah only hoped her boss didn't discover this fact. Because if he did, he would probably think she didn't have enough to do. Despite herself, she couldn't help but smile, albeit wanly, at the thought.

If she were honest with herself, she'd admit that she liked Hawk Bladehunter a great deal more than she was comfortable with. He was undoubtedly not only the most handsome man she had ever known, but possessed many other traits she admired tremendously—not the least of which were intelligence, ambition, drive, and self-confidence. Add to all this the undeniable and terribly sensual animal magnetism he exuded almost tangibly and, well, the combination was pretty lethal, Leah reflected sardonically.

She had to remain constantly on her guard against him. If she didn't, she might be in danger of making a complete fool out of herself by losing her head—not to mention her job—over him, and that would never do. Even if Hawk Bladehunter *weren't* her enemy—and so far, she had no good reason to believe he wasn't—she simply couldn't afford to jeopardize her position at MMI.

If she were to be fired from the company, it was extremely unlikely that she would ever be rehired. That would effectively put an end to any hope she had of seeing her adversaries duly punished for the crimes they had committed.

What to do about this last? Leah asked herself for the umpteenth time within the last hour. That was the sixty-four-thousand-dollar question.

Over the passing weeks, she had, as circumspectly as possible, carefully explored almost every single floor in the entire MMI skyscraper. From all the information contained in Roland Marlowe's attaché case, she had known that, at one point, her grandfather had resided in a penthouse apartment atop the MMI building. But that had been some years before the worldwide corporation had built the massive complex in which its headquarters were currently housed.

If Merritt Marlowe were still alive—and as yet Leah had no real, concrete grounds for assuming he was—he no longer lived in what had once been nicknamed "the Pentagon." As far as she had been able to determine, the top floor of the MMI skyscraper contained the executive offices of the company's board of directors, several different conference rooms, and the executive dining room, but nothing else.

According to those who claimed to be in the know at the corporation, her grandfather's latest residence was a penthouse apartment atop the Sand Castle hotel and casino. However, to date Leah hadn't been able either to confirm or to disprove this, because she hadn't been able to think of any plausible reason to explain why she was wandering around the upper stories of the hotel, in the event that she should be caught doing so.

She certainly had nothing business-wise to take

her there. Nor did she wish to give the appearance of having an assignation at the hotel, since that would hardly enhance her credibility on the job. In fact, she felt quite sure it would inevitably lead to her being terminated from MMI. Because in addition to warning her about Hawk Bladehunter's expectations for his employees, the personnel manager had stressed the importance the corporation placed on its people not falling victim to the lures of the hotel and casino.

"Of course, MMI is not in the business of regulating the personal lives of its employees, Ms. Tallcloud," the personnel manager had declared. "So we have no objections to your making use of the Sand Castle's attractions during your off hours. However, we hope you *do* understand that we expect our people here at MMI to maintain a certain degree of propriety during business hours. No one is going to fire you for occasionally dropping a quarter into a slot machine on your lunch hour. But we here at MMI *do* feel it would be best if behavior of that ilk did *not* become a habit."

"Yes, I quite understand," Leah had truthfully replied, for she had realized immediately the sorts of temptations the Sand Castle must offer MMI's employees—not just the opportunity to drink and gamble on one's lunch hour, but also to meet a colleague for a private rendezvous in one of the hotel rooms.

Still, she had felt quite certain that anything like that would have the manager of either the hotel or the casino placing a discreet call to the appropriate higher-ups at MMI, so the personnel manager had merely confirmed her suspicions.

Thus the only thing that had occurred to her was to openly rent a hotel suite at the Sand Castle for at least a week, claiming she was having her town house renovated and needed someplace to stay.

And actually, this *wasn't* a bad idea, Leah mused again now. If nothing more, it would give her the opportunity to explore the hotel and find out whether or not there existed at least the possibility that her grandfather *was* still alive and living on the premises.

It wasn't as though she couldn't afford a week in a suite at the Sand Castle. Thanks not only to the monetary nest egg her parents had so carefully guarded and nurtured for her over the years, but also to her own income and continuing successful investments, she was financially secure. Other than her town house and car, she had made no major expenditures since college, not knowing what kinds of things she might require funds for in pursuit of her goal.

So the only question seemed to be whether or not it would behoove her *truly* to hire some remodeling company to work on her town house while she was ensconced at the hotel. In the end, Leah decided this would, in fact, be her best avenue of approach, having learned that the most believable lies were always concealed in truths. Besides which, her town house *could* use a facelift.

Not knowing how she would explain a large inheritance when she ostensibly came from a relatively poor, working-class Native American family, Leah had been careful, when buying the property, to choose something in keeping with her current professional status. So the town house was in an older, albeit fashionable, portion of the city, one that appealed to upwardly mobile singles and couples of her generation.

Still, the property suited her, and it *did* possess some attractions that newer residences lacked, such as full-grown palm trees in its Mediterranean-style courtyard.

Unconsciously, Leah sighed heavily. Despite the fact that by temporarily moving into the Sand Castle, she knew she would at least be taking *some* positive action toward achieving her true aim at MMI, she still could not help but feel a strange, unnerving sense of unreality about it, too.

Not for the first time, she felt as if she had somehow got transported by mistake into a James Bond movie—except that unlike the heroines in those films, 007 hadn't shown up on the scene to rescue her and make everything turn out all right. Nor was he likely to do so. Instead, she was being compelled to do her own spying, and she didn't even have a Q to turn to for equipment.

It seemed terribly ironic to Leah that she should be working for MMI—manufacturer of some of *the* most sophisticated electronic devices in the world— and she couldn't even make use of anything currently under development. Security in the entire building was so tight that she felt certain even the most brilliant technological spy would have difficulty making off with the corporation's secrets.

Still, she supposed she *was* going to require *some* kind of gear. Otherwise, she didn't see how she was ever going to learn anything of consequence.

She wondered idly where one got espionage equipment. She thought she should get a pair of high-powered binoculars, at the very least, and maybe one of those microphones that picked up and amplified sounds yards away, even through concrete, and both a video camera and a tape recorder.

She would access the Internet and do a search for spy gear, she decided. But not here at MMI, where any of the higher-ups could monitor her activities on her computer. She would do it tonight, at home.

"Leah?" From the doorway that joined his office to that of his new personal assistant, Hawk Bladehunter gazed curiously at the woman seated behind the desk that dominated the room.

This was the third time he had called her name, only to have her remain oblivious of his presence.

In his short experience with her, that was just not like her at all. To date, he had found her more than punctual, not to mention extremely intelligent, hard-working, efficient, and professional. She was, in fact, quite the best personal assistant he had ever had.

The fact that she was also gorgeous and attracted him sexually was either a bonus or a drawback. He had yet to determine which, although if he were honest with himself, he'd admit leaning toward the former.

"Leah?" Hawk spoke again, this time loudly enough that she jumped in her chair before swiveling around hastily to face him. "I'm sorry. I didn't mean to startle you."

"That's all right. I'm afraid I was...momentarily lost in thought," Leah explained, trying to gather her composure and wondering uneasily if her boss could read her mind. No, of course he could not. That was a silly notion at best. Still, it demonstrated to her just how woefully inadequate she was at the role she had chosen to play, the goal she had set for herself at MMI. "What can I do for you?"

"It's just past noon, and I thought that if you weren't otherwise engaged, we could have lunch together. Once new personnel have settled into my department, I like to take the opportunity to chat with them and find out how they're coming along here at MMI. Since I've learned over the years that if I conduct such an interview in my office, some employees consider it something of an interrogation, it's become my practice to suggest lunch instead. That makes it much less formal, much...friendlier, if you will." Hawk smiled at her disarmingly.

At the sight, Leah felt her heart turn an unexpected somersault in her breast.

No man ought to be so damnably attractive! she thought, unnerved, and swallowed hard. Even under normal circumstances, it would have been difficult to remain immune to her boss. As it was, it was taking all her willpower not only to concentrate on performing her job to the best of her ability, but also to keep in mind her true purpose at MMI.

"Well, no, I...I don't have any plans for lunch," Leah managed to stammer at last. Then, bending her head to avoid what she had learned was Hawk's all-too-perceptive glance, she busily shuffled some of the papers neatly stacked on her desk. "Actually, I had intended just to get a sandwich from one of the vending machines and work straight through."

"Leah, I know I'm a demanding boss." Hawk grinned again, unabashed by the admission. "But even *I* am not such an ogre and slave driver as to insist that my employees stay chained to their desks during their lunch hours. Unless I miss my guess, given the long hours you've been working since you joined us here at MMI, you ought to have managed to catch up everything that had fallen behind while

I lacked a personal assistance. And even if you haven't, I think we're pretty well enough up to speed that one leisurely lunch is *not* going to prove a major setback.''

His words were charmingly spoken. Nevertheless, Leah realized that for all that her boss had phrased his invitation politely, he did not intend that it should be refused. It seemed that she was not going to be able to escape a tête-à-tête with him, after all. Inwardly, she groaned. The very last thing she wanted was to spend time in a more intimate atmosphere with Hawk Bladehunter.

Oh, for pity's sake, Leah! her conscience chided her crossly. *Anybody would think you were just sixteen years old again and giddy because some handsome, popular boy just noticed you. Stop being such a damned fool, and look at this as an opportunity to get to know your boss better so you can try to discover whether or not he's one of the enemy!*

"Very well," she said to Hawk, forcing herself to breathe deeply in order to steady her pulsing nerves. "Why don't you just give me a few minutes to clear off my desk and freshen up, and then I'll be right with you."

"Fine." Hawk nodded, then disappeared back into his own office.

After he had gone, Leah just sat there for a few minutes, thinking she must be out of her mind to have agreed to his invitation, despite the fact that he had really left her no alternative.

Since coming to work at MMI, she had gone out of her way to ensure that she was on distantly friendly, rather than intimate, terms with everybody, because she knew she simply couldn't afford to get close to anyone—especially her boss. Intimate relationships invited confidences she just wasn't in a position to make, and no matter how carefully she guarded her true identity and her tongue, there was always the chance of making an inadvertent slip.

"Nevertheless, it *is* only lunch, Leah," she muttered under her breath, in an attempt to reassure herself and bolster her courage. "And you're certainly never going to make any headway in achieving your *real* goal at MMI if you don't take *some* risks."

Still, as she slowly rose from her desk, she couldn't dismiss the unsettling notion that she was about to dine with an extremely dangerous tiger, which, while it seemed to purr and be on its best behavior, was entirely capable of turning on her ferociously at any time.

After retrieving her handbag from one of the bottom drawers of her desk, Leah made her way to the ladies' rest room to freshen up. Eyeing herself critically in the full-length mirror attached to one wall, she smoothed her rumpled white linen skirt and adjusted her short-sleeved jacket.

Then, knowing there was no longer any reason to

delay, she returned to her office, stepping into the doorway that adjoined it to Hawk's. "I'm ready now," she told him.

"Good." Picking up his telephone receiver and punching the intercom button, Hawk spoke to the secretary they shared. "Cammie? Leah and I are going to lunch now. We'll be at the Desert Rose if you need us." Hanging up the receiver, he rolled down his shirtsleeves, shrugged on his elegantly cut suit jacket, and straightened his foulard tie. "Shall we go?"

Eight

The Desert Rose

The desert shall rejoice, and blossom as the rose.

—*Isaiah,* 35:1

Once Hawk and Leah had locked their offices, they
took an elevator down to the main floor of the building. There, his hand lightly at her elbow, he guided
her through the lunch-hour crowds to the row of
upscale stores and restaurants that lined the large,
central courtyard.

"I don't know if you've had much of a chance
yet to explore this part of the complex," Hawk commented as they strolled along together, Leah pretending more than just a casual interest in the dis-

plays in the shop windows they passed. "We call this area and its counterpart in the opposite wing the Boulevards, and as you can see, we lease space here to any number of fashion boutiques, beauty salons, eating establishments, and so forth. This, along with the hotel and casino, is just one of the many ways in which MMI has expanded and diversified its business interests over the years. We in the research-and-development department aren't, of course, connected with any of this. Still, I thought you might enjoy seeing it."

"Yes, thank you," Leah replied.

Although there was nothing in the least improper about Hawk's hand at her elbow, she was nevertheless terribly conscious of their physical contact. Over the years, she had devoted herself so single-mindedly to pursuing her goal that she had had little time left over for a private life.

As a result, her relationships with the opposite sex had been few and far between and, ultimately, unsatisfactory. Because deep down inside, Leah had known she couldn't afford to get too serious about any of the men she had dated, to allow herself to be sidetracked from her chief aim in life by marriage, a husband, and children.

Still, her last breakup had proved so painful that, for the past few years, there had been no one in her life. She had almost forgotten what it was like to be an object of male attention, to feel the touch of a man's hand against her skin.

It was no wonder then, she told herself irritably, that she was finding Hawk's proximity so mentally disturbing, the feel of his flesh against hers so physically heated. Any other man would have had the same effect upon her. It was foolish of her to think otherwise, to believe that only her boss was capable of engendering within her the unsettling sensations she was currently experiencing.

If Hawk was aware of his impact upon her, however, he gave no evidence of it. Instead, he continued in the role he had temporarily chosen to play— that of congenial tour guide. Clearly in no hurry to reach their destination, he meandered along, pointing out this shop and that, recounting to her anecdotes about the various owners.

"For someone who spends all his working hours heading up MMI's research-and-development department, you're certainly very well informed about the businesses located here in the Boulevards," Leah observed at last, not only feeling as though she must contribute something to their conversation, but also curious and vaguely uneasy about the vast amount of data he seemed to possess about the corporation's other assets.

"Yes, well, I've always believed it pays to learn as much as possible about the company you work for," Hawk explained easily, "since you never know what may prove of value. As the saying goes, knowledge is power, and as I'm sure you're aware, I didn't get where I am at such a relatively early age by sheer luck alone.'' He grinned at her insolently, thereby letting her know that, at least as far as he was concerned, luck had actually had nothing whatsoever to do with how he had attained his position.

Despite the fact that Hawk's brashness was as appealing as everything else about him, Leah felt an icy shiver chase up her spine at his impudent grin. Because she could not help but wonder if he was, in reality, even more brazen than she realized, if there was an underlying message to his words that he believed her to be blithely unaware of.

Of course, it was entirely possible that he had meant only that his intelligence and hard work alone had been responsible for his meteoric rise at MMI. But what if they hadn't? What if the position he held at the corporation was due to his being one of the cadre of men she was after?

To her despair, Leah recognized that she didn't want to believe this last about her handsome boss— and that would never do. No matter how attractive he was, if he were guilty, he had to be exposed along with all the rest of his murderous cohorts! She could not afford any kind of weakness whatsoever. Otherwise, she would never accomplish her goal. She might even be putting her life at risk! Hadn't her parents drilled that lesson into her from the time she had learned her true identity?

The Desert Rose Restaurant was not at all what Leah had expected. She didn't know why, but since Hawk had chosen the Boulevards, she thought he would take her someplace trendy and swank, popular with the upwardly mobile crowd. But the Desert Rose was instead so quietly elegant, so understatedly upscale, that she didn't even need to see the menu to know it wasn't going to have any prices printed on it.

The maître d'hôtel greeted them courteously and cordially, obviously well acquainted with Hawk. "Monsieur Bladehunter, *mademoiselle*. Your table is ready. If you'll follow me, please."

Much to Leah's dismay, he led them to a secluded section of the restaurant, to an even more private booth. She had not counted on this, either—being so alone with Hawk, in such an intimate setting.

Still, she could hardly protest. She worked side-by-side with her boss five days a week, often behind closed office doors. How could she possibly—reasonably—object to eating lunch with him in a public place? She would look ridiculous.

So Leah settled herself on the plush, rose brocade banquette and accepted the large, leather-bound menu handed to her with a flourish by the maître d'hôtel. She opened it up. She had guessed correctly; there weren't any prices listed inside.

She wondered if Hawk planned on paying for this lunch himself. More likely, he was going to charge it on his company expense account. Either way, it wouldn't be cheap.

Was the fact that he could afford to dine in such a place indicative merely of the high position he held at MMI—or something more? She would be a fool not to use this opportunity to find out, she told herself sternly.

"What looks good to you?" Hawk inquired politely, startling her from her reverie.

"It all does, actually," Leah confessed honestly. "I don't know how I'll ever be able to make up my mind as to what to order. What do *you* recommend?"

"Ah." Hawk nodded sagely, then smiled knowingly. "As diplomatic a companion out of the office as you are in it. What to do, what to do? you are asking yourself, are you not? Should you choose one of the more obviously substantial entrées, as a man would, and have me wondering if you will always do the same where your own expense account is concerned? Or should you select some lighter, feminine fare and risk my thinking you would prove as frugal when entertaining clients for MMI?"

"I wasn't aware you read minds, Hawk."

"I don't. It's simply that I *do* understand the dilemma that faces every employee who is invited to lunch by the boss. I've been there myself, you see. It has been my own experience, however, that only the most astute employees think to ask their boss to recommend an entrée.''

''I'm glad I appear to have passed muster,'' Leah said rather stiffly, wondering if he was mocking her.

''You did that the first few weeks you worked for me. So why don't you relax, Leah,'' Hawk suggested expansively. ''Order what you want. I promise I won't think you're abusing your expense account if you spring for the roast duck à l'orange, or that you're parsimonious with clients if you prefer the breast of chicken instead.''

''Well, I'm certainly relieved to hear it. However, having never dined here before, I would still like to hear your own recommendation.''

''All right. I'll order for us both, then. But don't blame me if you don't like what comes on your plate.''

''Somehow, I don't think that will be a problem.''

At a signal from Hawk, their waiter, who had been unobtrusively hovering nearby, appeared at their table to introduce himself and to tell them about the day's specials, which weren't on the menu. Hawk listened attentively, never rushing the young man and, once or twice, politely soliciting his opinion. Finally, the order was placed, and the waiter gathered up their menus and disappeared.

"You must plan on our being here awhile," Leah observed with feigned lightness, for Hawk had ordered not only entrées, but also appetizers and salads, and he had indicated to the waiter that he would want to see a dessert menu, too, at the end of the meal.

"When one works through the lunch hour as frequently as you and I do, then one is entitled every now and then to a leisurely meal." Reaching into the inside pocket of his suit jacket, he extracted a pack of Marlboros and a lighter. "Do you mind if I smoke?"

"No, please, suit yourself."

Shaking a cigarette from the pack, he lit up, blowing a cloud of smoke into the air. "So, Leah, how do you like MMI so far?"

She was not deceived by his pleasant manner. Despite what he had told her earlier, she was cognizant of the fact that this interview *was* something of an interrogation. Large companies like MMI wanted employees who understood corporate politics, who knew how to fit in and be team players—not solitary mavericks, such as she knew herself to be, in reality.

Over the years, however, Leah had learned all the rules of this particular game and how to play it.

She had with every appearance of cheerfulness eaten her fair share of fried chicken and potato salad at annual company picnics. She had donned a T-shirt and jeans, and taken her turn at bat during softball games at annual company playdays. She had dressed to the nines and shaken dice at the craps tables during annual company casino nights. And she had downed at least one sociable drink and consumed a plateful of hors d'oeuvres at annual company Christmas parties.

She had also contributed to the various gifts for colleagues and to the charities favored by the corporations she had worked for. She had, in fact, become so adept at portraying the perfect employee that no one had ever been aware that she couldn't have cared less about any of this.

"I like MMI just fine," she told Hawk, forcing herself to speak calmly. "For the most part, all big businesses are fairly similar in structure and expectations. So it's really more of a matter—for me, at least—of having a position where the work offers a challenge and there's room for personal growth and advancement. Being at MMI has provided me with both, so I enjoy my job very much. I've also made some friends in the department. And—" swallowing hard, Leah compelled herself to take the verbal plunge "—I admit there's a certain fascination in being employed at a company started and owned by someone like Merritt Marlowe. Undoubtedly, he's a genius. He must be a terribly interesting individual. Have you ever met him?" She tried to make the question as casual as possible.

"No, I can't say that I have." He paused as the

waiter returned to their table, bearing the bottle of white wine Hawk had ordered earlier.

Leah could have wept with vexation at the interruption, because she felt sure that her boss had been about to tell her more. As it was, she could only curb her impatience while the traditional wine-tasting ritual was gone through, and then, following Hawk's approval, the waiter poured wine into two glasses.

"Well, I know Merritt Marlowe is famous for his eccentricities and reclusiveness," Leah said after the waiter had disappeared again. "But given his inventiveness, it's hard for me to imagine that he doesn't make even an occasional foray into the research-and-development department of MMI."

"Yes, that's a mystery to me, too, actually." Taking a long last drag of his cigarette, Hawk crushed it out in the crystal ashtray on the table. Then he sipped his wine. "But in all the years I've been with MMI, he's never once, to the best of my knowledge, stepped foot in the department. Of course, although he's still the chairman of the board, he's been semi-retired for quite some time now, and one presumes he's kept abreast of things by both the board of directors and written reports. Still, one would think he wouldn't be able to resist at least the occasional peek."

"Why do you think you haven't seen him there, then?"

Hawk shrugged nonchalantly. "Who can guess why Merritt Marlowe does or doesn't do anything? You obviously know, of course, that he's reputed to be at least half-crazy—although I believe it's safe to say that he's probably more idiosyncratic than anything else. Otherwise, he could hardly have built MMI into what it is today and continued to oversee its operations worldwide."

"No, one wouldn't think so," Leah remarked, careful to keep her face inscrutable.

"No, indeed. Suffice it to say, only various members of the board of directors at MMI have any direct contact with Merritt Marlowe. However, a rather interesting incident *did* happen to me some years back." Hawk smiled and shook his head at the memory.

"What was that?"

"I met a poor old man who *claimed* to be Merritt Marlowe."

"Really?" Leah was so startled by this unexpected piece of information that she nearly choked on her wine. Her pulse began to race. Was it possible her grandfather actually *was* still alive after all this time?

"Yes. It was a few days before I came to work at MMI. I was fresh out of college and had just completed my interviews with the personnel manager, as a matter of fact. And I was very hopeful that I was going to be hired on at MMI, in the research-and-development department, which has always been my area of interest.

"At any rate, I was returning to the city after being out at the Apache reservation to visit my grandfather. I was in a good mood and quite excited about my prospect of getting a job at MMI, so I'm afraid I was doing a bit of premature celebrating. I'd had a couple of beers with my grandfather and was drinking a third one while on my way back to the city. You know how wild young men are." Hawk grinned at her sheepishly at the admission that he had been drinking while driving. Then he continued.

"Anyway, it was a hot night. So I had the top off my Thunderbird, and I had the radio cranked up to a level I'm certain I would find deafening today. And I'm afraid that, like all wild young men, I was going quite a bit faster down the highway than the speed limit allowed. Not that under normal circumstances that would have been a problem, you understand?"

"Quite," Leah answered rather dryly, earning another discomfited grin from him.

"Well, there's nothing much beyond the city for miles but desert." Hawk pointed this fact out somewhat defensively. "So you can see practically forever, and this was back in the days when our good senators and congressmen—having no idea whatsoever about the amount of time it takes to get across a Southwestern state—had the speed limit reduced to fifty-five miles per hour, besides. Which was a totally unreasonable speed limit to begin with, as most of us west of the Mississippi River knew.''

"You're right, of course.'' Leah didn't even try to stifle the knowing smile that curved her lips at her boss's futile attempt to justify his driving far too fast. "So...you were wild and young, and you were drinking and speeding. I'm surprised you weren't pulled over by a highway patrolman.''

Hawk laughed outright at that. "*That* at least would have been expected—although not welcomed, by any means—given the situation. But what occurred instead was that as I was barreling along the blacktop, there suddenly appeared—out of nowhere, it seemed—an elderly man standing in the middle of the road. I don't mind telling you that he scared me to death, not only because I thought at first that he was a ghost, but also because I barely managed to get my convertible stopped in time to avoid running him over. If the highway department didn't periodically repave the blacktop, I'd be willing to bet that the skid marks my tires left for yards would still be visible to this very day.''

"Good grief!'' Leah exclaimed, shocked. "Did you actually hit the poor man?''

"No, but I came close enough that I was very badly rattled, as you may imagine. In fact, I just sat there in my car for a long moment, shaking. Then my temper got the better of me, and I barged out of the Thunderbird, shouting at the top of my lungs, to confront the old coot. He wasn't wearing anything but a white hospital gown, which was what had made me think he was a ghost, and as I approached him, he began to dance a crazy, gleeful jig, croaking something about being free and having escaped.

"Of course, I realized right then and there that he was as loony as a june bug. He had no concept whatsoever of the narrow brush he'd just had with my convertible, the fact that I had nearly mown him down. I didn't then, and still don't know where in the hell he'd wandered off from—one of the local sanatoriums, I suspect—or how he'd got so far out into the desert, either. But obviously, I couldn't just leave him out there."

"No, of course not," Leah agreed, her heart hammering. Was it possible the demented old man Hawk had nearly run over so many years ago *had* been her grandfather? "So what did you do with him?"

"Oh, I finally managed to coax him into my car, which wasn't as easy as you might think, because he was very suspicious of me, initially. He refused to tell me his name. But then, as he began to confide in me about looking for his mansion and his wife, I realized the poor old lunatic actually believed himself to be Merritt Marlowe!" Hawk laughed shortly at the recollection. "Can you imagine that?"

"No...no, I can't." Leah forced herself to join in

her boss's mirth. But inwardly, she was a bundle of nerves, dismay, and hopeful excitement.

Of course, if her grandfather *were* alive and being held prisoner, he would surely over the years have made one or more attempts to escape! What if he had actually, on at least one occasion, succeeded? What if he had, in fact, been the man Hawk had picked up on the blacktop?

"What...what ever became of him? Do you know?" she asked, her hands, which she now had concealed beneath the table, balling into fists from her emotional turmoil.

"No." Hawk shook his head. "He fell asleep in my car, thank heavens. Otherwise, I'm sure he would have been most upset that instead of driving him around the desert, as he'd wanted, to search for his lost mansion and wife, I took him straight to the nearest hospital and dropped him off at the emergency room."

"What hospital?" Leah almost bit her tongue off with annoyance when she recognized how sharp her tone had been. "I—I mean, well, *I* would have been curious myself to know what befell the old man afterward, that's all. Weren't you?"

"Oh, yes. Every now and then, whenever I happen to think about him, I confess I *do* wonder if I shouldn't have gone back to Our Lady of Mercy Hospital and checked on him. But in the end, he wasn't my responsibility, after all. I'd done what I could for him, which was all I *could* do under the circumstances. Anything more would have been just to satisfy my own curiosity.''

''Yes, I understand.''

It was all *Leah* could do to contain herself. Our Lady of Mercy Hospital and a crazy old man who had claimed to be Merritt Marlowe. It wasn't much to go on.

But still, it was a great deal more than she'd had just a few minutes ago.

Nine

The Would-Be Spy

The Soul unto itself
Is an imperial friend—
Oh the most agonizing Spy—
An Enemy—could send—

> *No. 683*
> —Emily Dickinson

Hacking into the computer system at Our Lady of Mercy Hospital had revealed that half a dozen John Does had been admitted to the emergency room during the year in which Hawk had first applied for a job at Marlowe Micronics, Incorporated. Of these men, three had died shortly after arriving at the hospital, two had been far too young to be Merritt Marlowe at the time, and one had been discharged after treatment, his true identity never learned.

Leah sighed heavily as she gazed at her computer screen. Despite all her hopes to the contrary, it seemed that she was still no closer toward reaching her goal than she had been before hearing her boss's story about the lunatic who had claimed to be Merritt Marlowe.

Tiredly, she wondered what she might be overlooking, what other avenues she ought to be exploring. If her grandfather had indeed been alive, had managed to escape from his captors and to elude them long enough to have been picked up on the highway by Hawk, then the consortium would have been desperate to find him, wholly uncertain about what he might say or do and whether or not anyone would believe him if he told his tale.

What would those men have done first, if they had discovered that Merritt Marlowe was missing? Leah asked herself, trying to reason the matter through. Well, surely, they would have checked with all the law-enforcement agencies and hospitals to see if her grandfather had turned up anywhere, she decided. The men she was after were all important, wealthy, powerful, ruthless, and efficient. They would have had some plausible cover story prepared in the event that they were asked hard questions.

No doubt they had carefully established a false identity for their prisoner, complete with all the necessary forged documents, just in case he should ever somehow succeed in slipping past his guards and the other security measures they most certainly had in place. That way, it would have been easy enough for one of the men to pass Merritt Marlowe off as an elderly, senile relative, Leah supposed, with no one the wiser.

Because no matter what, it would have been imperative for the men to locate and recapture her grandfather. They couldn't have risked just leaving him to wander around on his own, even if he were certifiably insane. So at least one of the men would have had to show up at Our Lady of Mercy to claim him, she deduced.

Maybe she was going about this all wrong, Leah told herself slowly. Maybe instead of looking for John Does, she should be combing the hospital's database for all the elderly men admitted to the emergency room during that same time. It would broaden the scope of her search pattern considerably.

Even so, she wasn't going to have to examine more than thirty days' worth of records at the most—and that only to make sure she didn't miss anything, in case Hawk's memory about the exact date of the incident on the highway was faulty. And she could limit her search to the evening hours, too, since, according to her boss, it had been nighttime when he had picked up his passenger.

Still, Leah sighed heavily as she once more applied her fingers to her keyboard. Her workload at

MMI had been such since she started there that, for weeks now, she had not got the amount of sleep she normally required. As a result, she was exhausted both mentally and physically, making it difficult for her to concentrate on the task at hand.

She ought to go to bed, Leah thought. But realistically, she knew that her schedule wasn't going to get any better in the near future. So she might as well press on, regardless of her weariness.

In the background, on the small television set in the spare bedroom that served as both her guest room and home office, CNN's *Headline News* kept her apprised of what was happening in the world as she diligently tapped away at her keyboard. The caffeine in more than one cup of strong black coffee helped to keep her awake as she studied the information she uncovered.

Eventually, Leah had a list of the names, addresses, and telephone numbers of all the elderly men admitted to the emergency room at Our Lady of Mercy during the time period she had specified. Then it became a matter of cross-checking those against the telephone directory she next called up on her screen.

One by one, she went through her list, deleting those names that matched up satisfactorily. What she was looking for, she suspected, was a fake identity, one that wouldn't show up properly during her search.

In the end, there were only three names that didn't match up. By hacking into the state's welfare system, Leah also managed to eliminate two of those, who were indigents. That left just one name: John Brown. A furtive foray into the birth and death records at city hall revealed that John Brown had been born and had died on the same day.

That was the way one usually established a false identity, Leah knew—by finding the name of a baby who had either been stillborn or who had not lived long after its birth. Seldom did anybody ever bother to check birth records against death records, which meant that one could get a birth certificate for the dead baby and build an entire new identity—however fake—from it.

Still, Leah was uncertain what she had managed to prove, other than that an elderly man apparently using an alias *had* been admitted to Our Lady of Mercy hospital at the same time as Hawk had dropped off his unidentified passenger there. But *had* that man, in fact, been Merritt Marlowe, as he had claimed?

Leah didn't know.

Even so, what she had discovered *did* fit her puzzle quite nicely. If her boss's unknown passenger *had* been her grandfather, then he would have been checked into the emergency room as a John Doe. Later, one or more of the cadre of men who had incapacitated him would have arrived to "identify" him and take him "home."

Emergency rooms were usually so busy that it was highly unlikely anybody on duty would have bothered to investigate the story very closely. The hospital staff would no doubt have been glad, in fact, to have had the matter taken care of, relieving them of any responsibility.

Returning briefly to Our Lady of Mercy's database, Leah observed that John Brown's hospital bill had been paid in full at the time of his discharge—in cash. That fact was further grist for her mill, because most people had insurance coverage, and those who didn't seldom had enough money to pay such a sum in total.

Whoever had taken John Brown away from Our Lady of Mercy had evidently either not wanted to file an insurance claim or else had been intent on leaving behind as little of a paper trail as possible.

Leah rather thought it was the latter.

Yawning and stretching, she rose from the swivel chair at her desk, making a futile effort to work the painful kinks and knots out of her neck and back. All the long hours she had spent sitting at a computer the past several weeks had wreaked havoc on her body. She couldn't remember the last time she had been to the gym for a workout. At this rate, she was going to wind up decrepit before she was even thirty-five years old, she thought ruefully.

Making her way to the kitchen, Leah refilled her stoneware cup from the coffeemaker on the Formica counter. Then, sipping the fresh, hot Colombian brew appreciatively, she walked back to the spare bedroom.

There, knowing she was still not finished for the night, she sat down again at her desk. Applying herself once more to the keyboard, she entered the URL for one of the Internet search engines that she liked best. Once the device had popped up on her screen, she typed in "spy gear" and pressed the efficient-looking gray Search button.

After a moment, a list of responses appeared.

Leah was so dumbfounded by the number of paragraphs displayed that at first she could only stare at them, not quite certain whether to laugh or gasp with dismay. Who would have believed there were so many places on the Internet from which to purchase spy equipment?

The new millennium was just around the corner, and Big Brother, it seemed, *was* indeed watching.

She clicked on the first blue hyperlink, for an online store called The Spyglass. She was further astonished as a sophisticated black home page gradually materialized on her screen. Red-hot neon typeface overlying a graphic of a modern-day spyglass presented her with a wide selection of choices. One by one, she went through the pages of the website, reading all about the various technological offerings.

Some of it, she knew, was hardly cutting-edge gear. But then, it didn't need to be. People wanting, for whatever reasons, to record their telephone conversations didn't need anything more than a simple tape machine they could buy just as easily at their local electronics shop. For those aspiring to emulate James Bond, however, the equipment available was absolutely amazing.

MMI had had a hand in the design and development of quite a bit of it, Leah recognized, feeling slightly sick at the thought. With some time and a couple of hundred dollars, a suspicious wife didn't even need to hire a private detective. She could get the goods on her cheating husband herself. And if one were willing to invest even more time and thousands of dollars in surveillance gear, one could get the lowdown on just about anybody anywhere, it appeared.

Uneasily, Leah wondered how much of the equipment she was looking at was legal. Probably it could all be sold. Whether or not it could be legitimately employed, however, was doubtless a different matter altogether.

Still, she wasn't interested in legalities at the moment, she reminded herself sternly. Her first and foremost task was to determine whether or not her grandfather was even still alive, however she had to do that. If he *had* been Hawk's mysterious passenger, then there was a good chance that the consortium of men she hoped to expose had *not* killed him.

A great deal of reflection had convinced her that while it *would* have been risky for the men *not* to have murdered Merritt Marlowe, it would have been equally as dangerous for them to have done away with him. After all, they might have needed to produce him at some point. And even someone surgically altered to look like her grandfather wouldn't have possessed his technological genius and, therefore, wouldn't have stood up to more than a cursory examination.

Not knowing exactly what she would require, Leah spent more than two hours perusing all that was offered by the top ten websites that sold spy gear. Carefully, she compared models and prices of everything she thought she might need. Then, once she had decided on all her purchases, she added them to her shopping cart at each website, paying by credit card, confident that the on-line encryption services would prevent anyone from grabbing her American Express number off the Internet.

After that, so weary that she could scarcely keep her eyes open despite the amount of coffee she had drunk, Leah powered down her computer and shut off the small television set in the spare bedroom. Then she traversed the short distance down the hall to her own bedroom.

Despite her tiredness, she forced herself to spend

several more minutes in her adjoining bathroom, dutifully washing her face, cleansing away every last trace of makeup, and brushing her teeth. Then she stripped off her clothes and tossed them into the wicker hamper in one corner before donning her nightgown.

Snapping off the bathroom light, Leah staggered into her bedroom and collapsed gratefully upon her king-size bed. The sense that she had forgotten something nagged at her unsettlingly as she drifted into slumber. But her exhausted brain refused to remember what it was that she had failed to do. And presently, as sleep claimed her, it ceased to matter.

In her unnerving dreams, she had become a detective with all the finesse of Peter Sellers's Inspector Clouseau—which was to say that she possessed absolutely none at all.

She stumbled around the rooms and corridors of the immense MMI complex like a complete buffoon. Then, in the crazy way of nightmares, she somehow wandered out of the skyscraper and onto the desert highway, where Hawk Bladehunter deliberately ran right over her with his 1966 Thunderbird.

Ten

Late for Work

Do not shorten the morning
by getting up late;
look upon it as the quintessence of life,
as to a certain extent sacred.

Counsels and Maxims
—Arthur Schopenhauer

Leah awoke to the sound of imperative ringing.

Groaning at the deeply unwelcome noise, she reached out blindly to punch the Snooze button on the alarm clock that sat on her night table. But much to her dismay, this failed to produce the desired effect. The ringing continued, seeming to grow even louder and more jangling, frazzling her nerves. Fumbling for the telephone, she lifted the receiver and placed it to her ear.

"Hello," she murmured sleepily, only to hear the bewildering buzzing of the dial tone in response— and the ringing persisting, reverberating down her hall.

Managing to pry her eyes open at last, Leah returned the receiver to its cradle. She was absolutely horrified as she did so to observe the large green digital numbers on the face of her alarm clock.

"Oh, my God!"

Wholly unable to believe the time, she leaped out of bed, her heart hammering frantically as she raced into her bathroom. From the hook on the back of the bathroom door, she jerked down her sleek white satin robe and drew it on. Her hands trembled as she tied it at her waist.

It was almost noon! She should have been at work nearly four hours ago!

"I'm coming! I'm coming!" Leah called as she hurried toward her front door, from where she now—belatedly—realized the tenacious ringing was emanating. To her distress, it was being accompanied by a furious pounding that threatened to break down the door—and the unmistakable sound of Hawk Bladehunter's voice shouting her name.

Her hands still shaking, she quickly punched the code to her alarm system into the pad by the door. Then she unlocked the dead bolt and wrenched open the door itself.

Her boss stood impatiently on the front porch. At

her appearance, his worried black eyes filled visibly with first relief, then anger. And then, as they raked her assessingly from head to toe, taking in her disheveled, unbound hair, which hung nearly to her waist, her lack of makeup, and her state of dishabille, they began to smolder with something more than just ire.

"Usually when my employees decide to take the day off, they notify me in advance, Leah," he drawled by way of greeting, abruptly hooding his gaze so she could not guess his thoughts. "Do you know what time it is?"

"Yes, yes, I do," Leah replied breathlessly, startled to see him standing there. "And I'm—I'm so terribly sorry, Hawk! I can't believe this happened! I'm afraid I don't have any excuse at all to offer, except that I was—I was so tired last night that I apparently forgot to set my alarm clock. Obviously, I've overslept."

"That is the understatement of the year," he observed dryly. "I've been trying to call you since eight-thirty this morning. Do you sleep with earplugs in or something?"

"No, I don't. But I—I often *do* shut off the ringer on the telephone in my bedroom during the weekends so I won't be disturbed and can sleep late. I guess—I guess I forgot to turn that back on, too," she confessed lamely. Then, nervously, she bit her lush lower lip, blithely oblivious of the effect that this produced upon Hawk.

He wanted to nibble that lip himself, to trace its contours with his tongue before tasting her sultry mouth. One of his measures of a woman had always been how she appeared when she was rousted out of bed in the morning—and to his way of thinking, Leah Tallcloud looked mighty damned good.

What must he be thinking of her? she wondered, hideously embarrassed at being caught in such an unprofessional situation.

As though in answer to her unspoken question, Hawk's glance fastened on the tiny pulse fluttering erratically at the hollow of her throat. Then his gaze slowly traveled down to her full, round breasts. Beneath his half-shuttered lids, his dark eyes suddenly blazed like twin embers again, and his indrawn breath was a sharp hiss.

It was the only warning Leah had that during her haste to reach her front door, the sash at her waist had loosened and now had come totally undone, allowing her robe to fall open.

The negligee she wore beneath was of white satin that matched the robe. But unlike the latter, which was rather mannishly tailored, the former had spaghetti straps and a bodice cut in a deep, seductive V that revealed more than a glimpse of the generous swell of her breasts. The narrow sheath clung like a second skin to her lithe, curvaceous figure, clearly delineating her nipples, and the floor-length skirt, slit on one side to the thigh, fully exposed one long, graceful leg.

Blushing crimson with mortification as she abruptly realized she was half-naked before her boss, Leah once more drew her robe tightly around her, this time tying the sash at her waist securely.

"Well, are you going to keep me standing out here on your front porch all day, or are you going to invite me in?" Hawk inquired, sorry she had closed her robe. "I mean, I don't mind giving your neighbors the wrong impression if you don't. But if I don't check in with Cammie at the office pretty soon and let her know you're all right, she's liable to start worrying that something's happened to me, too, and call the police, and I left my cellular telephone in the car." He motioned toward his Thunderbird, parked in the driveway.

As she stared at the convertible, Leah suddenly remembered her disturbing dream last night, in which Hawk had deliberately run her down on the desert blacktop. For a moment, frightened, she was reluctant to let him inside. He could be the enemy. She mustn't ever let herself forget that, not even for an instant.

Unbidden in her mind rose terrifying visions in which—having somehow discovered her true identity—Hawk came inside her house to attack, rape, and murder her. After all, who would know he had done it? She hadn't shown up for work this morning, and from what he'd said, it was clear the secretary they shared had grown concerned about her. He could claim he'd driven over to learn what had become of her and found her dead.

"As much as the idea holds a certain amount of appeal, I'll admit I really don't intend to fling you down and ravish you, Leah." Hawk's sensual mouth curved into a mocking half smile, as though he had read her mind and was amused by her fears.

"I...I didn't think you did." She forced herself to speak the lie calmly. "My concern was rather that you intend to fire me."

"There's always that possibility, of course," he agreed impassively, nodding. "But as I've told you before, although I'm a hard taskmaster, I'm also a fair one, and it's not my usual practice to terminate excellent employees just because of one mistake. Do you *really* want to discuss this on your doorstep, Leah? I wasn't joking when I said that Cammie would call the police. You've come in early so many mornings since you began to work for me that she's convinced you're either deathly ill or have been knocked in the head by an intruder."

"Please, won't you come in, then?" Opening the door fully, Leah at last stepped aside to permit Hawk entry into her house, unable, as she did so, to prevent herself from wondering if she were behaving like the proverbial simple shepherd, inviting the wolf into the sheepfold.

Involuntarily, she shivered at the thought. Fortunately, however, her boss had his back turned to her and so didn't observe the unwitting reaction.

"Nice place you've got here," he remarked politely as he glanced around with interest at his surroundings.

Being familiar with the neighborhood, Hawk knew the house had to be more than fifty years old. Still, it had been well kept up, and it was tastefully decorated with an eclectic mixture of furniture, several pieces of which were plainly antiques. In the living room to which Leah led him, an overstuffed, camelback sofa upholstered in a soft shade of blue brocade sat with equally substantial chairs covered in a coordinating striped fabric. An armoire and matching tables of dark wood gleamed against the white stucco walls, where paintings he recognized as the work of local artists hung. White plantation shutters covered the windows, and an Aubusson rug lay upon the dark wood floor.

"Why don't you make yourself comfortable—" Leah indicated the couch "—while I go and get dressed."

"I need to call Cammie first," Hawk reminded her. "So if you could just point me toward a telephone..."

"Of course. How silly of me to have forgotten.

Obviously, this just isn't my day,'' she observed ruefully as he followed her across the foyer to the dining room, then through a swinging door that opened onto a bright, cheerful kitchen. "The telephone's over there.'' She pointed to one wall, where the instrument was mounted. "Now, if you'll excuse me, I'll try to make myself presentable.''

"Forgive me for saying so, but I kind of like you just the way you are.'' Hawk grinned at her impudently as he reached for the receiver.

Leah didn't bother to answer that. Instead, feeling the heat of her cheeks as they flooded again with color, she turned and fled from the kitchen.

Oh, was there ever a more disastrous day? she asked herself, horribly upset as she hurried down the hall to her bedroom. Despite her boss's earlier reassurance to the contrary, she would surely be lucky to keep her job after this! And if he fired her, all her plans and hard work over the years would be for naught! What would her parents say? She would rather die than disappoint them after all their efforts on her behalf, their scrimping and hiding, the life they had endured for her sake, in order to keep her safe.

How *could* she have forgotten to set her alarm clock last night? And why, oh, why hadn't she awakened at her usual time, anyway? Then none of this would ever have occurred! She must have been utterly exhausted to have slept for so long!

In her bathroom, Leah turned on the taps in the shower so the water would get hot while she divested herself of her robe, nightgown, and French-cut panties. With her brush, she swept her hair back from her face, then haphazardly twisted it up loosely and secured it with pins. Opening her large jar of Pond's Cold Cream, she generously slathered the thick white cream all over her face. Then she stepped into the steaming shower, knowing from experience that the combination of heat and cream helped to keep her skin moist and soft in the dry desert.

Normally, Leah lingered in the shower in the mornings, considering this a vital necessity with which to begin her day. But there was no time now for anything but the most cursory of scrubbings. She was in and out in ten minutes flat, when she usually spent thirty, vigorously employing soap and a loofah to her entire body.

A hot washcloth removed the now nearly liquid cold cream from her face. But after that, she was forced to stop for a moment, to take several deep breaths in order to steady her hands so she didn't make a mess of her makeup, lining her eyes unevenly and smearing her lipstick.

The knock on her bathroom door almost made her jump out of her skin.

"Leah?" Hawk called. "Leah, are you in there?"

"Yes." Suddenly, vividly aware that she was

standing stark naked at her bathroom counter, she grabbed hastily for her discarded robe and hauled it on. Then she hesitantly cracked open the door.

"Sorry," he apologized tersely as he caught sight of her. "I didn't mean to wander into your bedroom and interrupt you at your morning ablutions. But I *did* think you'd like to know that I spoke with Cammie. After assuring her that there was nothing more awry at your house than an unset alarm clock and a ringer turned down on the telephone in your bedroom, I informed her that you wouldn't be in at all today and that I wouldn't be back, either. On the off chance that you had, in fact, simply overslept, I brought what we need to work on this afternoon from the office. So I just wanted to tell you that you needn't rush and that you should feel free to dress casually."

"Thanks. I appreciate that," Leah said with heartfelt gratitude. "I guess that means I still have a job at MMI."

"Yeah, you do. In fact, to be perfectly honest, Leah, I'm surprised that this didn't happen sooner. And in a way, I suppose, it's *my* fault. I'd noticed that you looked especially tired the past several days. That's one of the reasons why I took you to lunch yesterday and told you that we were pretty much all caught up and that you'd more than met my expectations as an assistant. But I guess I left it a little late."

"No, I...I had trouble sleeping last night, that's all." Leah wasn't about to tell him that she had been up until the wee hours, hacking into Our Lady of Mercy's database and ordering equipment from on-line spy stores.

"Yeah, well, I know from experience that that often occurs when you've been pushing yourself to the limit. You get wound up so tight that no matter how exhausted you are, you still have difficulty getting to sleep. And then whenever you finally *do* drop off, you end up slumbering like the dead. You probably wouldn't have heard your alarm clock or the telephone under any circumstances."

"You may be right about that," Leah admitted reluctantly, knowing that might indeed have been true. "Nevertheless, I remember what you said about punctuality on the job, so you can be sure that this won't ever happen again."

"Perhaps not," Hawk conceded, smiling. "Still, I don't want you to worry about it. After all these weeks of working side by side with you, I'm well aware that you're a professional and that this was an out-of-the-ordinary event. Now, if you don't mind me poking and puttering around in your kitchen, I thought I'd make coffee and something to eat while you finish up in here."

"You don't have to do that," she protested.

"No, I know I don't. But I confess that my motives aren't *entirely* altruistic. Breakfast is the most important meal of the day, they say, and not too many people concentrate very well on an empty stomach, besides. Even though we're not going to be working at the office today, we've still got quite a bit to do. In fact, I may be here half the night, seeing as how most of my morning was taken up by Cammie's repeated interruptions, listening to her insist that she was going to call the police unless I consented to drive over here to make certain you were still alive and kicking.''

"Hawk, I am truly sorry for being the cause of your being put to so much trouble. No one knows better than I what a busy man you are." Leah bit her bottom lip again contritely.

"I really wish you'd stop doing that...nibbling on your mouth that way. It was bad enough when I knew you had something on beneath that robe. But now that I feel sure you're not wearing *anything* under it, your doing that is making me crazy!"

For the third time that morning, Leah flushed bright red. "You—you shouldn't say such things to me," she insisted, abruptly pulling the edges of her robe more closely together, as though that would offer some protection against him. "It's—it's most unseemly!"

"So?" He shrugged nonchalantly, his eyes dancing wickedly, his mouth curving into an insolent grin. "Sue me for sexual harassment. At the very least, stop chewing your lip and get dressed. Otherwise, I might be tempted to find out whether or not I'm right about your not having anything on beneath that robe but your birthday suit!''

At that, with a small gasp of shock, Leah quickly shut the bathroom door and locked it, her heart thudding furiously in her breast with a mixture of outrage and perverse excitement. Feeling as though her knees were about to give out from under her, she leaned against the door, one ear pressed to it, listening intently.

Despite the fact that her common sense told her she was allowing her wild imagination to run rampant, Leah nevertheless envisioned Hawk breaking down the door to get at her. Instead, his soft laughter echoed mockingly in her ears as he departed from her bedroom beyond.

Strangely enough, she didn't know whether she felt relieved or disappointed as she heard the light tread of his footsteps grow distant.

"You had better get a grip, my girl," she muttered severely to herself. "Because the very last thing you need is to fall head over heels for your boss and wind up out on the mean streets, unemployed, with nothing to recommend you but the fact that you allowed yourself to become another notch on Hawk Bladehunter's bedpost! Not to mention that the man might be your mortal foe, to boot!''

Still, it was unnervingly clear to Leah that whatever attraction she felt for her boss was evidently mutual.

So far, however, despite the fact that he was plainly as predatory as his name, Hawk had done little more than talk, letting her know, even if it were only in a teasing fashion, that he was interested in her. But...what if he persisted in his attentions? What if he grew physical, actually made a pass at her? What would she do then?

Unbeknown to her boss, Leah was in a position neither to file a lawsuit against him nor to quit her job because of his advances. She couldn't afford to rock the boat at MMI, to instigate anything that might conceivably cause her employment to be terminated, or to leave there of her own free will, either.

And on top of all that was her *own* damnable attraction to Hawk. Deep down inside, Leah knew that *that* was what really disturbed her. The fact that she couldn't trust her own reaction to her boss if ever he were to take her in his arms and kiss her....

Just the idea ignited a flame of desire at the very core of her being, a slow-burning heat that licked through her whole body, making her feel flushed and feverish. A hot flood of moisture seeped between her thighs, leaving them sticky, as though she had not just minutes ago stepped from the shower.

Angry and impatient with herself—and a great deal more frightened by her powerful emotions where Hawk was concerned than she wanted to acknowledge—Leah snatched the pins from her hair. Energetically, she worked her brush through it again. Then, with less than her usual deftness, she plaited it into the French braid she normally wore when she was not at work.

In her bedroom, Leah firmly closed and locked the door before stripping off her robe and slipping into a lacy, strapless bra and a clean pair of French-cut panties. A short-sleeved, oversize pink T-shirt, which sported a wide boat neck that revealed her graceful shoulders, and matching leggings appeared to fit the casual-clothes bill, as did huaraches on her bare feet. Tiny gold studs in her ears completed her ensemble.

Lightly, she sprayed herself with just enough cologne to produce a subtle scent. Then, remembering at the last moment to put on the glasses she didn't need, and drawing a deep breath, she braced herself to join Hawk in the kitchen.

Eleven

Perceiving the Possibilities

> How shall the dead arise,
> is no question of my faith;
> to believe only possibilities,
> is not faith, but mere philosophy.
>
> *Religio Medici*
> —Sir Thomas Browne

The enticing aroma of freshly brewed coffee greeted Leah in the hall, causing her mouth to water.

On a normal day, the very first thing she did upon rising each morning was to make her way drowsily to the kitchen, where her coffeemaker, which she always prepared late the evening before, would automatically have turned itself on at the same time as her alarm clock sounded in her bedroom. Pushing the Snooze button on her alarm clock gave her ten extra minutes in which to rouse herself fully to consciousness, and by then, the Colombian coffee she favored would have finished dripping into its glass carafe.

But last night, just like setting her alarm clock, Leah had forgotten to ready her coffeemaker, as well. And this had turned out to be anything but a normal day. So by this time, she was feeling more than a trifle desperate for caffeine.

In the kitchen, she drew up short as she observed that Hawk had done far more than simply fix coffee and a bite for her to eat. He had, in fact, gone to a great deal of trouble.

The French doors leading from the kitchen to the courtyard beyond stood wide-open, as he had apparently decided that they should dine outside. The verdigris table that reposed beneath the shade of a huge palm tree had been covered with a white, lace-trimmed cloth and attractively set with stoneware from her cabinets. Napkins that matched the tablecloth had been laid at both places, and in one of her crystal vases, he had arranged fresh-cut flowers from her garden. A glass pitcher whose open top was protected by another napkin from insects was half filled with what she knew was freshly squeezed orange juice. A large stoneware bowl boasted peaches, grapes, and strawberries.

"Will it suit?" Hawk asked as he turned from the stove to see her standing there.

"Yes. In fact, it's far too much, really. I would have been content with just a cup of coffee and a slice of toast."

"*You* might have been. I, however, would not. And in case you've forgotten, most of the working crowd is eating lunch right about now."

Leah smiled ruefully at that. "Please. Don't remind me. I feel bad enough already. I'll probably be apologizing to you for weeks."

"Don't. Twice was more than sufficient, I promise you. Besides which, I'd certainly be less than honest if I didn't confess that wasting half my day *has* had more than its fair share of enjoyable compensations." His eyes appraised her meaningfully, causing her to blush again for the umpteenth time that morning. "I shan't soon forget the sight of you in bewitching dishabille. And lunch with you two days in a row can count as nothing less than a treat."

"You really must *not* continue to say such things to me," Leah declared.

"Why not? And don't try to tell me it's because you're not as attracted to me as I am to you. I know better."

"Do you?" She forced herself to ask the question lightly, casually. "Or is it only that arrogance and conceit are to be numbered among your faults?"

At that, Hawk grinned hugely at her, unabashed. "That, too."

"No matter," Leah stated firmly, refusing to return his smile. "The fact remains that you are my boss, and it would therefore be both foolish and unprofessional for me to become involved with you."

"On the other hand, it could be the best thing that ever happened to you," he rejoined smugly.

"Oh, now you are brazenly boasting about your prowess, too, are you?"

"Could be."

"What is uncertain is whether or not it is, in fact, something about which you *can* boast!"

"There's only one way for you to find out, isn't there?" The glance he gave her was deliberately provocative, and his voice held more than a note of challenge.

"While I am indeed flattered by your offer, it would simply not be politic for me to do anything other than decline," she reiterated determinedly.

"Ah, yes, corporate politics. You're more than just a little deft at those, Leah, aren't you?"

"I try my best."

"And your best is very good, indeed. It's one of the things that makes you such a valuable assistant to me. You know exactly who at MMI requires being kowtowed to, who can safely be given the brush-off, and who needs to be sent away with a bee in his bonnet."

"Well, I would be a very poor assistant if I didn't know those things, wouldn't I."

"Yes, so please don't get me wrong. I'm not complaining—not by a long shot. I'm just...curious about such single-minded devotion to the job. It's relatively rare to see that kind of one-track mentality in women where a career is concerned. Even the most driven of them usually have some kind of a relationship in their lives and a desire for children."

"We've covered this ground before, I do believe. And my answer now is still the same as it was then. My private life is none of your business, Hawk."

"Even if I want to be a part of it?" he queried bluntly.

Leah was flustered by the frank admission; she had not expected it. "I've—I've already told you more than once. I'm simply not interested in having an affair with anybody I work with—especially my employer. I just don't think it's ever a very good idea to mix business with pleasure."

"Yes, well, that all depends on the two people who are doing the mixing, I've always believed. However, we'll leave it. For now. I'm hungry, and unless I miss my guess, this omelette is just about done to perfection."

Lifting from the stove's burner the pan he had been adroitly manipulating as they talked, he slid its contents onto the stoneware platter that sat to one side on the counter and on which were already a second omelette, several strips of bacon, and some sausage patties. From the toaster oven he withdrew hot croissants, arranging them, too, on the platter. Then he poured the steaming-hot black liquid from the coffeemaker's glass carafe into her silver-plated coffeepot.

"Let's eat," he said. "You grab the coffee. I'll bring the food."

"It's a deal."

Outside in the courtyard, Leah filled their stoneware mugs with coffee, then carefully placed the pot on its Sterno-heated base, which Hawk set to burning with his lighter.

"Everything looks wonderful," she announced as he ladled one of the Southwestern-style omelettes onto her plate, along with rashers of bacon, a sausage patty, and a croissant. "But, please, that's more than enough. I'll never be able to eat all this!"

"Try. I'm willing to bet you're a good deal hungrier than you realize, and fresh air is always conducive to the appetite, too."

To her surprise, Leah soon discovered that he was right, that she was, in fact, starving. It was hours since she had last eaten, and she had hardly had any supper the previous evening, besides, having contented herself with just a ham sandwich while she had worked at her computer.

Little by little, she ate her way through all the food on her plate, not even bothering to protest when, voicing his approval, Hawk peeled and sliced a peach for her, and insisted on her having some of the grapes and strawberries, as well. He kept her coffee cup and juice glass filled, also.

"I like your home," he told her as they dined. "It's got a lot of charm and character, which is something most new houses these days seem to be extremely short on. Oh, you might get at least a courtyard, of course, the Southwest being what it is architecturally. But most of the time, it won't have all these gorgeous old palm trees and full-blown flower beds."

"Yes, those are some of the things that encouraged me to buy this place." Pushing her plate away at last, Leah settled back in her verdigris chair to savor her coffee. "Still, there are drawbacks to an older home, too. In fact, I've been wanting to have this one remodeled for quite some time now. I was planning on getting estimates from contractors shortly, actually."

"What are you wanting to have done?"

"Well, for one thing, I'd like to have the rooms opened up more, give the house an airier feel. Older homes are almost always boxy inside. And both the bathrooms and the kitchen could use facelifts, as well. They're awfully dated. I'm not sure what will be involved in redoing all that. But...I was thinking...wondering, really...if it would pose any kind of a problem if I moved into the Sand Castle for a while—just through the worst of the remodeling? I mean, I know that, at some point, I probably won't be able to cook in my kitchen. And the hotel would be convenient.''

''Yeah, it would,'' Hawk acknowledged as he peeled and sliced another peach, eating this one himself. ''No, I wouldn't have any trouble with that, if that's what you're asking. And I don't think the hotel manager is going to be placing any discreet calls to anybody else in the upper echelons at MMI, either, if that's what's worrying you.''

''It is. The personnel manager made MMI's policy about the hotel and casino very clear to me when I hired on. So I don't want to violate any unwritten rules in that regard.''

''Well, what you're proposing *is* a little different from drinking and gambling in the casino or arranging a rendezvous in the hotel. So you go ahead with your plans. If anyone should object, I'll take care of it.''

''Thanks. I appreciate that.'' Leah wondered if she dared bring up Merritt Marlowe again, especially so soon after probing about him only yesterday. She didn't want to arouse her boss's suspicions. On the other hand, she needed to find out about her grandfather, and surely her question would seem natural enough under the circumstances. ''I understand that Merritt Marlowe lives in the hotel.''

''So they say.'' Hawk nodded. ''Apparently, the

top floor of the hotel wing is a private residence, complete with its own elevators, both of which, I'm told, require keys and codes in order to operate. However, it's always difficult to confirm anything where Merritt Marlowe is concerned. He's so eccentric and such a recluse that he could just as easily be residing incognito in the Bahamas or something, while the paparazzi waste their time hanging out at the Sand Castle, hoping to catch a glimpse of him. It's been decades since he's agreed to speak to the media. The press conferences he deigned to hold were always infrequent, in any case, and the personal interviews he granted were even rarer. Not that I blame him for not wanting to become grist for the tabloid mills—especially after what happened to Princess Diana. But as a result of his avoidance of the media, I imagine that, these days, even a photograph of Merritt Marlowe, no matter how poor, would probably be worth a fortune.''

"I hadn't thought about that."

For the first time since embarking upon her mission in life, Leah was assailed by doubts. Hawk's observations all made a great deal of sense to her. It *was* logical to assume that someone as idiosyncratic and private as her grandfather had always been *would* wish to avoid the media at all costs.

Was it possible, Leah now asked herself slowly, that Roland Marlowe had been wrong all those years ago to suspect that a consortium of powerful, unscrupulous men had seized control of MMI and either murdered or incapacitated his father? Roland had, after all, been very young—only twenty-five years old at the time of his tragic death.

Perhaps Merritt Marlowe *had* been angry at his son, *had*, in fact, deliberately cut off all contact with him. Maybe the alleged attempts on Roland's life, even the explosive car crash that had finally killed him, had, in reality, all been nothing more than accidents, into which first Roland and then the Tallclouds had read more than had actually been there.

Her heart sinking, Leah knew she must acknowledge the fact that, although the likelihood appeared to be remote, there *was* some possibility, however slim, that she had undertaken a wild-goose chase.

Nevertheless, the fact remained that there was only one way to find out—and that was to get to her grandfather if he was still alive.

Her resolve thus bolstered, Leah swallowed the last of her coffee. Then she rose from her chair and began to clear the table.

"Here, let me help you with that," Hawk offered.

"No, no." She shook her head staunchly, indicating that he should remain seated. "You cooked. That means the clean-up detail is my duty. It'll only take me a moment, and I'm sure you'd like to smoke a cigarette, besides. As I understand it, the one following a meal is especially enjoyable."

"Yeah, it is at that. And I wouldn't find another cup of coffee at all amiss, either."

Reaching for the coffeepot, Leah courteously refilled Hawk's empty mug, while he withdrew a pack of Marlboros and a lighter from one pocket. Shaking loose a cigarette, he tamped it briskly against the tabletop for a moment. Then, settling back in his chair, he lit up, inhaling deeply before blowing a stream of smoke from his nostrils.

Having gathered and stacked the dirty dishes, Leah carried them inside to the kitchen. Running water in the sink, she set them to soaking, as was her usual practice before loading them into the dishwasher. No matter what manufacturers claimed to the contrary, she had yet to see a dishwasher that truly *could* clean off every single trace of hardened food.

Making space on a shelf in the refrigerator, she slid both the glass pitcher of orange juice and the stoneware bowl of fruit inside to keep their contents cold and fresh. Then she rejoined Hawk in the courtyard, resuming her seat and pouring herself another cup of coffee.

"You said that you brought what we needed to get done today from the office. Did you want to work out here?" Leah asked tentatively. "I'm afraid my home office is in my spare bedroom, so there's no table space available in there, only a small desk. The other options are the dining-room table and the kitchen table. Or, I suppose, we could use the coffee table in the living room, if you prefer.''

"The dining room would probably be best... rather like our working in the conference room at the office, I expect."

"Yes, that was my own thinking, as well."

"Good. I'll just fetch my attaché case from the car, then we'll get started."

While Hawk was outside getting what they needed from his Thunderbird, Leah carried the silver-plated coffeepot, its Sterno base, and their mugs into the dining room, arranging everything on the Mission table. Rummaging through the drawers in her china cabinet produced a heavy glass ashtray. Not knowing what all they might require, from her spare bedroom cum home office she brought out notepads and pens, as well as paper clips, Scotch tape, a pair of scissors, a stapler, and a calculator.

By that time, her boss had returned. Setting his briefcase down on the table, he opened it, hauling file folders and other materials from inside, tossing them into various piles. He also removed a small black leather case and a tiny black electronic device that somewhat resembled a pager.

"What's that?" Leah inquired curiously, pointing at the latter.

"That, my beautiful, efficient assistant, is a new prototype for what is popularly called a 'code breaker.' It is, in fact, the main item on our agenda this afternoon. Greyson assures me that it works, and he gave me a brief demonstration this morning to prove it." Greyson Phillips was one of the "techies" in MMI's research-and-development department. "But it hasn't yet been tested in the field, and as I was compelled to drive over here today to find out whether or not you were still among the living, I thought it might come in handy if I were forced to break down your front door and, in doing so, set off your alarm system, should you happen to have one installed."

"As a matter of fact, I do," Leah confirmed.

"Good. Then we'll shortly discover whether or not the boys and girls in R and D's back rooms are up to snuff. Where's the keypad to your system? In the foyer?"

"Yes."

"Come along, then."

Grabbing the small case and the electronic device, Hawk led the way. There, he surveyed the keypad mounted on the wall just inside her front door.

"Tsk, tsk." He eyed her askance. "From someone in my employ, I really expected better, Leah. This is hardly the most sophisticated of alarm systems. In fact, I'm afraid it won't prove much of a challenge at all to our little code breaker."

"Well, my house is scarcely Fort Knox, Hawk." Leah pointed out this fact somewhat dryly. "So all

I really require is basic protection from burglars and other intruders.''

"True. Still, we need to see what we can do about getting you a better system. I'm sure I don't have to tell you that crime is unfortunately all too rampant these days and no longer confined to just the city's mean streets, either. Besides which, government security agencies don't have a lock anymore on all the latest technological advances. Believe it or not, even plain old ignorant crooks can buy just about anything on the black market these days, while the more knowledgeable types can actually *build* it themselves. Hell. That's why Third World countries are constructing chemical-warfare plants and testing nuclear bombs. Not to mention the fact that we now live in a world in which even twelve-year-old whiz kids are capable of hacking their ways into some of the most sensitive computerized databases in existence.''

At that, Leah thanked God that her boss had his back turned to her. Otherwise, he would unquestionably have wondered at the guilty crimson flush that stained her cheeks hotly as she thought about having spent most of last night breaking into various computer systems.

No matter how she tried to tell herself that the end justified the means, Leah knew she had technically joined the ranks of the criminal element with her forays into the databases she had so illegally searched last night.

Having unzipped the black leather case he held—which proved to be a miniature tool kit—Hawk had removed a small Phillips head screwdriver. He was now employing it on the tiny screws that fastened the cover plate of her keypad in place. Freeing them at last, he laid the screws and the cover plate on the floor, along with the tool kit.

"Now we'll see whether or not Greyson knows his business," he announced, motioning for Leah to step closer to him so she could observe what he was doing. "I realize this isn't your own particular forte, my otherwise invaluable assistant. But a few lessons in this area won't come amiss, either. Activate your alarm system, and then watch closely."

Leah did as he had bidden her, punching her code in so the monitor light on the keypad switched from green to red.

From the electronic device Hawk had retrieved from the floor, he unwrapped two lead wires, which he showed her how to clip onto the now-exposed inner workings of her keypad. Then he pressed a button on the small black box, and instantly, a series of digital numbers began to appear on the lighted display panel, running at a high rate of speed that, to Leah, seemed incredibly fast.

Much to her dismay, although she had known that such things were indeed possible, within moments the code for her alarm system appeared on the display panel, and the monitor light changed from red to green.

"Not much of a test, I'll admit," Hawk commented. "But had I evil designs upon your house or person, your system would now be effectively disabled."

"I've seen things like that in the movies." Leah sighed heavily with distress at how easily her system had been overcome. "And, of course, I'm well aware that MMI's R-and-D department develops all kinds of equipment of this ilk. Still, actually seeing a piece of gear like this in action is something else again. What makes this particular code breaker different from all the others that must surely be in existence?"

"Its speed, for one thing, and its size, for another. Basically, the idea is not just to build a better mousetrap, but also to make it much faster and smaller than anything else on the market. Not that this device will be sold to the general public, of course, for obvious reasons. It would enable burglars and other intruders to bypass even the most sophisticated alarm systems."

"I assume that it works not only on alarm systems, however, but any kind of security device that requires an electronic code."

The wheels in Leah's mind churned furiously as she perceived the possibilities. Her boss had said that the elevator leading to the top floor of the Sand Castle's hotel wing needed both a key and a code to be rendered operational. If she had this code breaker, then all she would have to acquire was a key, and then she could find out whether or not her grandfather was indeed ensconced at the hotel.

Somehow, she would have to steal the code breaker.

That much was clear.

It was, however, highly unlikely that she would be able to make off with it from right beneath Hawk's handsomely chiseled, aquiline nose. And even if she *were* able to, he would know immediately that she had taken it, and that would never do. That meant she would have to filch it from MMI's R-and-D department itself.

To do that, she would, Leah realized with trepidation, have to get much closer to her boss than she had ever intended. Because somehow, she would have to obtain his own key, the one that gave him access to all areas of MMI's research-and-development department.

Twelve

Summer Wine

A Book of Verses underneath the Bough,
A Jug of Wine, a Loaf of Bread—and Thou
Beside me singing in the Wilderness—
Oh, Wilderness were Paradise enow!

The Rubáiyát of Omar Khayyám
—Edward FitzGerald

Hawk was attracted to her. He had made that plain.
And whereas Leah had previously considered this a
curse, she now saw it as a blessing instead, something that could be used to her advantage.

Still, he wasn't stupid. To the contrary, he was an
extremely intelligent and astute man. So he would
at the very least be intensely curious if, having protested all day that the last thing she wanted was an

affair with her boss, she now abruptly did an about-face where he was concerned. At worst, he might even grow suspicious of her motives, and that would never do.

She would have to proceed carefully, Leah told herself. Still, his arrogance would help her. She had never met a man yet who wasn't susceptible to having his male ego flattered and stroked, and Hawk was probably more accustomed to that than most, being so handsome, powerful, and financially well-off.

Having undoubtedly had more than his fair share of women, he would surely be expecting her to eventually succumb to his desire, no matter how she demurred.

And if that's what it took to accomplish her goal, well then, she would just have to do it, Leah resolved, conveniently thrusting to the back of her mind the fact that sleeping with her boss had never, until now, been a part of her plans. Still, it wasn't as though she were a virgin or physically repelled by Hawk.

Of course, if she could get his key without going to bed with him, then she would. But otherwise, the only method of obtaining it that she could think of was to lift it from his wallet while he lay deep in slumber, exhausted from an evening of hot, wild sex.

Or, possibly, she could drug him. Leah brightened

significantly at that thought. But then her spirits just as quickly sank again as it occurred to her that the inherent risk in that notion was the fact that she knew little or nothing about pharmaceuticals. What if she gave him a drink laced with sleeping pills and accidentally poisoned him—or, God forbid, even killed him—with an unintentional overdose?

Further, she knew absolutely nothing at all about Hawk's medical history. What if he were highly allergic to barbiturates or something? She didn't want to be arrested for murder.

Maybe she could ply him with alcohol until he passed out, Leah thought, continuing to speculate on the ways and means of temporarily incapacitating her boss. That would at least be worth a try. If it didn't work, if he proved to have a hard head for liquor, she could always fall back on her original idea of sleeping with him. Because no matter what, she dared not take the chance of mistakenly causing his death through her own ignorance of both drugs and his medical history, she reluctantly decided.

"Leah? Earth to Leah..." Hawk's amused voice finally penetrated her consciousness, jolting her from her reverie. "Where'd you go? The moon's not up yet."

"Sorry." She forced a rueful smile to her lips, hoping he wasn't able to guess her thoughts. "I guess I was just momentarily distracted by the extremely unpleasant idea of that tiny black box falling into the wrong hands. One likes to think one is safe in one's own home, you know. It was just... upsetting, I suppose, to realize how vulnerable I actually am here, despite the fact that I *have* taken all the right precautions—alarm system, dead bolts, thorny bushes under all my windows.... About the only thing I lack is a dog. But after much consideration, I decided that I really didn't have the necessary time to devote to a pet, to take care of it properly. So it simply wouldn't be fair of me to own one."

"Don't worry. Like I said before, we'll get you set up with a better alarm system. I promise you that," Hawk reassured her. "Now, shall we get down to business?"

Under ordinary circumstances, Leah would have been dismayed and resentful at the amount of work that Hawk expected them to accomplish before the day was out. But having overslept, and thereby effectively wasted his entire morning and half his afternoon, too, she was hardly in a position to complain.

Besides which, the longer he stayed at her house, the greater her opportunity would be to put her scheme to acquire his corporate key into action—regardless of how the idea continued to unnerve her.

In fact, as matters turned out, the two of them wound up laboring very late, pausing for a break only after eight o'clock, when they realized they hadn't yet eaten any supper. Hawk suggested that they send out for a pizza. But in keeping with the plan she had determined upon, Leah insisted on cooking instead.

"No, I won't hear of you ordering anything in," she declared firmly. "You've fed me twice already in the past two days. Now it's my turn. I've got all the fixings for an Italian salad and spaghetti and meatballs on hand, as well as a loaf of garlic bread, and it won't take me long to prepare if you can spare me from all this paperwork for about thirty minutes or so."

"I think I can manage that," Hawk replied, grinning. "To be honest, an Italian salad, spaghetti and meatballs, and garlic bread sounds a whole lot heartier and more appetizing to me than a fast-food pizza any day of the week."

"It will be, I promise you."

So Leah busied herself in the kitchen, while her boss continued to apply himself to all the file folders and other materials he had earlier dragged from his attaché case.

It occurred to Leah, as she cut up lettuce and boiled pasta, that there was a not wholly unwelcome domesticity to the scene, which both unsettled and yet, strangely enough, comforted her. She and Hawk might have been a typical married couple, with her playing the wifely role, readying supper in the kitchen, while her husband pored over work brought home from the office.

That image was only reinforced when, after a while, Hawk rose from the dining-room table to wander into the kitchen.

"Smells good," he observed as he lifted the lid of one of the pots on the stove and sniffed its contents appreciatively. "Such was the savory aroma emanating from the kitchen, in fact, that I was finding it difficult to concentrate. Is there anything I can do to be of assistance?"

"No." Leah shook her head. "Thanks, but I've got it all under control, except—"

"Except...what?" Hawk quirked one thick black eyebrow upward inquisitively.

"Nothing. Never mind. I *was* going to suggest that you could open a bottle of wine. But I don't know how much longer we'll be working, and I need to have a clear head for that." She laughed lightly, as though sharing a joke, knowing she was about to employ an age-old feminine wile he would be almost certain to take advantage of. "I drink so seldom that I'm afraid even just a couple of glasses of wine is more than I can safely handle. And having already blackened my slate by oversleeping this morning, I wouldn't want to do any further damage by also being drunk on the job!"

"I don't believe there's any danger of that. It *is* after hours, and the truth is that we've already got through everything of any real importance. In fact, *I* was going to suggest that we call it an evening and finish up the rest tomorrow morning—provided, of course, that *you* don't forget to set your alarm clock again tonight and oversleep once more! Or at least, if you do, I'd like to think it'll be because you have a much more...pleasant reason for doing so than utter exhaustion.'' He gave a soft, low, mocking laugh as he eyed her intently.

A blush stole up Leah's cheeks. There could be no mistaking his meaning. Still, tonight was not the time to tumble headlong into bed with him—if it came to that. No, she must wait until the new prototype of the code breaker was safely back in the research-and-development department, so Hawk wouldn't suspect that she was the one who had taken it.

"I really *do* wish you wouldn't persist in coming on to me," she told him, but took the sting from the words by smiling at him with feigned shyness and confusion. "You were right, you know, when you said earlier today that I'm attracted to you. I am. And I don't want to have to keep reminding myself that you're my boss."

"So...don't."

"I don't want to lose my job, Hawk."

"Would it help if I promise you that no matter what happens between us, you won't?"

"Probably. But still, how can I trust you? How

can I be sure that you'll keep your word, that you're not just saying that to get what you want from me?''

''I think you know me well enough by now to have a pretty good idea what kind of man I am. I don't have any reason to lie to you, Leah.''

''Unless it serves your purpose, of course.''

''Would it? Really? You know, somehow I don't think so. After all, it would be rather a sticky wicket for me if I didn't keep my promises and you decided to cry foul afterward. It's not as though you don't hold a position of some power and importance yourself at MMI. You're my personal assistant, and unlike some corporations, at MMI that title happens to mean that you're a great deal more than just a glorified secretary.''

''I know that. But still, I've only been employed at MMI for a matter of weeks—''

''Which have now added up to more than three months.'' Hawk pointed that fact out calmly.

''Yes, but even so, that's not a very long time at all, realistically speaking, and you know it!''

''Nevertheless, it's still long enough for you and me to have got to know each other fairly adequately, to realize we work extremely well together, and to acknowledge that we're highly attracted to each other. And there's no reason for that to change if we should decide to become intimate. We're both adults—and professionals, as well. I think we can handle it.''

"Maybe. But it's a big step...and one I'm still unsure about."

"Take your time. I can wait," Hawk asserted. Then he grinned at her insolently, both that and his next words letting her know he wasn't as patient as he pretended. "Now, where's that wine?"

Leah pointed her wine rack out to him, then turned her attention back to the stove, so he wouldn't guess how he had just played right into her hands. A surreptitious glance informed her that her boss had chosen a bottle of good Bordeaux, one that was fairly potent. Obviously, he hoped she would get, if not outright drunk, at least tipsy from the wine, since that was what she had deliberately— however falsely—led him to believe.

As every woman who had ever used alcohol as an excuse for her misbehavior knew, it was a rare man who failed to take advantage of a female who had drunk enough to no longer be thinking clearly or to put up much of a genuine resistance. Leah would not, in reality, be made even slightly light-headed by a few glasses of wine. But she fully intended to allow Hawk to gain that impression.

In that way, she would be able to satisfactorily account for how her defenses against him had apparently developed serious weaknesses, thus quelling his curiosity about her capitulation and allaying any suspicions he might otherwise have had.

The supper they ate together was as hearty and

appetizing as Leah had promised it would be, and she consumed more than her fair share of it, knowing how food in the stomach greatly slowed the absorption rate of alcohol. So, despite the fact that Hawk kept her wineglass assiduously filled to the brim, she actually drank less than he realized and was scarcely affected by the liquor.

The coffee she served with dessert—spumoni ice cream pulled from her freezer—helped, too, in keeping her relatively sober.

Afterward, it seemed the most natural thing in the world that they retire together to her living room, Hawk bringing along the wine bottle and glasses.

"Why don't we listen to some music?" he suggested.

"All right. What would you like to hear?"

"Something slow and mellow would be nice."

Leah hadn't intended to play anything other than that. Still, she laughed, fancying that she had struck just the right giddy, tinkling note. "Seduction music, is that it?"

"Yeah, something like that." Hawk's mouth curved into a sensual half smile.

"I'll say one thing for you," Leah announced as she moved to her stereo and began to program her CD player, knowing from memory what each of its three cartridges contained and thus able to make her selections without difficulty. "You don't give up easily."

"No, I don't. I learned early in life that Calvin Coolidge was right, that persistence and determination alone *are* omnipotent."

"Is that so?"

Her hips swaying with a deliberate but subtle sexiness, Leah went to sit beside her boss on her wonderfully comfortable, overstuffed sofa as the sweet strains of Bob James and David Sanborn's version of "You Don't Know Me" filled the air. The song was her private, ironic joke on Hawk—although he was blissfully unaware of it.

He didn't know her. He didn't know her at all.

The woman he *thought* he knew was Leah Tallcloud, his personal assistant in the research-and-development department at MMI. But in reality, she was Angelina Marlowe, the sole heiress to her grandfather's entire global enterprise and billion-dollar fortune.

Tonight, for the first time in her whole life, Leah abruptly and truly felt that.

The wine she had drunk at supper must have affected her more than she had believed, engendering within her a kind of Dutch courage. Because all of a sudden, she felt extraordinarily powerful, almost invincible. Capable of outwitting Hawk Bladehunter, regardless of how brilliant and clever he was. Capable of outwitting the entire cadre at MMI, in fact.

"Have some more to drink." From the now nearly empty wine bottle, Hawk refilled her glass.

"I think I've probably had more than enough already," she protested. "I *told* you I hardly ever drink and that I don't handle alcohol very well as a result. I feel a little dizzy, and I've got a bit of a headache coming on, too."

"Maybe I can help with that."

Reaching out, her boss gently drew her closer to him. But much to Leah's surprise, instead of attempting to take her into his arms, he shifted her on the sofa so her back was to him. Then he tugged the coated elastic band from the end of her long hair and, little by little, worked the French braid loose, spreading the black silky tresses across her shoulders.

Without warning, one of Hawk's hands slipped around to cover her face, blinding and momentarily panicking her before she realized he was intent only on removing her spectacles, not suffocating her into unconsciousness for some nefarious purpose of his own. He laid the tortoiseshell glasses on the coffee table.

"Close your eyes and relax." His voice in her ear was low and husky, his breath warm against her skin, raising the fine hairs on her nape and sending a tingle of excitement down her spine.

Somehow unable to resist, Leah did as Hawk instructed, involuntarily sighing with pleasure despite herself as his fingers began slowly to massage her temples.

This was not what she had expected or planned. She had thought to be the proverbial femme fatale, to have complete control over the situation, not to find it inexplicably sliding from her own grasp into that of her boss. But that was without a doubt what was happening.

"Hmm…" Had that soft, low moan of delight really issued from her own throat?

"Feels good, does it?" Hawk inquired, his lips brushing her hair.

Or had she only imagined that?

"It feels *heavenly*," she replied truthfully.

No, she had *not* just imagined the feather-light kiss, because now it was not only being repeated, but his mouth was continuing on down the strands of her hair to the incredibly sensitive place where her nape joined her shoulder. Softly, he pressed his lips to the highly responsive spot. His tongue stabbed her there delicately with its heat.

Instantly, Leah felt her nipples tighten and harden, straining against the thin cotton of her T-shirt. Another unwitting moan escaped from her throat.

To her mingled dismay and excitement, Hawk continued to kiss and nibble her shoulder, his tongue teasing her unbearably, making her shiver uncontrollably. As he did so, he slid his fingers slowly from her temples to caress her arms lingeringly before running his palms lightly across her breasts, leisurely circling the twin peaks taut and engorged beneath her T-shirt.

Then, finally, one hand cupped her chin, turning her face and tilting it up to his own.

His mouth descended on hers, touching lightly, gently at first, brushing her lips as tenderly as he had kissed her hair just moments ago. Once, twice, he kissed her, his tongue darting forth to trace the contours of her lips lingeringly before at last deliberately compelling them to part and insinuating itself inside.

Although she had intentionally set into motion the events that would bring about precisely this occurrence, she had nevertheless badly misjudged her own reactions to it, Leah thought ruefully in some dim corner of her mind. Having stoutly assured herself that submitting to Hawk's advances was only the necessary means to a vital end, she had believed she would have better control over her emotions. She had counted on that, in fact.

Quite wrongly, it appeared.

She had never expected her body's swift, leaping response to Hawk's kiss, the way in which her mouth yielded pliantly, as though it had a will all its own, to the enticing, exploratory invasion of his tongue. She had not counted on being unable to resist when his fingers slowly crept up to tangle themselves in her hair, silently urging her to shift her position subtly on the sofa. She was like wet clay in his hands, his to mold and shape as he pleased. She was hardly even aware of her compliance as she turned to face him fully, allowing herself to settle against the back of the couch, giving him free access to her body.

With a low groan, Hawk deepened the kiss, his mouth growing harder and hungrier as he devoured her, his tongue searching out every honeyed, secret crevice of the dark, moist cavern it plundered, which opened to him like an unfurling rose to reveal the nectar at its heart.

The taste of her was sweeter than the rich red wine the two of them had shared earlier. He wanted to drink of her just as fully, taking his time, savoring her. Over the years, he had had many women, but none of them had been like Leah—beauty combined with brains, reserve coupled with refinement.

She was, in truth, everything he had ever dreamed of in a woman. It was as though, somehow, that long-ago day at the corner grocery store at the crossroads, she had seared her image into his very soul as surely as the bright-burning sun had scorched the desert.

The thought came unbidden into his mind that he had searched for her forever, that in every woman's face he had looked for Leah's own.

And now he had found her.

He wanted her—and he meant to have her. It was as simple as that.

The fact that by becoming personally involved with her he would be breaking his own strict rule about not entering into a relationship with a female in his department, Hawk determinedly shoved from his brain. He had worked with her long enough, got to know her well enough by now to realize she was different from all the other women of his acquaintance.

Special.

Worth making an exception for.

He wrapped his arms around her, pulling her tightly into his embrace, groaning again as she whimpered involuntarily beneath his encroaching mouth and pressed her softness against him.

She was crazy, Leah thought blindly. She could not remember ever being kissed in quite this fashion before, with a passion and expertise designed to crumble all her carefully erected barriers, to scatter all her senses, so she could no longer think, but only feel.

Of their own volition, her arms swept up to lock around Hawk's neck. As his own had earlier, her fingers tunneled through his thick, gleaming black hair, clenching into fists as his tongue continued to assail her parted lips, teasing and twining with her own tongue. He swallowed her breath, along with the little, incoherent sounds of delight and desire that issued from her throat and seemed to inflame him, even as he enkindled her.

Like Leah's, Hawk's breath had begun to come harder now, labored rasps that mingled with her own quick, shallow gasps. With each unsteady, indrawn respiration, her breasts, now swollen and aching with passion, heaved alluringly against her pink T-shirt. She was agonizingly conscious of her rigid nipples, how they peaked against the thin material, a visible sign of her arousal.

Hawk was highly aware of them, too. As his mouth traveled ardently across her cheek to her temple, his hand glided down to cup one breast. His thumb rotated deliberately, erotically, across the stiff bud, causing Leah's breath to catch raggedly in her throat. Like ripples in a disturbed pool of molten ore, white-hot waves of pleasure radiated from the center of her breast to course through her body.

In response, deep in the hidden core of her womanhood, a savage, burning longing ignited, blazing up like a wildfire. Instinctively, she yearned for assuagement, and as though cognizant of her fierce need, Hawk trailed his hand sensuously down her belly to the juncture between her thighs. Boldly, he stroked her there, so the fabric of her leggings rubbed intimately against the soft, secret heart of her, stimulating her unendurably. A flood of wetness dampened her thighs, and the musky woman's fragrance of her filled the air, fusing with her sweet perfume.

It was the wine, Leah told herself.

It was only the wine that caused her to feel so headily intoxicated, so flushed and feverish that she felt as though her every muscle and nerve and sinew was an exposed live wire, writhing and sparking with electric current.

Her entire body seemed to be a mass of shockingly exquisite sensation, flaring and jolting at every demanding kiss, every inciting lick, every thrilling caress that Hawk pressed upon her. He had her T-shirt pushed up now. His breath was hot against her flesh as his mouth moved fervidly over her breasts, his tongue delving deep into the hollow between them.

Before Leah even realized what he intended, he unfastened her strapless bra with an adroit flick of his wrist, tugged it away, then tossed it aside. Released from their lacy restraint, her breasts sprang free, full and heavy, burgeoning with desire, their nipples puckered and roseate. His palm captured one breast, squeezing it possessively and pressing it high for his seeking lips.

They closed over its crest, sucking strongly and greedily.

Rather than as a clear thought forming in her mind, Leah sensed intuitively that, in moments, Hawk would be roughly divesting her of her clothes and urgently pushing her down onto the sofa to thrust himself hard and deep inside her.

She must not let that happen! She simply couldn't allow herself to become nothing more to him than a one-night stand. Otherwise, she would never get the code breaker, and then perhaps she would never learn the truth about her grandfather and MMI.

"Hawk...please stop...please..." Leah murmured, trying desperately to gather her wits, push him away, and pull down her T-shirt.

"Hmm. Are you quite sure?" Raising his head, he kissed her mouth again ardently, deeply, his hands caressing her intimately. "Are you?" His voice was low, hoarse with emotion.

"Yes... Yes, I'm sure...please...."

At first, she was half-afraid Hawk intended not to heed her dictates. His black eyes smoldered dangerously, hot and dark with passion as they raked her appraisingly, lingering on her bare breasts and setting her heart to pounding even more furiously.

Hurriedly, Leah yanked down her T-shirt. "I'm so sorry. I never meant for anything like this to happen." She cast her eyes down demurely, so he would not guess how she lied—although she had not intended for things to go as far as they had. "I—I told you I couldn't drink. I should never have had all that wine at supper. Please, Hawk. It's grown very late, and I think you should go now. We both have to work tomorrow, and I—I don't want to accidentally oversleep again. My boss might not like it,'' she said lightly, teasingly, to lessen the barb of her rejection.

With obvious reluctance, he slowly released her, giving her a crooked smile to show he understood. "Oh, I don't believe he'd be too angry if he were the cause of your lateness. But you're right. It *is* late, and tomorrow *is* a workday. But...how about this weekend? Are you free then, Leah? I'd like to take you out on a proper date if you'll let me."

She didn't know what to say to that. One more thing she hadn't expected. If this evening had been a baseball game, she would have struck out every time at bat! It was not like her to be so extraordinarily unperceptive.

Her initial instinct was to turn him down. But how could she? She needed him.

Or, rather, she needed the code breaker, Leah amended hastily.

Even now, despite everything, she didn't want to admit to herself how carried away she had been by Hawk's kisses and caresses, how strong her physical attraction to him had proved. So overwhelming, in fact, that she—who was normally so cool and composed—had momentarily lost all command of herself and her emotions.

She couldn't remember ever being so swiftly and powerfully aroused by a man, and she simply couldn't afford to be distracted from her primary purpose. But how would she ever manage to get the code breaker without Hawk's corporate key?

It seemed she was damned if she did and damned if she didn't, Leah thought ruefully. What was that old saying...something about he who rode the tiger not being able to dismount? Somehow, she had the uneasy feeling that continuing this particular relationship with her boss was going to amount to pretty much the same dilemma. After all, hadn't he reminded her of a tiger that first day in his office?

"Well, I can see that my invitation has left you speechless," Hawk observed casually. "I only wish I knew whether that's because it's filled you with such stunning delight—or just the opposite."

"It just...took me by surprise, that's all," Leah confessed truthfully. "I told you I—I just don't believe in becoming involved with men I work with, especially a man who's also my boss."

"I'm not just going to walk away and forget tonight ever happened, Leah. And what's more, if you're honest with yourself, I don't think you'll be able to, either. As I've said, the attraction's mutual and we both know it—particularly after tonight. So why don't you agree to go out with me? I promise I won't push you for anything more than you want to give. And no one at MMI need know we're developing a personal, as well as a professional, relationship, if that's how you want to play it."

"I must be out of my mind." Extremely conscious now of the fact that she was minus her bra, naked beneath her T-shirt, Leah crossed her arms over her breasts in a woman's age-old defensive gesture. Fervently, she wished there were some other solution to her problem than employing Hawk to gain her ends. But she couldn't see one. "All right. I'll go out with you."

"Great. How does Saturday night suit you? I just happen to have two tickets to one of the best shows in town."

"Fine. That sounds wonderful, in fact."

"Shall we say seven o'clock, then? That'll give us plenty of time to enjoy a leisurely supper together before the show starts. And then, afterward, maybe we'll try our luck at one of the casinos."

"I'll look forward to it."

"I hope you will, Leah." Hawk's voice had suddenly lost its bantering tone. His eyes, when he gazed at her, were serious, without guile as his hand cupped her chin and he kissed her briefly, tenderly, once more. "Well, I'd better be on my way."

After they had gathered up all the file folders and other materials still spread out on the dining-room table and packed them neatly away into Hawk's briefcase, Leah walked him to the front door.

"I'll see you tomorrow morning," she said.

"On time." He grinned to take the sting from the words.

"Yes, on time." Leah nodded, returning his

smile. "And, Hawk, thanks for being so understanding about my oversleeping today. I really *do* appreciate it more than you know."

"Just don't let it become a habit," he warned lightly.

"No, I won't."

For a moment she thought he was going to kiss her again. But instead, to her relief and perverse disappointment, he only bade her good-night. Then he strode down the sidewalk to the driveway, where his Thunderbird was parked. Leah stood in her doorway, watching him depart. Only after he had driven away did she shut the door, lock it, and switch off the porch light.

"Leah, you're a damned fool!" she chided herself sternly as she leaned drowsily against the closed door, replaying the day's events in her mind. "I don't care how you're attempting to justify starting up a personal relationship with Hawk Bladehunter. Because deep down inside, you know that the code breaker is just an excuse. You're falling head over heels for that man!

"No, I'm not...no, I'm not," she muttered defiantly in answer.

Ruefully, she bit her lower lip. Good God! She was talking to herself now, actually carrying on a two-sided conversation. Maybe, given the deadly game she had entered into at MMI and the severe strain she had been under since beginning work there, she really *had* gone off the deep end! Or perhaps the wine truly *had* affected her more than she had realized. As this last thought crossed Leah's mind, one hand stole irrepressibly to her mouth.

No, it hadn't been the wine, after all.

The exhilarating taste of Hawk still lingered.

Book Three

High Stakes

Whose games were empires
and whose stakes were thrones,
Whose table earth—
whose dice were human bones.

The Age of Bronze
—George Gordon, Lord Byron

Thirteen

At the Sand Castle

Lives of great men all remind us
We can make our lives sublime.
And, departing, leave behind us
Footprints on the sands of time.

A Psalm of Life
—Henry Wadsworth Longfellow

The Neon City, The Southwest, The Present

Leah's hands trembled with both fear and excitement as, with a sharp X-Acto knife, she sliced through the packing tape that bound the boxes that had just been deposited on her front doorstep by the United Parcel Service delivery truck.

The various labels on the packages informed her that they contained all the spy equipment she had ordered from the on-line spy stores. With ironic humor, she wondered if she could deduct and depreciate all of it on her income taxes, claiming it as a legitimate business expense. But somehow, she just didn't think the Internal Revenue Service would see it in the same light.

Uncle Sam had absolutely no sense of humor.

One by one, she opened all the boxes, removing the gear. Not knowing what she might need, Leah had ordered a wide variety of items, including a small video camera, an audio amplifier, a miniature tape recorder, a pair of night-vision binoculars, and a black leather attaché case with a cleverly concealed false bottom.

This last would certainly come in handy, she thought now, when she took the code breaker from MMI. Not that she was actually going to *steal* it, precisely. In reality, she was only going to borrow it. If all went well, she would return it immediately after using it on one of the two private elevators that led to the top floor of the Sand Castle's hotel wing.

Of course, she still hadn't figured out how to acquire whatever key was also necessary to operate the elevators. But she would cross that bridge when she came to it, Leah had decided.

One thing at a time.

What was important at the moment was to spend

a week or more at the hotel, surveying the top floor where Merritt Marlowe might—or might not—be located, if he were even still alive, and determining who, if anyone, was accessing those private elevators.

Once Leah determined this last, then she would at least know who possessed keys to run them. After that, she would try to come up with some kind of a plan to get her hands on a key. That was, if anything, going to prove much more difficult than filching the code breaker.

Despite the fact that no one was there to see her, she still flushed guiltily at the thought of how she intended to use Hawk. It was wrong. Deep down inside, she knew that. What made it even worse was the realization that no matter how hard she had fought against it, and continued to do so, she had developed strong feelings for him.

He had taken her out more than once the past few weeks, and despite herself, Leah had enjoyed herself immensely. If she didn't have her perilous goal at MMI hanging over her head, she would, she recognized, be growing serious about her boss. Even knowing she could not let that happen, she nevertheless found herself fantasizing and dreaming about him endlessly, imagining being free to love him, even to marry him.

"Face it, Leah," she lectured herself. "You don't want Hawk to be the enemy, and you don't want to betray him, either, by lifting his corporate key in order to steal the code breaker. But what other choice do you have? It's just too dangerous for you to reveal your true identity to him, and you have to learn whether or not your grandfather is still alive.''

She sighed heavily. In the end, everything always came back to this last. If Merritt Marlowe *was* alive and being held prisoner on the top floor of the Sand Castle's hotel wing, it was her duty to rescue him and expose what had befallen him.

But this, Leah thought, would be the easiest task of all, requiring nothing more than that she get her grandfather down one of the elevators, out of the hotel, and into her car, which she would have waiting for them in the Sand Castle's parking garage. Then all she would have to do would be to drive straight to the police station, where she and her grandfather would tell their story to the authorities.

After much reflection, Leah had decided it would be necessary for her to simultaneously alert the media. That way, the consortium of men she was after wouldn't somehow be able to hush everything up, as they had managed to do now for more than thirty years.

She gazed at all the spy equipment strewn around her on the floor, amid the empty boxes and discarded packing material. There was no excuse now for not proceeding with her plan. While it might leave a lot to be desired—and indeed, Leah feared that it did—it was still all she had, and better than nothing.

First thing Monday morning, she would start calling remodeling contractors and arranging to get estimates on the cost of renovating her house. Then, once that job was under way, she would move into the Sand Castle.

"Will you be staying with us long here at the Sand Castle, Ms. Tallcloud?" the efficient young man at the reservations desk asked politely.

"At least a week...and possibly even two or more. I don't know. I'm having some remodeling done on my house, and I'm not quite certain how long things are going to be torn up to the point where it's not really practical for me to be in residence," Leah explained, using her carefully rehearsed story.

Not that it was necessary for the desk clerk to be informed of her plans, of course. But still, she wanted to establish her credentials, just in case the hotel manager should decide to check, since she *was* an employee of MMI.

"You asked for a suite on the top floor, I believe?"

"Yes, something overlooking the courtyard, please."

Taking a deep breath, Leah forced herself to count to ten to quell her rising anxiety. If she weren't assigned a room with a courtyard view, she wouldn't be able to survey the top floor of the hotel wing, which was where her grandfather would most likely be, if he were anywhere on the premises. And then all her costly machinations to get herself installed in the Sand Castle in the first place would be a complete waste of time and money!

"Ah, yes, here we are...the Painted Desert Suite—one of our best. I guess it pays to have connections in the right places at MMI," the desk clerk announced.

"I do work for MMI, yes," Leah confirmed slowly, puzzled. "But I've already explained to my boss about staying here because of the renovation being done on my house—"

"Please forgive me, Ms. Tallcloud," the young man apologized, reddening. "I didn't make myself clear, and so you misunderstood. I wasn't insinuating that there was any breaking of MMI's rules involved in your being here. To the contrary, in fact. I have a note here from the hotel's manager, attached to your reservation. It seems that your boss, Mr. Bladehunter, has already called ahead to explain your situation and specifically requested that you be given the Painted Desert Suite."

"Oh. Well, that was very kind and considerate of him."

Leah could not help but be touched by the gesture. Despite the elaborate scheme she had concocted to account for her presence at the hotel, she had still worried that a discreet telephone call might be placed about her to the higher-ups at MMI, resulting in a sticky situation for her at the very best and the loss of her job at the very worst.

But Hawk had effectively circumvented any such unpleasantness for her—which made her feel even guiltier where he was concerned. Despite her several more dates with him during the passing weeks, she had yet to spend the night with him. Still, Leah knew that, realistically speaking, it was only a matter of time before she would succumb.

She could not keep holding him at bay. Sooner or later, he was inevitably bound to insist on their sleeping together. He might even issue an ultimatum in that regard. Despite how he had managed to contain, if not wholly conceal, his growing frustration and impatience about not sharing her bed, Leah felt reasonably certain that the day of reckoning would come sooner rather than later.

After placing her electronic room key in an envelope, the desk clerk pounded vigorously on the bell that sat on the reservations desk and was used to summon the bellhops.

"Have an enjoyable stay here at the Sand Castle, Ms. Tallcloud," he said.

"Thank you. I'm sure I will." Actually, Leah was certain of exactly the opposite. But of course, she didn't voice that thought aloud.

A bellboy appeared and began to load her luggage onto the wheeled garment rack cum baggage carrier that he trailed in his wake.

"Ms. Tallcloud is in the Painted Desert Suite, Eddie," the desk clerk informed him.

"Right." The bellhop nodded. "If you'll follow me, please...it's this way, ma'am."

After an elevator ride that had her feeling as though her stomach had somehow been left behind on the first floor, and a short walk down a winding corridor, Leah was comfortably installed in the suite.

There, a huge bouquet of English-garden flowers was waiting for her on a table in the sitting room. On the small, accompanying white card, written in what she recognized as Hawk's own bold scrawl, was his first name, nothing more.

Not that she had expected him to write "With love," Leah assured herself hastily. Still, it would have been nice if there had been some message....

Good Lord! What was she thinking of? She didn't want any love notes from Hawk. She didn't even want any flowers from him. It was bad enough that she had been compelled to become involved with him in the first place. Going out with him, attempting to hold him at arm's length and keep a tight rein on her own desires and emotions at the same time was wreaking havoc on her nerves.

The more Leah saw of him, the more strongly attracted to him she seemed to grow, and the harder it was for her to remember that no matter how much she hoped otherwise, Hawk might be her mortal enemy.

What she was going to do if he turned out to be one of the men making use of the Sand Castle's private elevators to the hotel wing's top floor, she didn't know. Just the thought filled her with dismay—proof enough, if she needed any, of how far gone she was where her boss was concerned.

Tucking the card back into its envelope, Leah replaced it on the plastic holder carefully arranged amid the fragrant flowers in their crystal vase.

She didn't have time to stand around like some silly, moonstruck schoolgirl, daydreaming about Hawk. As the saying went, she had things to do and places to go.

From the sitting room of the suite, she made her way to the adjoining bedroom, where the bellboy had put her luggage. After hefting two of the three matching bags up onto the bed, she unlocked and opened them, beginning to remove her clothes. Leah loathed living out of a suitcase, and since she was going to be at the Sand Castle for at least a week or more, she wanted to be comfortable.

She hung her workaday and dress garments in the closet, where, on the shelf over the hanger bar, she also neatly stashed her purses and shoes. Her casual clothes and lingerie she folded into the drawers of the ornate dresser that stood against one wall.

The third bag contained all the spy equipment Leah had bought, and she didn't dare unpack this. Not only did she not want any of the maids to see the gear and wonder what she was doing with it, there was also the possibility that one of them might steal it.

The equipment was worth quite a bit of money, and it was just the sort of thing that was easily fenced or sold, regardless of whether or not it was "hot."

Laying the suitcase on its side, Leah shoved it onto the floor of the closet. Then she placed the other two bags on top of it. That ought to deter all but the most brazen of thieves, she thought, for getting to the suitcase that contained the spy gear would entail time—the one thing hotel thieves usually lacked.

Asking to have the bag locked up in the Sand Castle's luggage room was out of the question. She wanted to attract as little attention to herself as possible, and constantly requesting access to her suitcase was not the way to accomplish that goal.

Firmly, Leah shut the closet doors. Then, feeling like a fool but knowing she could not leave anything to chance, she plucked a single strand of black hair from her head. Licking it to moisten it, she pressed it across the seam between the closet's louvred doors, just the way she had seen done more than once in various spy movies.

Now, should anyone open the closet, she would know about it—or so Leah hoped. Who knew whether or not such a trick actually worked in real life? Or what she should do about it in the event that she discovered someone *had* tampered with her closet in her absence?

She glanced around the bedroom to be certain she had not left any of her possessions out in plain sight. Then, satisfied that there was nothing that revealed anything about her or her mission at the hotel, Leah grabbed her purse and the electronic key to her suite, tucking the latter into the pocket of her cotton trousers.

It was time for her first foray around the Sand Castle.

As an additional security measure, she turned on the television set in the bedroom, leaving the door slightly ajar so the sound would filter into the sitting room, as well, making passersby believe there was someone in the suite. When she exited from the sitting room, she placed the suite's Do Not Disturb placard on the handle of the door.

It was highly unlikely that the maids would be making their rounds this early in the day to turn down beds and leave chocolates on pillows, but Leah didn't want to take any chances.

Slinging the leather strap of her purse over one shoulder, she strode down the corridor to the bank of elevators that would take her back to the lobby.

Once there, she headed toward the indoor boulevard housed on the first floor of the hotel wing.

It was Saturday afternoon, so there ought to be especially heavy crowds of traffic to conceal her movements...gamblers looking to spend their winnings, hotel guests milling around the courtyard and swimming in the pools, people eating late lunches or having early drinks in the restaurants, women having their hair or nails done in the salons, shoppers in search of bargains in the stores, and tourists out sightseeing.

Leah hoped she didn't run into anybody she knew. But if she did, well, she was just one more person looking to run up her charge card. That was scarcely liable to raise anyone's suspicions. After all, it wasn't as though the two boulevards housed in the MMI complex weren't just as popular with the locals as they were with out-of-towners.

Still, although it seemed wholly improbable, just in case she were being watched, Leah took her time, moving along casually. Now and then, she paused to window-shop and even to go inside more than one store to examine the various wares offered.

What Leah was really in search of, however, were the two private elevators alleged to lead to the top floor of the hotel wing.

Common sense dictated that she was not apt to find them here, where they would be exposed to the crowds of people who frequented the boulevards.

Nevertheless, she had to make sure. For all she knew, they could be concealed somewhere in the concrete corridors by which means deliveries were made to all the establishments in the boulevards.

Once she had finished a complete promenade of the first floor, Leah stood uncertainly for a moment, glancing at her wristwatch. It had taken her three hours to explore the boulevard from one end to the other—and that was just the first level. She hadn't even made it to the concrete corridors yet. Nor had she taken the glass escalator up to the mezzanine level, where more restaurants and shops were located.

She sighed heavily. As much as she would have liked to carry on with her investigation, the time grew late. It was now past four o'clock, and she had a date with Hawk tonight, for which she must get ready. She would have to continue her sleuthing tomorrow, she reluctantly decided. Otherwise, she would not be on time when her boss showed up for their evening together.

After returning to her suite, Leah performed a careful check of her closet. Much to her relief, the strand of black hair she had placed on the louvred doors was still there, apparently undisturbed.

She hadn't realized just how on edge her nerves were until she abruptly laughed out loud, wondering crazily if she would go bald before checking out of the Sand Castle.

"Get a grip, Leah!" she muttered sternly to herself. "Even if you're obviously *not* cut out for this, you can't afford to lose your nerve and fall apart! Otherwise, you'll never learn the truth about your grandfather and MMI."

She knew that—didn't need to be reminded of it, in fact. Still, she couldn't help wishing that the dangerous burden of exposing the consortium hadn't fallen squarely on her shoulders.

But there was no one else.

Her parents were getting on in years, and even if they hadn't been, it was possible that one or all of the men who were part of the unscrupulous cadre had long memories. They might remember the Tallclouds and the fact that Jim and Faith had once worked for Roland and Natalie Marlowe.

Leah knew there was even a slight risk to herself, using the last name Tallcloud at MMI. But after much discussion, she and her parents had decided that was still the best course of action. It would look even more suspicious if she got hired on at MMI under a false name and someone inadvertently discovered that fact.

Tallcloud was a common enough Native American surname in this region, and there was nothing on her employment application to connect her to Jim and Faith. So if anyone should dig deeply enough to learn who her parents were, it would be more than likely that she had somehow already aroused suspicions at MMI, anyway, Leah had reasoned.

Flicking on the light in the bathroom, she started water running in the bathtub. A basket of complimentary toiletries sitting on the counter yielded a small plastic bottle of bubble-bath oil, which she poured into the bathwater. There were also containers of shampoo and conditioner, and even a disposable razor and shaving gel.

The Sand Castle, it appeared, had thought of everything its guests might require in the bathroom. But then, of course, the hotel could afford to be generous. Millions of dollars a year were gushing into its coffers—and not just from its suites and rooms, but also from the casino.

This latter was where Hawk was taking her tonight, having learned a few days ago that Leah had yet to see it.

"I'm afraid I've just never been one for gambling," she had confessed to him with a rueful laugh, her thick, sooty lashes sweeping down to veil her turquoise eyes, so he wouldn't guess that she had, in fact, embarked on a game of stakes far higher than any played in the casino.

"Nevertheless, a little flutter at cards, a few throws of the dice, and a couple of pulls on a slot-machine handle aren't going to kill you, Leah," he had insisted.

And because she had thought it would behoove

her to scrutinize this aspect of MMI's holdings, as
well, she had not protested. A lone woman in a casino was a target for drunks and high rollers looking
to get laid—and she didn't need that kind of hassle
on top of everything else.

It would have to be a very inebriated or brazen
man indeed who would accost her while she was in
Hawk's company. His six feet three inches of lithe
but powerful muscle were enough to give anybody
pause, not to mention his authoritative, predatory de-
meanor and his silent, tigerish way of moving, as
though capable at any moment of springing on an
opponent and rending him limb from limb.

Despite the heat of the bathwater she had now
settled into, Leah shivered at the image involuntarily
evoked in her mind. If she succeeded in stealing the
code breaker and her boss not only found out she
was the culprit who had taken it, but also how she
had managed its theft, there was no telling what he
might do to her.

Especially if he were one of the enemy.

In the latter case, the possibility existed that Hawk
would kill her. She would be the world's biggest
fool not to acknowledge that fact, not to be prepared
for it, Leah thought as she lathered herself generously with the sweet-scented soap.

After all, he had not hesitated to draw a knife in
response to Skeeter Greywolf's producing a like
weapon that day so many years ago in the parking

lot of the grocery store at the crossroads. It wasn't logical, then, to assume that her boss would be capable of any less. He was older now and, if anything, a good deal harder and more experienced than he had been that long-ago day when she had first seen him.

Perhaps he would slit her throat without so much as batting an eyelash.

Fourteen

The Casino

Urge no healths;
Profane no divine ordinances;
Touch no state matters;
Reveal no secrets;
Pick no quarrels;
Make no comparisons;
Maintain no ill opinions;
Keep no bad company;
Encourage no vice;
Make no long meals;
Repeat no grievances;
Lay no wagers.

> *The Twelve Good Rules*
> —ascribed to Charles I

Leah and Hawk had eaten supper in the casino's theater, and watched the first performance that evening of a popular stand-up comedian who had warmed up the audience for an even more famous singer.

Now, she and her boss strolled through the huge casino, which was filled to bursting with crowds of people who tried their luck twenty-four hours a day in the city that never slept. Everyone from tourists on dream vacations to professional gamblers met and mingled, all with one single aim in mind—to win a fortune at the Sand Castle.

The noise was deafening. The air reverberated with loud talk, raucous laughter, the ceaseless whirring and ringing of slot and video poker machines, and the piped-in music whose driving beat subtly, psychologically, encouraged bettors to crank the handles of the one-armed bandits as hard and as fast as possible.

"It's like something out of *Alice Through the Looking-Glass*," Leah observed, astonished as her gaze took in her surroundings. "Unreal…a world gone mad."

Hawk laughed. "Yeah, well, gambling fever has a way of doing that to people. You'll notice there are no clocks on the walls, and no windows, either. Nothing to let anyone present know what time it is, or even whether it's day or night. People who really get hooked in places like this can spend hours, even days gambling. I've seen fortunes won and lost here in a matter of seconds…addicts and high rollers on a lucky streak finally cleaned out.''

"I just can't believe it." Leah shook her head, joining in his laughter. "I've never seen anything like it before—except in the movies, of course. The few casinos that I ever stepped foot in before tonight were nothing like this…I guess because they were much smaller and had very low betting limits.''

"Well, here at the Sand Castle, one can play for quite high stakes. That's part of the attraction," Hawk explained. "So, Leah, what would you like to try first? The slot machines, video poker, blackjack, baccarat, keno, craps, roulette? The list is practically endless, and the Sand Castle offers it all.''

"I don't know. Believe it or not, I've never even so much as stuck a quarter into a one-armed bandit. I have no idea why. I've just never been terribly tempted, I guess. It's like buying a lottery ticket. I've never done that, either. The odds of winning have simply always seemed so astronomical, I suppose, that I've inevitably figured you might as well set fire to your money since it's all going to go up in smoke, anyway.''

"You're sadly missing the point, Leah." Hawk glanced down at her with unconcealed amusement, his black eyes dancing devilishly. "Yes, deep down inside I expect that, just like you, most people feel certain they are going to lose their money. After all, none of the odds are in their favor. Otherwise, casinos would go broke in short order. Still, there's always that one-in-a-million chance that one will get lucky. But one can't take advantage of that unless one puts a quarter in a slot machine or buys that lottery ticket.''

"I guess not," Leah conceded ruefully.

"So...what's your pleasure?''

"Oh, the one-armed bandits, I suppose. They look easy enough to master. I mean, all you have to do is shove a token in the slot and pull the handle, right?''

"Right. Come on, then. The first thing we've got to do is get some tokens and chips.''

Hawk took her hand in his, leading the way to one of the several booths scattered throughout the casino where money could be traded in for tokens and chips. Presently, Leah found herself in possession of two plastic cups filled nearly to overflowing with tokens, while Hawk sported a tray stacked with chips.

Carrying their bounty, the two of them then meandered through the casino in search of a bank of slot machines that were not currently being employed. At last they managed to find a one-armed bandit not in use, and Leah's boss instructed her to grab its seat quickly.

Obediently, she sat down on the vinyl stool, placing her cups in the convenient holders for that purpose.

"Well, have at it," Hawk urged, grinning broadly at her hesitation. "I promise I'm not going to kill you if you lose all my money."

It was all Leah could do not to shudder at his choice of words, and she devoutly wished he had chosen some other means of expressing his sentiments.

"Are you quite certain?" she inquired lightly, forcing herself to smile up at him brightly. "After all, I haven't worked side by side with you these past months without becoming aware of the fact that you have something of a wicked temper. So...how do I know you're not going to unleash it on me should I inadvertently cause you to go broke in here?"

"Oh, I don't think there's much chance of that. I'm hardly a pauper, you know. Besides which, I assure you I never bet more than I know I can comfortably afford to lose. So you can consider yourself safe from my 'wicked temper,' as you called it. I swear I won't even scalp you if you wind up not winning at a single game all night."

"Okay, then. Here goes."

Despite herself, Leah could scarcely repress her excitement as she dropped a token into the one-armed bandit's wide slot and yanked the handle down to set the cylinders in motion. Practically everything these days was computerized, and the slot machines at the Sand Castle were no exception. Still, they simulated the sounds of the old-fashioned one-armed bandits, and her pulse raced as the cylinders whirled, chirring and then clanking to a halt.

Much to Leah's surprise and delight, she had struck a winning combination and a shower of tokens clattered from the slot machine into its winnings tray.

"I won!" she crowed, laughing. "I can't believe it! I actually won!"

"Beginner's luck," Hawk declared, laughing with her. "So don't get too cocky. The night is young yet. We've only just got started."

As the evening wore on, Leah couldn't remember when she had last had such a good time. No matter how she tried to keep a close check on her emotions, to remind herself that the odds always favored the house, she was still bitten by the gambling bug. With increasing eagerness, she tried her hand at everything Hawk suggested. He patiently explained to her the rules of each game, almost all of which she had been only vaguely familiar with before tonight.

Once she and Hawk finally abandoned the one-armed bandit, they played several rounds of video poker. From there, they moved on to blackjack and then to the baccarat tables. When Leah threw a set of snake eyes at the craps tables, Hawk took her place, insisting she blow on the dice for him as he took a turn at rattling the bones.

"But I was terrible at this game," she protested, shaking her head.

"Nevertheless, tradition dictates that a man's luck at craps is always improved by having a gorgeous woman blow on the dice for him."

So Leah did as he requested, and whether due to that or merely to chance, Lady Luck smiled on Hawk and he enjoyed quite a winning streak before finally gathering up his chips and stacking them neatly on his tray.

"The number-one rule of gambling," he informed her, "particularly when you're playing for high stakes, is always to quit while you're ahead. Otherwise, you're inevitably bound to lose your shirt sooner or later. Now, on to the roulette wheel."

Leah was having such a good time, and by now had drunk so many more Tom Collinses than she realized, that it was several long minutes before she observed that she and Hawk were not the only MMI employees gathered at the one of the tables boasting a roulette wheel.

For a moment, taken completely by surprise, she could only stare at the tall, distinguished, silver-haired man standing directly across the wide expanse of green felt from her. At the sight of him, she felt the fine hairs on her nape involuntarily prickle and her spine tingle icily. She had never before actually seen him in the flesh.

But still, she recognized the man immediately.

Over the years, his handsome picture had gazed out at her from the slick, sophisticated pages of countless MMI annual reports and well-known business magazines. His name had tortured her endlessly whenever she had riffled through the contents of Roland Marlowe's black leather attaché case, for one of the things her birth father had written down in his journal was a list of those movers and shakers at MMI whom he had considered prime suspects in the secret coup that he had believed had cost Merritt Marlowe his empire and possibly his life.

Winston Pryce was one of the names on that short list.

In Roland Marlowe's day, Pryce had been one of the undisputed golden boys at MMI, an extremely ambitious, up-and-coming young executive with friends and mentors in high places.

Today he sat on the board of directors as the powerful president of MMI.

Handsome, rich, and exceedingly influential, Pryce wielded an authority that stretched around the world. One had only to look at him to know he was a person of significant wealth and importance.

He was dressed in an elegantly tailored suit that Leah guessed had cost at least a couple of thousand dollars, if not more, and his tie was by one of the top designers. His well-manicured fingers sported more than one diamond-and-gold ring. An expensive Rolex watch encased his left wrist. She couldn't see his feet, but she was willing to bet her last Sand Castle chip that he was wearing handmade Italian shoes.

Although Pryce was a married man, his wife was nowhere in evidence. Instead, he was surrounded by a bevy of revealingly clad young women—cocktail waitresses and showgirls, mostly, from the looks of them—all vying for his attention. Amid the females were also a number of businessmen, all of whom treated Pryce with obvious deference.

Nor was the casino staff slow to respond to his slightest gesture. He had only to wave a hand and his every wish was catered to instantly. Hand-rolled cigars and Scotch on the rocks flowed as freely as the chips he stacked on the green felt of the roulette table whenever it was time to place bets.

Instinctively, Leah loathed him on sight.

She told herself that the feeling was irrational, born of Roland Marlowe's suspicions and perhaps even his jealousy of a supreme rival at MMI. After all, her biological father had been only twenty-five years old at the time of his death, and thus, no doubt subject to all the failings of youth, including the competitiveness that men seemed never to outgrow.

It was therefore foolish to make a snap judgment about Pryce.

But no matter how attractive he was, how jovial and charming he appeared, Leah couldn't help noticing that his smile never quite reached his gray eyes, which glittered like steel and were just as hard.

Of course, a man didn't reach Pryce's pinnacle in life by being a softy. But as she studied him covertly, it seemed to her that his good-natured bantering with those who flocked around him actually bore a cruel, cutting edge. And he commiserated rather a shade too heartily for her liking with the others' losses, as though taking secret delight in their bad luck.

After some minutes, as though finally sensing her gaze upon him, Pryce suddenly looked straight at her. For what seemed to Leah like an eternity, but which was in reality no more than seconds, their eyes met and locked.

Without warning, she had the hideously chilling impression that she was staring into the cold, pitiless eyes of death.

A violent, involuntary shudder racked her body. She had a horrible, desperate urge to tear her glance away. But despite that overwhelming longing, she couldn't seem to make herself comply with the frantic prompting of her brain. It was as though she were frozen where she stood, mesmerized by Pryce's sharp, penetrating gaze.

At last, in response to some comment directed at him by one of his entourage, he looked away, and the strange, inexplicable spell he had cast upon her was broken.

"Leah, are you all right?" Hawk asked, jolting her from her musings.

"Yes," she managed to get out, forcing herself to gather her wits and summon her tongue. "Just suddenly terribly tired and overcome by a bit of a headache, I'm afraid. A combination of too much excitement, too much to drink, and too much noise, I expect. Would you mind if we called it a night now, Hawk?"

"No, not at all," he said politely after a moment, beginning to collect his winnings, adding the chips to the large pile already stacked upon his tray. "I'd say that we've had more than our fair share of luck tonight, anyway. No sense in pushing it."

They turned from the roulette table—only to be confronted by Winston Pryce.

Unwittingly, Leah gasped, horrified, and swayed unsteadily on her feet, nearly bumping into him. As swiftly as a snake striking, his hand shot out, grabbing hold of her arm to brace her.

"My apologies." He smiled at her disarmingly. "I didn't mean to startle you."

Yet, somehow, Leah had the distinct, uneasy feeling that he *had* intended to do just that. His hand seemed to burn like a hot iron against her skin, making her yearn fiercely to wrench away from him. But his grip was too staunch, as though he sensed her desire and was taking a perverse delight in thwarting it.

"Hawk, how are you?" Releasing her at last, Pryce extended his hand to the younger man. "Or need I ask? From the looks of this beautiful woman you're with and that mile-high stack of chips weighing you down, it would appear that you're doing just fine."

"I can't complain, and that's a fact." Securing the tray against one hip, Hawk shook the older man's hand. "Winston, I don't believe you've had the pleasure of meeting my new personal assistant in the R-and-D department. Leah, allow me to present Winston Pryce, the president of MMI. Winston, this is Leah Tallcloud, one of MMI's best and brightest."

Leah wanted nothing more than to run pell-mell from the roulette table. Her mouth had suddenly gone so dry that it tasted like stale bread, and her heart was hammering so loudly that she could hear it in her ears. Her palms were perspiring profusely. Surreptitiously, she wiped them along the sides of her dress before forcing herself to courteously offer Pryce her hand.

To her horror, instead of shaking it firmly as she had expected, he raised it to his lips in the gallant manner of an old-fashioned gentleman, and kissed it. Leah's skin crawled with revulsion at the gesture, making her feel sick to her stomach, as though she were going to throw up.

Fervently, she wished she hadn't had so much to

drink this evening. Maybe then she wouldn't be feeling so nauseated now.

With difficulty, she choked down the bile that rose in her throat, compelling herself to smile at the man whom she suspected of being, if not the ringleader at the time, at least one of the participants in the murder of her birth parents.

"It's a pleasure to meet you, my dear." Still retaining his hold on her hand, Pryce patted it in what she knew he perceived as a dapper, congenial, and even fatherly fashion. "I always enjoy getting to know our employees at MMI—especially when they're as pretty as you. I hope you don't mind my saying so, Ms. Tallcloud, but you've got just about the most beautiful eyes I've ever seen. They're quite unusual in color...very striking, that remarkable shade of turquoise."

It was the kind of flattering comment any man might have made upon meeting her for the very first time. But somehow, as she stared again as though hypnotized into Pryce's own narrowed, steely gray eyes, Leah knew instinctively that he was seeing not her, but Natalie Marlowe.

Fifteen

Dreams

Now o'er the one half-world
Nature seems dead;
And wicked dreams abuse
The curtained sleep.

> *Macbeth*
> —William Shakespeare

Leah never knew how she managed to get through that incredibly panicky meeting with Winston Pryce.

She could not remember ever having been so frightened in her entire life. Not even that long-ago day at the corner grocery store at the crossroads, or later, when a drunken Skeeter Greywolf had run her parents' truck off the road.

"Leah, are you quite certain you're all right?"

Hawk inquired as he handed her the electronic key to her suite with which he had opened the door. "You're as white as a ghost."

"I'm sorry," she murmured, trying but failing to regain her composure. "I'm afraid my head has really started to pound something fierce, and it's making me feel horribly queasy. Thank you so much for the flowers and for the evening, Hawk. I had a wonderful time. But now, if you'll excuse me, I think I'd better call it a night."

"You surely can't imagine I'm going to leave you alone here until I know you're all right. For all we know, you could have a case of food poisoning or something. Maybe I should phone downstairs to the front desk and request to have the hotel doctor sent up."

"No, no, that isn't necessary, I assure you. Really. I've told you before that I don't handle alcohol well. It's given me a migraine that's upset my tummy, that's all," Leah lied, because while she actually *did* have a splitting headache and a sick stomach, the liquor she had drunk wasn't the cause of either.

"I'll tell you what. Why don't you go on into the bedroom and get ready for bed?" Hawk suggested, a frown of concern still knitting his brow. "In the meanwhile, I'll look around the suite, see what I can find in the way of aspirin or sodium bicarbonate, since you don't want a doctor."

"There's no need for that—" Leah began to protest, only to be firmly cut off.

"Maybe not, but still, I'm afraid I have to insist. You ate that filet mignon medium rare, and you had shrimp scampi with it, besides. Either one might have been tainted, and these days, with all the E. coli and salmonella contaminating our foods, it just isn't safe to take chances. People have died from eating undercooked meat and polluted seafood, Leah."

Hawk's dark visage now bore upon it the implacable expression that she recognized from experience meant he would brook no argument. She knew it was useless to object further.

Besides, it wasn't as though he intended anything of an amorous nature. He wasn't the kind of depraved male to press his advances on an obviously ill woman—or at least, she sincerely hoped he wasn't.

"All right. Just give me a few minutes. Please?"

"Take all the time you need. Like I said, I'm not going anywhere until I know there's nothing seriously wrong with you."

In the bathroom, Leah gratefully unpinned her hair from its usual classic and sophisticated French twist. She rubbed her throbbing right temple tiredly. Now that she was no longer face-to-face with Winston Pryce, she had begun again to be assailed by doubts.

What if she *was* letting her fears and her vivid imagination run away with her, thinking the president of MMI had associated her with Natalie Marlowe and, as a result, now suspected her true identity? After all, even though turquoise eyes weren't particularly common, there were a lot of women who boasted them nowadays, thanks to all the colored contact lenses on the market designed to alter the shade of eyes completely.

She should have got some of those herself, Leah thought glumly, ones that would have made her eyes appear to be dark brown instead of turquoise. But without her tortoiseshell spectacles, she had worried that her resemblance to both her birth parents would have been all the more pronounced. Besides, people would have been curious if she'd worn both contact lenses *and* glasses.

After diligently brushing her teeth, she debated removing her makeup, too, as was her usual practice. But vanity prevented her from letting Hawk see her without it again. Like many beautiful women, Leah was secretly highly insecure when it came to her looks, and she didn't want her boss to see her as anything other than gorgeous and eminently desirable.

Stripping off the sexy, short red dress she had worn that evening, she hung it up carefully in the closet. Then she donned her nightgown and robe, tying the sash of the latter firmly about her waist.

The maid had been in earlier to turn down the bedcovers and to leave one of the Sand Castle's chocolates on the pillow, along with a napkin that read "Sweet Dreams." It was a gesture many hotels indulged in, but one that Leah always found especially delightful.

Wrapping the chocolate up in the napkin to eat later, she set it aside on the night table. Then she climbed into bed and pulled the blankets up around her just as Hawk knocked peremptorily on the door.

"Leah, are you in bed yet?"

"Yes," she called.

Opening the door, he stepped into the bedroom. In one hand, he carried a glass half-full of clear liquid that fizzed and foamed, so she knew it was Alka Seltzer.

"I couldn't find anything in the sitting room. I guess the hotel's amenities don't extend to medications. So I phoned down to the drugstore in the lobby and asked them to send up some sodium bicarbonate," he explained. "Although one sometimes tends to forget the fact, there *are* some advantages to living in a city that never sleeps." He handed her the glass. "Be a good girl and drink it all down, now."

Leah smiled wanly. "Whatever you say, Boss."

"Yes, I *am* your boss—but only in the office. I thought we had agreed upon that. So at the moment, I'm simply a friend—a *close* friend, I hope—who's worried about you and wants to be certain you're okay."

"I'm sure I'm fine."

She could not help but be touched by Hawk's kindness and concern, which made her plan to filch his corporate key from him so she could steal the code breaker seem all the more treacherous. To hide what she knew must be the guilty expression upon her face, Leah upended the glass he had given her and obediently swallowed the Alka Seltzer in three long gulps.

"Thanks." She handed the empty glass back to him. "I imagine I'll feel better presently."

"Maybe so. But I'm going to hang around here for a little while longer, anyway. I'll be out in the sitting room, stretched out on the sofa, if you need me." Reaching out to smooth her long black hair gently back from her face, Hawk bent and planted a tender kiss on her forehead. "Close your eyes and get some rest, now. Do you want me to leave the bedside lamp on for you?"

"Yes, please. I'm so tired that the light won't bother me, and besides, I need to be able to see in case I have to get up in the night."

"All right. Sweet dreams, then." Her boss unwittingly echoed the words printed on the napkin that now held her bedtime chocolate. "Call me if there's anything else I can do for you." He turned to go.

"Hawk?" Leah murmured drowsily.

"Hmm?"

"I'm really sorry our evening together ended on such a note." Much to her surprise, she realized she spoke no less than the truth.

"Yeah, me, too," he admitted ruefully. "Good night, Leah."

"Good night."

A few hours later, Leah awoke with a violent start, terrified and screaming, clammy with sweat, her heart thudding so hard that she thought it would burst from her breast.

A dark, amorphous shadow hovered over her, and at first, highly disoriented and beset by blind panic, she lashed out at the figure defensively, thinking she was under attack.

She had been dreaming, a hideous, crazy nightmare in which Winston Pryce had chased her through the casino, his steely gray eyes shooting bolts of silver lightning at her, like the unnatural monster in some gruesome Playstation game. Finally catching up to her, he had flung her onto one of the roulette tables and strapped her to the wheel, which, in her horrible dream, had been several times its normal size. Then the roulette croupier had set the red-and-black wheel into motion, flicking the ball into the 00 slot.

But instead of being its usual size of a marble,

the ball had been as large and heavy as a cannonball, and it had pounded Leah mercilessly as it had bounced from slot to slot in the roulette wheel, battering and bruising her. The whole time, Pryce had stood watching and placing bets on whether or not she would survive the ruthless pummeling.

Now, barely conscious, gasping desperately for breath, she battled frantically against her assailant, using her fists to hit him wildly around the head, shoulders, and chest. The recipient of this barrage of blows grunted and swore savagely, doing his best to shield himself. Then he finally grabbed her wrists and gave her a hard, rough shake.

"Leah!" Hawk snapped again for the umpteenth time in the past few minutes. "Wake up, damn it, and stop fighting me! I'm not going to hurt you. Do you understand? You were having a bad dream...a nightmare. I heard you screaming and came to investigate. That's all. Leah! Do you hear me?"

Gradually, his words penetrated. Her eyes slowly focused on his face, illuminated faintly by the dim light of the bedside lamp, its fabric shade casting its rays downward to form a glowing pool on the night table.

"Hawk! Oh, God, I'm so sorry.... I didn't—I didn't realize it was you. I thought someone had broken into my suite, that I was under attack...." Leah's voice trailed away awkwardly.

She was embarrassed and stricken that she should

have beaten her boss, however unintentionally. She longed to bury herself under the bedcovers in shame. It was a wonder he hadn't taken more aggressive measures to restrain her, she had behaved so hysterically.

"It's all right, Leah," Hawk reassured her soothingly. "I know you weren't responsible for your actions, that you weren't yourself."

"What are you—what are you still doing here?" She glanced at the alarm clock on the night table. "It's after four o'clock in the morning. I would have thought you'd gone home by now."

"I should have. In fact, I *would* have," he insisted. "Only it seems I was more tired than I realized. I fell asleep on the sofa out in the sitting room. That's why I'm still ensconced in your suite. It was your screams that woke me up. I only hope they didn't rouse the rest of the floor, or we'll have security up here shortly, demanding to know what's going on. And *that* could prove a little awkward for us both. I, for one, don't want the whole of MMI to think I was somehow abusing my personal assistant in the wee hours of the morning, and you probably don't want anybody wondering what I was doing here at such an hour in the first place."

"No, you're right. I don't," Leah conceded quietly. "You know I'd rather our personal relationship wasn't grist for the gossip mill at MMI."

"Yes, I do."

Abruptly rising from the bed, Hawk strove over to the minibar that stood in one corner. Turning the key in the lock, then opening the door, he rummaged around its shelves for a minute, finally producing a cold can of Coca-Cola. He checked the ice bucket on top of the small refrigerator. Finding it empty, he deftly dumped ice from the two tiny trays inside the freezer compartment into it, then dropped several cubes into a glass and filled it with Coke.

"Here." He handed the glass to Leah. "It probably ought to be brandy, to calm your nerves. But I figure you've had enough to drink already tonight, and I don't want you to get another upset stomach."

"Thanks. This will be fine." She sipped the cola gratefully, suddenly becoming aware of how hot and flushed she was.

And no wonder. She had forgotten to take off her robe before falling asleep. The combination of it, her nightgown, the bedcovers, and her profuse perspiration as a result of the bad dream had all overheated her.

As Leah drank the Coke, her boss sat down on the edge of the bed again, his face wearing the same expression of concern she had witnessed earlier.

"I apologize, Hawk. I seem to have caused more trouble than I'm worth tonight," she noted lightly.

"That's okay. I don't mind. I'm just glad I was here to help. But I *am* beginning to wonder if maybe you're working too hard again, Leah. You look as though you're under a strain, and nightmares are often an indication of that.''

"No, it was just a bad dream, that's all," she lied. "Probably nothing more than the result of my getting so keyed up earlier, to the point that I felt sick. And, of course, I don't think anybody ever sleeps too well in an unfamiliar bed." She pointed this last out with relief, glad to have hit upon an explanation he would likely accept.

As she had hoped, he nodded in agreement.

"Yes, you're right about that," he said. "I should have thought of it myself. But at least it looks as though our good luck is going to hold. If someone on this floor had heard you screaming and called down to the front desk to report it, security would have been here by now."

"I expect that's so." Leah set her now-empty glass down on the night table.

"Do you want some more?"

"No, but thanks for asking."

"Do you mind if I just finish out the night on the sofa in the sitting room? It's almost dawn now, so there doesn't seem much point in my hurrying on home at this late hour. Besides which, I'd kind of like to stick around in case you have another nightmare."

"So you can be mistaken for a bogeyman again?" Leah laughed softly, ruefully. "You're a braver man than most, Hawk."

"I try my best."

He gazed at her silently for a long moment. Then, without warning, he stretched out one strong, slender hand and wrapped it in her long, unbound hair. When she did not demur, he drew her gently but inexorably toward him, wordlessly making his intention clear.

Still Leah did not protest.

In the face of her mute acquiescence, Hawk's black eyes abruptly darkened with passion, smoldering like twin embers as he slowly but determinedly lowered his mouth to claim her own.

Sixteen

Desire in the Painted Desert Suite

> From the desert I come to thee
> On a stallion shod with fire,
> And the winds are left behind
> In the speed of my desire.

> *Bedouin Song*
> —Bayard Taylor

Hawk kissed Leah tenderly, leisurely at first, his tongue tracing the outline of her lips before thrusting deep between them to explore her mouth, touching and tasting, delicately wreathing her own tongue.

Her pulse leaped erratically in response, and her nipples pebbled as a sudden, wild thrill of desire shot through her. A low moan escaped from her throat. In some obscure chasm of her mind, she realized dimly that it was growing increasingly harder for her to resist him.

She wanted him. And not just because she needed him as a means to an end. She had only been kidding herself about that, trying to find some excuse to justify becoming personally involved with her boss. He was more than that to her. Deep down inside, she had known that all along; she just hadn't wanted to admit it to herself.

But now, tonight, she must, Leah thought. She couldn't keep on stalling him, stringing him along. It simply wasn't right. Even though Hawk had not yet said as much, he must care for her in some fashion, must want more from her than just sex. He wouldn't have remained in her suite otherwise to look after her, worried about her well-being. Instead, he would have kissed her good-night at the door, then headed back down to the casino to find more willing prey.

Of their own accord, her lips yielded pliantly to the intrusion of his tongue, opened even wider, drinking him in as though she still thirsted, had not been sated by the cola. He tasted of cigarettes and the smoky Scotch he favored, things that, for whatever unknown reasons, Leah had always associated with potent males. He smelled subtly of sandalwood soap and cologne, equally masculine aromas that were heady in her nostrils.

As she wound her arms around his neck, she became aware for the first time that Hawk's long, glossy black hair hung free, warrior fashion, in a way she had not seen it since that day years ago at the corner grocery store at the crossroads. When she tunneled her hands through it, tightening them amid the loose mane, it felt inconceivably soft and silky to her touch, rippling like liquid silver through her fingers.

Sometime after she had gone to bed, he had also stripped off his suit jacket, tie, and belt, and unbuttoned his crisp cambric shirt, pulling its tails from his trousers. His broad, muscular, bare chest gleamed coppery in the half-light, sprinkled with fine black hair that trailed enticingly down his firm, flat belly to disappear beneath his unfastened waistband.

He was incredibly sexy, Leah reflected hazily as Hawk's carnal mouth began to move on hers more demandingly. Increasing the pressure of his hold on her, he pulled her even nearer to him, kissing and caressing her in ways designed to inflame them equally. Wildly, his lips blazed a trail down her throat to her breasts, fierce and feverish, tormenting and titillating her unbearably, his breath hot against her skin.

The animal magnetism he exuded was almost tangible, causing both fright and excitement to surge through her giddyingly as she felt the power of him, the strong, rock-hard muscles that sensuously bunched and rippled in his arms and back as he crushed her to him. In comparison, Leah felt fragile and helpless—and as dizzy as though she were inebriated or drugged. Her head reeled. Her thoughts drifted in her mind, chaotic, oblivious, scattered by his unstill mouth and tongue and hands.

They continued to roam over her expertly, as though they had every right to do so, knew every soft, susceptible spot to taste and tease and touch in order to raise her desire for him to a feverish pitch. So skillfully that Leah wasn't even aware of it, Hawk's fingers untied the sash at her waist and slipped her robe from her body. Then he deftly eased the short sleeves of her nightgown down to bare her breasts, swollen and aching with passion.

His palms cupped them possessively, squeezing and kneading, his thumbs rubbing and circling her hard, rosy nipples, stimulating them to even greater heights. His every savage kiss and searing caress, his every tantalizing lick and taunting bite, sent electric tingles coursing through her, as though the heat lightning that sometimes shattered the night sky above the desert mountains and bluffs now erupted within her.

Leah trembled uncontrollably with swiftly spiraling desire, clutching him, clinging to him, swept away by the exquisite sensations and emotions he was arousing within her.

"God, you're sweet," Hawk muttered hoarsely

against her lips. "And I've ached for you since the very first moment I ever saw you. That was years ago at the old crossroads. Do you remember? I was in a knife fight that day, and you watched from the porch of the corner grocery store. You looked so fine and beautiful standing there...something infinitely rare and precious in that dusty, one-horse town. I wanted like mad to take you away someplace private and make love to you, to teach you what it was to have a man...."

"Teach me now...." Was that really her own voice, Leah wondered, so soft, so husky, so tremulous with passion?

Moments later, somehow—she wasn't quite sure how—she was wholly naked, as was Hawk. And he was sliding into bed with her, his dark body moving urgently to half cover her own pale one. His head was at her breasts, his mouth capturing first one flushed, rigid nipple and then the other, his teeth nibbling them erotically, his tongue stabbing them with its heat, sending waves of delight flooding through her.

His hand was between her thighs, spreading them wide to expose the hidden heart of her. Lingeringly, he stroked the tender, mellifluous folds that burgeoned at his touch and opened to him of their own volition, sweet and wet, like succulent, ripe fruit bursting and dripping with sugary juices. He found the concealed little nub that was the secret to her pleasure, languidly rubbing and teasing it until it was hard and throbbing.

At the very nucleus of Leah's being, an unendurably hollow ache seized her, so she longed instinctively to be filled and assuaged by him. Sensing her burning need but deliberately taking his time, torturously protracting the action, Hawk eased one finger fully inside the molten core of her, only to withdraw it just as unhurriedly, wringing a tiny, frantic mewl of dismay and craving from her lips.

"You need that...now...don't you, my sweet?" he queried, his voice low and thick as he resumed his earlier lazy fondling of her, tugging gently at downy curls and spreading quicksilver heat with each flick of his thumb against the tiny, taut crux of her.

"Yes...please..." Leah whispered, pushing exigently against his hand.

In answer to her entreaty, he slowly pushed two fingers as deep into her as he could, stretching and opening her even more completely to him as, after a moment, he started to thrust them forcefully in and out of her. Her body arched and shuddered unrestrainedly at the inciting motion. Her thighs spread even farther apart for his penetrating onslaught.

And all the while, his thumb goaded her on, and he kissed her hard and hungrily on the mouth, his tongue mimicking the urgent movements of his hand.

Leah was a mass of quivering sensation, straining desperately toward the climax she felt she must attain or die. Her head thrashed. Her nails dug into the sheets as the agonizing tension built within her. Then, at last, she came, exploding violently. The orgasm was like a lightning bolt striking her, electrifying her, blotting out all coherent thought, engendering only raw, atavistic feelings that were like a primeval storm wind sweeping through her.

She was only barely conscious of Hawk poising himself above her, looking like some barbaric Indian warrior in the half-light, his long black hair streaming over his shoulders and down his back. The powerful muscles in his steely arms flexed beneath his weight as, calling her name, he drove into her so suddenly and forcefully that Leah's breath caught in her throat. Then she cried out, a high, keening sound that he smothered with his lips as he impaled her fully.

For a moment, he lay still atop her, reveling in the feel of her slick, liquid heat engulfing him, her muscles clenching spasmodically around him as she writhed in the throes of her climax. Then, compelled by sheer blind need, Hawk began to move within her. As he thrust in and out of her, he ground himself against her, causing Leah to experience a series of multiple orgasms that left her mindless and gasping for air.

Harder and faster he rode her, his body quickening urgently against hers until his own release came. The climax ripped through him savagely, causing him to shudder long and violently against her, his low groans of fulfillment mingling with her own whimpers of delight. He collapsed atop her, his breathing harsh and labored, and his heart hammering furiously against hers.

After several long minutes, not wanting to crush Leah with his weight, Hawk rolled off her onto his back. Then, drawing her snugly into his embrace, he cradled her head gently against his shoulder, stroking her damp, tangled hair lightly.

With his free hand, he reached out to retrieve his trousers from the floor, where he had tossed them earlier. Removing his lighter and a half-crumpled pack of Marlboros from one pocket, he extracted a cigarette and lit up, blowing a cloud of smoke into the air.

"You okay, Leah?" he asked quietly.

"Yes...better than okay, actually," she confessed shyly, for in truth, she couldn't remember ever having been made love to before in a way that had sated her so gloriously and completely.

"I'm glad to hear it. I wanted it to be good for you." He paused for a moment, dragging on his cigarette again. Then he continued. "You know, I really didn't stay here tonight intending to take you to bed. But in all honesty, I'm not sorry it happened. How about you, sweetheart? Do you regret it?"

"No...no. I thought I might, but the truth is that I don't."

"Good." He fell still once more, as though lost in contemplation, gathering his thoughts. Then he said, "I realize I haven't exactly told you before, but I *have* come to care for you, Leah. I want you to know that."

"Shh." She placed her hand lightly against his mouth to silence him, for such was her nature that she would rather hear bitter truths than sweet lies. "I'm a big girl, Hawk. You don't have to say such things to me just because we wound up making love tonight."

"I know that. And I assure you that I am *not* in the habit of telling a woman whatever she wants to hear just so I can get her into my bed—or so I can keep her there, either. Whether you believe me or not, I'm serious about you, my love—and I can't remember ever telling any woman *that* before. I want more from you than just a one-night stand, Leah...much more. You're everything I've ever desired in a woman. I've thought so for quite some time now."

"I—I don't know what to say, Hawk." She was startled and touched by his words.

He smiled down at her tenderly, ruefully. "Well, you *could* tell me that you care for me, too, even if it's only just a little."

"I do. It's just that...I've never been good at relationships—especially long-term ones—with men. I suppose I've always been too busy building my career to devote the necessary time and energy to sustaining any kind of a private life.''

"Join the crowd." Momentarily, Hawk grimaced. Then he brightened again. ''But that doesn't mean things can't change if we both want them to and are willing to make an effort where each other is concerned. Does it, Leah?''

"No, of course not. And I'd like that—provided that my slave-driving boss can be persuaded that it's not in either of our best interests to continue working sixty and seventy-two-hour weeks.''

Hawk laughed. ''Somehow, I don't believe that's going to present much of a problem, my sweet.''

Taking a long, last drag of his cigarette, he ground it out in the glass ashtray on the night table. Then, turning back to Leah, he cupped her chin with his hand and tilted her face up to his, his mouth descending to cover her own possessively once more, his tongue plunging deep.

As dawn broke on the horizon, they made love again, and then yet a third time, passionately, feverishly, until they were both utterly drained and exhausted. The sun had climbed into the morning sky by the time they at last fell into a deep, dreamless sleep together, a tangle of naked, sweating bodies, Leah with her head resting on Hawk's chest, listening to the steady, reassuring beat of his heart as she drifted into slumber.

Seventeen

Deceptions and Revelations

The essence of lying is in deception,
not in words.

Modern Painters, vol. I
—John Ruskin

Sleeping with Hawk had been a terrible mistake.

She shouldn't have weakened and given in to her desire for him, Leah thought for the umpteenth time that day, sighing heavily. By doing so, she had accomplished nothing but to distract herself from her primary purpose in life and complicate matters horribly. She should have stuck to her plan and pursued it with an utterly ruthless single-mindedness designed to rival that of the consortium.

Three days had passed since Leah had gone to

bed with Hawk, and during that time, she had made little or no progress whatsoever toward achieving her aim at the Sand Castle hotel. Instead, when she wasn't working, she frittered away the vast majority of her off hours with her boss-now-turned-lover. She might as well have never checked into the hotel in the first place.

To date, all she had managed to complete was her survey of the lower levels of the hotel wing. There were, indeed, two private elevators that led up to the top story. However, these were located on the second floor, in the hotel proper, above the mezzanine and away from the busy shopping areas where Leah's presence might go undetected.

Both elevators were extremely secluded—a circumstance that precluded her from simply hanging around the hallway, pretending she was on her way to her own room. Much to her dismay, in fact, one of the elevators would be totally impossible to watch, being at the end of a short corridor that opened onto nothing else. Across from the other elevator, however, was one of the second-floor storage rooms used by the maids, where items such as fresh towels and the hotel's complimentary toiletries were kept.

Obviously, she couldn't conceal herself in the storage room for hours on end, Leah had realized. There was too much activity during the daytime hours, with the maids constantly coming and going as they performed their daily cleaning routines.

However, a quick perusal of the storage room when it was open had revealed a possible place of concealment for the video camera Leah had purchased from one of the on-line spy-equipment stores. There was a large ventilation duct with a grill located directly over the door of the storage room. If she could somehow manage to mount the video camera inside this duct, directly behind the grill, then she would have a bird's-eye view of the elevator across the hall.

Leah had known she would have to do it in the wee hours, when the maids were not on duty. But Hawk had stayed over in her suite every night since they had become lovers, unwittingly interfering with her scheme. And every time she had attempted to find some excuse not to spend the evening with him, she thought of how passionately he would make love to her later, and hadn't been able to get the words out.

"Face it, Leah," she muttered to herself reprovingly, feeling both annoyed and guilty. "After all your years of hard work and plotting to get where you are at MMI, you've now gone and thrown a monkey wrench into everything by falling for Hawk like a ton of bricks! And you don't even know whether or not he's the enemy! There's just no getting around it. You've acted like a damned idiot! A woman in your position can't allow her emotions to get the best of her—and you *know* that. Some spy you've turned out to be! You'd better get hold of yourself in a hurry before you slip even worse than you already have and wind up dead!''

Sighing deeply once more, Leah turned away from the wide bank of windows in her office and resumed her seat at her desk. She tried to concentrate on the information that appeared on her monitor, but unfortunately, since the columns of figures were the cost projections for the code breaker, all they did was remind her of how foolishly she had behaved.

How could she take advantage of Hawk now to steal the device? she asked herself. How she planned to use him had been bad enough when she had only been attracted to him. Now that she was in love with him...

Unexpectedly at that thought, Leah buried her face in her hands. Of course. It was more than just an infatuation.

She *was* in love with him!

She hadn't wanted to admit that before, to acknowledge how deep her feelings for him really did run. Instead, she had unconsciously decided that as long as she didn't use the word *love* in connection with her boss, she could pretend that what she was experiencing with him, no matter how serious it might seem, was *still* nothing more than the equivalent of a giddy, schoolgirl crush.

But now Leah could no longer go on fooling herself. What on earth was she going to do? she wondered, dismayed. How could she betray Hawk, caring for him as she did?

How could she not?

If she didn't obtain the code breaker, she would never be able to operate the private elevators that led up to the top floor of the hotel wing. She would never learn whether or not her grandfather was still alive and being held captive in the MMI complex.

Much to her despair, the high-powered binoculars and night-vision glasses she had bought had proved of little use. The windows on the uppermost story of the hotel wing were coated with some kind of reflective material that effectively prevented her from seeing inside, either during the day or the night. So she hadn't even managed to get a glimpse of the interior of the hotel wing's top floor.

However, the fact that none of the other windows in the MMI complex were similarly treated gave her hope that the reason for the protective shielding of the hotel wing's uppermost story was that Merritt Marlowe was indeed within.

"Leah, are you done analyzing those cost-projection figures for the new code breaker yet?" Without warning, Hawk appeared in the doorway connecting their two offices.

As she glanced up to spy him standing there, so tall, dark, and handsome, her heart did flip-flops in her breast, and her pulse raced. No wonder she had fallen in love with him. He was everything she had ever dreamed of, she realized abruptly. He just *couldn't* be the enemy!

"Yes, almost…give me fifteen more minutes and I'll have them on your desk," she replied.

"Good. Are we on again for tonight?"

Everything inside Leah longed desperately to answer yes. But deep down inside, she knew that if she kept giving in to her desires where her boss was concerned, she would wind up wasting all her time at the Sand Castle hotel, and she just couldn't afford to do that. There was too much at stake.

"No…no, not tonight," she forced herself to say reluctantly. "I'm so sorry, Hawk, but I promised my folks I'd have dinner with them this evening. My mother hasn't been feeling well recently," she lied guiltily, unable to go on meeting his gaze. "So I'm a little worried about her."

"Yes, of course. I can imagine. I hope it's nothing serious."

"I don't think so. But you know how parents are. They often want to protect their children by not telling them the truth about such things. So I'd like to see for myself how Mom really is."

"Well, I can't say as how I'm not disappointed," he confessed, a crestfallen expression on his dark visage. "But naturally, I understand. Tomorrow night, then?"

"It's a date." Somehow, Leah managed to smile at him brightly. "Now, if you want the analysis of these cost-projection figures for the new code breaker, you'd better let me get back to work. You're a terrible distraction—and I don't believe my boss would like that."

"Your boss likes it extremely well, actually." Hawk grinned at her insolently. "And he is finding you equally distracting, sweetheart. But you're right. Business before pleasure. So it's back to work for both of us, I guess."

After he had disappeared into his own office, it was all Leah could do to concentrate on finishing the analysis he required.

She had never felt so deceitful, miserable, and guilty in her entire life. She knew Hawk was serious about their relationship. More than anything, she wished she were free to love him without reservation, to marry him, if that was what he had in mind, and to have his children.

But she wasn't.

No matter what, she mustn't forget that.

As she crept furtively down the corridor to the second-floor storage room of the hotel wing, Leah's heart beat so fast and horribly that she was afraid it might actually burst from her breast.

Even though it was now nearly midnight and the hallway was deserted, she still feared that her clandestine foray would be observed by someone—a hotel guest at best, an MMI employee at worst. And in the case of the latter, how she would explain her presence here, she hadn't any real clue. Any MMI personnel wandering this particular corridor of the Sand Castle could only have one purpose for doing so: to take the private elevator up to the top floor of the hotel wing.

Being caught here would do nothing but arouse the suspicions of anyone who might happen to see her. Still, Leah had prepared as best she could against that possibility, dressing in an old sweatsuit. If need be, she hoped to say that she had simply been in search of some quiet area where she could jog without disturbing any of the other hotel guests. It was a lame explanation, but better than none at all, she guessed. In any event, it would have to serve.

In front of the door to the storage room, she paused, glancing around again anxiously. This was the most crucial moment because, no matter what, there could no be believable excuse for her breaking into the hotel's housekeeping facilities.

Setting down the bag in which she carried her paraphernalia, Leah tried the doorknob. She had hoped it might have accidentally been left unsecured. But it hadn't. With heart sinking and hands shaking, she reached into the concealed inner pocket of her jogging pants for the set of lock picks she had ordered.

She had watched the lock-picking video and practiced on her own doors at home endlessly. But now that she was actually being put to the test, Leah wasn't at all certain she would be able to pick the lock of the storage-room door.

Inserting one of the slim picks into the lock, she began the appropriate maneuvers. Her heart still thudded at an alarming rate, and her palms sweated so profusely that she could scarcely maintain her grip on the pick.

Then, finally, after what seemed an eternity but was in reality no more than a few minutes at most, she heard the soft click as the tumblers in the lock fell into place. Heaving a huge sigh of relief, Leah quickly grabbed up her carryall and slipped into the storage room, shutting the door gently behind her.

Once inside, she leaned against the door in the darkness, waiting for her eyes to adjust to the lack of light and for the hideous pounding of her heart to slow. Then, locking the door behind her, she carefully unzipped her bag and fumbled around within it for her flashlight. Locating it at last, she snapped it on, training the beam around the storage room.

Removing one of the hotel's fluffy towels from a stack on the shelves, Leah rolled it up and pressed it into place along the bottom of the door to ensure that no light would escape. Only then did she flick on the overhead light.

After that, she got swiftly to work, knowing there was no time to waste, that anyone from the house-keeping department could show up at any moment, in search of blankets or towels for guests making late-night complaints and demands.

In the wall at the far end of the storage room was a low grill that gave access to the ventilation system. Employing her battery-powered screwdriver to un-fasten the grill, Leah set it aside, then climbed into the large duct, dragging her carryall with her. Shin-ing her flashlight up into the recesses of the vertical shaft revealed that she had several feet to ascend.

Physically, she was in excellent shape. Still, she groaned inwardly, knowing it was no easy task that lay ahead. But there was no help for it. One way or another, it had to be done.

Positioning her bag on her lap, Leah determinedly wedged her back against the rear of the duct and her feet against the front. Then she began tediously to inch her way upward, fervently praying that her strength would not give out halfway up, causing her to fall.

That would be a disastrous turn of events, one that didn't even bear thinking about. At best, she would be bumped and bruised. At worst, she would wind up breaking her neck.

Fortunately, nothing like that befell her, and after

several long minutes had passed, Leah managed to squirm her way into the horizontal shaft. For an instant, she just lay there, catching her breath and waiting for the burning of her muscles to subside. Then, shoving her carryall before her, she crawled toward the grill at the end of the duct, the one she knew looked out onto the corridor beyond and the private elevator leading to the top floor of the hotel's wing.

Once there, Leah worked as rapidly as she could in the cramped quarters, drilling holes and screwing into place the mounting bracket for the surveillance video camera she had bought. Finally, she had it in position and the camera itself installed in the bracket.

She was just getting ready to creep back along the horizontal shaft when, through the grill, she abruptly spied someone coming down the hallway. She froze in place, her heart hammering so loudly that she could hear it in her ears, her pulse racing as one ghastly scenario after another popped into her head.

If it were someone from the hotel's housekeeping department, she would be discovered and no doubt arrested! Pulling herself forward as stealthily as possible in the duct, Leah peeked surreptitiously through the grill.

Dear God! It was Winston Pryce!

She didn't know whether to be relieved or horrified as she rapidly ducked down, praying desperately that he hadn't seen her, that he wouldn't notice the video camera through the grill.

There was not a single doubt in her mind now that he was a member of the consortium. Probably, early on, he had been one of the younger, ambitious, up-and-coming executives who had taken orders from the higher-ups. But today, as president of MMI, he was unquestionably the cadre's ringleader.

Pressed as flat as possible against the floor of the horizontal shaft in order to avoid detection, Leah listened intently for the sound of the elevator bell that would inform her that its doors had opened to admit Pryce. Only when she heard the soft chime did she dare to risk glancing covertly through the grill once more.

Pryce had stepped into the elevator, seemingly unaware that he was under observation. Taking his corporate key from his pocket, he ran the magnetic strip of the plastic card down the slot of the keypad in the elevator, then punched in a number code. In response, the elevator doors closed, and the car whooshed upward.

Only then, as she expelled it heavily, did Leah realize she had been holding her breath. She had to get out of the storage room immediately! There was no telling whether or not Pryce would be upstairs for any length of time, or only a few minutes. He could return at any moment. She couldn't chance remaining where she was until he came back down again because she might be discovered by someone from the housekeeping department in the interim!

Hurriedly, Leah checked to ensure that she had actually turned on the video camera and set it to record. She had. Its battery would run for twelve hours, as would its eight-millimeter cassette tape. Then she would have to make another furtive foray into the storage room to retrieve the film and replace both it and the battery.

She shuddered at the thought. Tonight had sorely strained her nerves. She wasn't cut out for this kind of clandestine—and, in many respects, illegal—activity. Further, she didn't know how she could continue it, especially now that she felt quite certain Winston Pryce was her mortal foe.

But there was no other way. Leah knew that her grandfather *was* alive and being held captive on the top floor of the hotel wing! Why else was there a need for two private elevators requiring both a key and a code to operate—and for Pryce to be employing one of the cars in the dead of night?

Quickly, Leah slithered through the duct and inched her way back down the vertical shaft. She replaced the grill she had used to gain access to the ventilation system, making certain it was screwed on securely. Then, looking around the storage room to be sure she hadn't forgotten anything, she carefully folded up the towel with which she had sealed the door and returned it to the shelf.

Flicking off the overhead light, she cracked open the door, peering furtively down the corridor. To her vast relief, it was deserted. Nor did she hear any sounds to indicate that the private elevator was descending, bringing Pryce back down to the second floor.

From her carryall, she withdrew a knee-length tunic that she slipped on over her sweatsuit to hide the fact that she was coated with grime from the interior of the ventilation system. Then, locking the storage-room door behind her, Leah slung the wide strap of her carryall over one shoulder and sprinted lightly down the hallway, making as little noise as possible in her running shoes.

She was trembling so violently when she reached her suite that, once she was inside, her knees abruptly gave out and she collapsed on the floor, wishing fervidly that she was anybody's granddaughter but Merritt Marlowe's.

Eighteen

Betrayal

When lovely woman stoops to folly,
And finds too late that men betray,
What charm can soothe her melancholy?
What art can wash her guilt away?

The Vicar of Wakefield
—Oliver Goldsmith

During the next several days, so she could periodically return to the storage room to retrieve the film from her video camera and replace both it and the battery, Leah continued her pretense of her mother's illness in order to avoid spending all her nights with Hawk.

She felt terribly guilty at the deception, and longed to take him into her confidence and beg for his assistance. But even before she talked the idea over with her parents, she knew deep down inside that she simply couldn't take the risk that revealing her true identity to Hawk entailed.

"Oh, Leah." Faith sighed heavily as she gazed at her daughter, seated at the Tallclouds' kitchen table. "I know all this has to be an unbearable strain for you, and more than anything, I wish you weren't having to go through it—especially alone. I can tell that you've come to care for this man and that you'd like to be able to trust and rely on him. But you just *can't* afford to tell him who you really are. It's much too dangerous! What if he's one of the enemy?"

"Your mother's right, Leah." Jim spoke as he joined his daughter at the table, carrying the coffee-pot to refill her cup. "It's bad enough that you suspect Winston Pryce may be aware of your true identity. That worries your mother and me no end, I don't mind telling you. If he's the ringleader of the cadre, as you believe, your very life could be in jeopardy! Maybe we should just give all this up now and go to the police."

"With what evidence, Dad?" Leah asked, more tartly than she had intended. "I don't yet have any more proof than my birth parents did. And even if we got the police to persuade some judge to issue a search warrant for the hotel, the consortium would find some means of whisking my grandfather off the premises before an investigation could be carried out. Then, afterward, Pryce and his cohorts would claim the three of us had concocted this story in an attempt to blackmail the corporation or something.''

''I guess you're probably right about that.'' Jim's face was glum. ''I really *do* wish we could be of more help to you, Leah. But I'm afraid that, by stepping into the picture, your mother and I would only be creating more difficulties and danger for you. If Pryce knew we were your parents...''

''Well, he doesn't—or at least, I hope he doesn't.'' Leah sipped her steaming coffee, not wanting Jim and Faith to see how even just the thought of Pryce upset her terribly. ''Tallcloud's a common enough Indian name, and there's nothing to lead him back to you. So while I think he *does* know who I am, he's still only guessing. He can't be sure, and I don't believe he'll risk acting against me until he is. After all, for all he knows, I'm not even aware of my own true identity.''

''That may be so, Leah,'' Faith said, removing from the oven the chocolate-chip cookies she had baked earlier and beginning to scoop them off the aluminum tray onto a plate. ''But still, there are billions of dollars at stake, and for all *we* know, Pryce may be the man who planted whatever miniature device it was that blew up the Mercedes and killed your birth parents that horrible night. Because if you're right about him, he would have been one of the lower men on the totem pole back then, probably one of the cadre who had to do all the dirty work in order to prove himself to the higher-ups.''

''Yes, I know, Mom.'' Leah plucked a hot cookie off the plate her mother set on the table. ''That's why I'm being so careful—and why I wish I had someone at MMI to confide in, as well. Because if something should happen to me, there's a good chance that Pryce and the rest will never be brought to justice.''

''No, in that case, your father and I would come forward and tell what we know,'' Faith insisted stoutly. ''Even if we had to make it public via one of those dreadful tabloid newspapers.''

''In which event, no one of any intelligence would believe it, Mom.'' Leah smiled wryly. ''The story would probably appear right next to one about some poor woman giving birth to an alien's baby, or else a talking chimpanzee that passed a Mensa test. And then, Pryce and company would make sure you and Dad suffered some fatal accident or else simply disappeared.''

''Still, Leah, you have no good reason to trust this boss of yours.'' Jim pointed out that fact quietly but firmly. ''And until you do, it would be most unwise of you to take him into your confidence. In your heart, I think you know that. Maybe in time, if he somehow manages to prove himself to you, things will be different. But right now, there's just too much at stake, and the danger to you is too great.''

"I know you're right, Dad," Leah agreed slowly, reluctantly. "It's just that I...I don't *want* Hawk to be the enemy!"

"Oh, Leah, of course you don't." Faith reached over to squeeze her daughter's hand both lovingly and reassuringly. "You love him. Your dad and I would have to be blind not to see that. And you *deserve* to be able to fall unreservedly in love with someone and have a chance at happiness. But the truth is that no matter how much all of us wish you could have that opportunity, you're *not* just plain old Leah Tallcloud. You never were. You're Angelina Marlowe, and you're entitled to all that entails, too. Only, promise your dad and me that you'll be careful, that you'll leave MMI and go straight to the police should you feel yourself threatened in any way."

"Don't worry, Mom. I will. I promise. Thanks for the coffee and cookies." Rising, Leah gathered up her handbag and car keys. "And remember, should anyone happen to ask, you're not feeling very well, Mom."

That brought a smile to Faith's lips, although her eyes were still filled with concern. "I might even be forced to take to my sickbed." She tried hard to interject a light note into her tone.

"You take care, Leah." Jim spoke gruffly as he hugged his daughter tightly. "And don't you worry about that boss of yours. I'm sure that in the end, he'll turn out to be an all-right fellow—because you wouldn't have fallen in love with him if he weren't.''

But her father was dead wrong, Leah discovered to her heartbreak that night in her hotel suite, after she had retrieved the latest cassette tape from the video camera.

For that night, it was not Winston Pryce who stepped into the private elevator leading up to the uppermost story of the Sand Castle.

It was Hawk.

Ever since Leah had discovered that her boss was part of the conspiracy at Marlowe Micronics, Incorporated, she had been sick with despair.

She felt as though she had built a sand castle as beautiful as that for which the hotel had been named, only to see it washed away by an ugly, destructive wave. She didn't know what to do, where to turn. She felt like a damned idiot, wounded to the core and angry at herself for being so stupidly caring and trusting in the first place. She had known better, had warned herself over and over that there was always the possibility that Hawk was the enemy, her mortal foe.

And now, Leah knew for certain that he was—in league with Winston Pryce and probably every other department head and member of the board of directors. In fact, all the upper echelons of the entire corporate structure at MMI were no doubt riddled with those who would not only oppose her at every turn, but who would also murder her if they ever learned her true identity.

To think she had been on the verge of revealing that piece of information to her boss, perhaps even *would* have done so had her parents not counseled her otherwise!

Oh! How could she have been such a complete fool? Leah asked herself bitterly as she crammed the last of her belongings into her luggage, in preparation for checking out of the hotel and returning home.

The remodeling on her house was nearly finished and, realistically, there was nothing more she could uncover here at the hotel. Since viewing last night's tape, she had learned all she needed to know.

Hawk's corporate key not only unlocked all the security measures in MMI's research-and-development department, it also operated the two private elevators to the top story of the hotel wing. She would simply steal his key, retrieve the prototype of the new code breaker, and rescue her grandfather.

She need do nothing more than that. Once she had Merritt Marlowe safely away from the MMI complex and ensconced in a police station, telling his own story in concert with hers, the authorities would know what steps to take next, how to investigate and implement the appropriate legal measures against the criminal consortium at the corporation.

Indeed, given the company's global nature, its worldwide business dealings and manufacturing of sensitive technology, Leah wouldn't be at all surprised if even the CIA and its various foreign counterparts became involved.

Previously, she had felt guilty about deceiving her boss, using him to gain her own ends at MMI. But now, her heart breaking, she felt as though he deserved whatever he got. She had foolishly fallen in love with him, and he had repaid her by turning out to be among the ranks of the enemy.

Although the notion seemed far-fetched, Leah thought it was even possible that Winston Pryce was routinely kept informed about all new employees—at least those at the MMI complex. Perhaps he had seen her name—Tallcloud—on the employment application and been suspicious about her from the very start. Maybe he had even instructed the personnel manager to hire her and Hawk to pursue her, with the aim of discovering her true identity and purpose at MMI.

As she rang downstairs for a bellboy, Leah's vivid imagination ran wild, and her heart pounded with fear. There was no telling what Pryce, Hawk, and the rest of the cadre intended, whether they were as yet unsure who she really was or merely biding their time, waiting for her to slip up, to make some fatal mistake that would confirm their suspicions about her.

She had to act quickly, Leah recognized. Like sand through an hourglass, her time could be running out while she remained oblivious of that fact.

To delay would be only to postpone the inevitable. She simply *had* to assume that her grandfather was alive and being held captive on the uppermost story of the Sand Castle. Nothing else made any sense. There was just no other logical reason for the two private elevators with their heavy security, as well as the furtive, nighttime visits being made by MMI's president and various other powerful, strategically placed executives within the corporation—including Hawk.

She had another date with him this coming Friday evening. She would carry out her scheme then, Leah decided resolutely. The sooner, the better. It was going to be hard enough for her to behave naturally around him until then as it was, to pretend that there was nothing wrong, that she had never learned what she now knew about him.

Her boss was extremely intelligent and astute. That was one of the reasons she had fallen in love with him. But now, perversely, those very same traits would serve her ill, Leah realized with dismay. Hawk was not a man who would be easily fooled, and if his suspicions became aroused, she would be in even more peril than perhaps she already was.

When the bellhop arrived to take her baggage downstairs to the lobby, she made a final check of her suite to be certain that she had not left any of her possessions behind. Then, pulling the heavy door firmly closed behind her, she followed the bellboy down the long corridor to the bank of elevators that led to the lobby several floors below.

While she and the bellhop waited for an elevator to convey them downstairs, Leah securely tucked into her purse the plain white notecard that had accompanied the flowers Hawk had sent her that day she had checked into the Sand Castle.

In light of everything she had discovered, why she still wanted it, she could not have said.

She knew only that she did.

Nineteen

False Pretenses

Necessity hath no law.
Feigned necessities, imaginary necessities...
are the greatest cozenage that men can put
upon the Providence of God,
and make pretenses to break known rules by.

To Parliament
—Oliver Cromwell

Hawk's kiss was tender, hesitant at first, as though, despite all of Leah's attempts to behave as usual this evening, he still sensed that there was something wrong between them.

It had actually been much easier than she had expected to deceive him all week at Marlowe Micronics, Incorporated. Work had caused her to remain principally in her own office, and those times when she had needed to consult with her boss, she had kept things strictly business, lightly turning aside his veiled attempts to interject a more personal note into their day-to-day relations. And in the end, Hawk had sighed, grinned at her crookedly, and let it go, seeing how determined she was not to mix business with pleasure.

Or so Leah had allowed him to believe.

But tonight, at her house, things had proved a great deal more difficult. In fact, the more brightly she had chattered while showing him the remodeling, and the harder she had tried to entertain him all through the supper she had cooked for the two of them, the more silent and watchful he had appeared to grow.

Leah, too, had eventually fallen still and then finally, uneasily, had asked quietly, "Hawk, is everything all right?"

"I don't know. Why don't *you* tell *me*, Leah?" he had suggested soberly, gazing at her curiously with concern—or had it been suspicion she had glimpsed in his glittering black eyes? "You just...don't seem to be quite yourself this evening. If I didn't know better, if we hadn't been seeing each other on a fairly regular basis since we first began going out together, I'd think my being here was actually making you nervous."

"No...no, it's not that." She had forced herself

to smile at the lie. "I guess I'm just keyed up. You know, excited about all the changes I've had made to my house. Everything's turned out so well, even better than I expected. As I told you earlier, the last of the work was completed just this afternoon, so that's why I wanted to fix supper for us here tonight, to celebrate."

"So you said. I'm sorry, sweetheart," Hawk had apologized after a moment. "I must be more tired than I thought. As you're well aware, it's been a long, hard week at the office. Of course you're delighted to be back in your own home, to have all your remodeling finished at last, and to your satisfaction. And you're right. It all looks wonderful. I just…I don't know. I was afraid that perhaps I had flustered you in some way."

"No more than usual," Leah had compelled herself to respond lightly. "So why don't you pour us some more wine? Maybe we both can use it."

Afterward, they had retired with brandy to her living room, where she had turned on her CD player. Earlier, before Hawk had arrived, she had guiltily programmed it with the most seductive music she could find in her collection, knowing she was deliberately setting a provocative mood not for the reasons her boss would assume, but for her own nefarious purposes.

Now, as he kissed her gently, Leah thought with distress that perhaps she had failed in her attempt to beguile him so completely that he would be driven to making mad, passionate love to her, so exhausting himself that he would fall into a deep slumber afterward.

She had also hoped that the wine and brandy—of which she had carefully drunk very little—would help to make him both amorous and sleepy. But it was difficult to discern whether or not this had affected Hawk. As she had learned, he had a hard head for liquor.

As lightly as the gossamer wings of a butterfly flicked against the petals of a flower, his lips continued to brush hers, making Leah impatient for more. She didn't have all night, she told herself. She needed to get him into bed, so that, after he had fallen sound asleep, she could take his corporate key and steal the code breaker.

She didn't want to admit to herself that the longer he teased her in this fashion, the more all the defenses she had forced herself to erect against him seemed to be crumbling, leaving her hungry for him and his lovemaking—instead of cold and calculating, as she had planned.

Until this moment, Leah had not recognized that, despite what she had learned about him and how he had unwittingly broken her heart, her boss would still possess the power to cause her to respond to him physically. That realization unnerved her and,

perversely, seemed to make her even more susceptible to his advances.

When she did not demur, made no effort to pull
away from him as Hawk had appeared to expect, the
pressure of his mouth gradually increased, growing
less controlled, more demanding.

His tongue followed the full, generous contour of
Leah's lips, then inexorably insinuated itself between them, driving deep, touching, tasting, making
her shiver irresistibly with an abrupt rush of yearn-
ing. She swayed against him, momentarily bracing
herself by placing her hands flat against his chest
before, of their own volition, they slid up to twine
around Hawk's neck.

Her fingers tunneled through his thick, glossy
black hair, tightening into fists as his tongue continued to explore her moist, parted mouth.

His breath had become more laborious now. Leah
could feel it warm against her skin as his mouth at
last left hers, searing across her cheek to her temple,
the strands of her hair. His tongue was like a feather,
tickling her ear; his teeth nibbled her lobe, sending
an electric thrill shooting through her. She was vividly cognizant of how her nipples tightened at the
sensation, straining visibly against the thin cotton of
the simple sundress she wore.

Hawk was highly conscious of it, too. His hand
glided slowly up from her thigh to cup one breast,
his thumb circling the stiff peak languidly, sensu-

ously, making Leah's breath catch in her throat. A low moan escaped from her lips.

"Do you know how much I want you, baby?" Hawk asked huskily, his eyes like twin embers beneath hooded lids as he gazed at her. "I missed you all those nights when you were away from me, spending time with your mother. I'm so glad she's better now."

"Yes, so am I," Leah whispered tremulously, desperately wishing she had far better control over herself and her emotions, that her body didn't leap like a hot, wild flame at the slightest touch of his hands and mouth.

Deep down inside, she understood that there could never be anything between them now, except this. But if she were honest with herself, she knew that, right or wrong, she still wanted him—this man who was her boss, her lover, and her enemy. Tomorrow, she would be sorry for that, and even sorrier for all that was yet to come....

No, she would not think about regrets now, Leah told herself sternly, in some dim corner of her mind. She would think only about what needed to be accomplished in order to free her grandfather and see the consortium of men who had imprisoned him, stolen his company, and murdered her birth parents brought to justice.

Hawk might not be guilty of any of this firsthand, but he was certainly an accessory after the fact. Why was it so difficult for her to remember that when his mouth claimed hers again, his tongue plunging deep?

Without warning, as though he had read her thoughts, Hawk abruptly gathered Leah up in his arms, swept her from the sofa, and carried her into the bedroom, illuminated only by the silvery moonlight streaming in through the windows. There, he laid her on the bed, staring down at her silently as he stood over her, beginning to unbutton his shirt.

The white cotton sundress she had on reminded him of the one she had worn that long-ago day. With its eyelet lace and filmy skirt, it was like a diaphanous cobweb woven delicately around her, so she appeared to Hawk like some fairy-tale swan as she lay there before him, her skirt stirred gently by the ceiling fan overhead.

Earlier, he had taken the pins from her long black hair, and now it tumbled in sexy disarray around her oval face, gleaming like jet against her pale, creamy skin bathed with the soft glow of the moonlight. Her body was beautifully proportioned, her full, generous breasts swelling gently against the bodice of her dress, her slender waist flaring into narrow hips and long, graceful legs like those of a ballet dancer. In moments, they would be wrapped around him tightly as he made love to her fiercely, passionately.

Hawk was mesmerized, tantalized by the picture his mind conjured. In a million years, he had never thought to find someone like her. Growing up on an Indian reservation as he had, he had not known her kind, except from afar—as he had watched and wanted her that day at the crossroads. That she was his now still slightly surprised him whenever he thought about it. When he had spied her standing on the wooden porch of the corner grocery store all those years ago, he had never dreamed that, one day, she would belong to him.

In later years, as he had risen in the ranks at MMI, Hawk had enjoyed more than his fair share of women and had taken his pick as he pleased. Still, none had been Leah. It was as though, somehow, without his being aware of it until this moment, he had measured them against his vision of her—and found them all wanting.

Dimly, it occurred to him as he gazed at Leah that she had somehow unwittingly branded her image deep in his mind that day, becoming the epitome of his ideal woman. He had expected that attaining her would prove a challenge, and it had. Even now, Hawk was not quite certain of her and her emotions toward him.

That was a new and unfamiliar experience for him.

Tonight, he had found himself vaguely disquieted by her behavior, had felt as though she had withdrawn from him somehow, was once more holding him at arm's length. And that had made him all the more determined to possess her, to break through the barriers she had erected around herself and her heart.

Hauling off his boots and socks, he slipped into bed beside her. Wordlessly, he pulled her into his embrace again, his mouth capturing hers hotly, his tongue insistently compelling her lips to part for his invasion. Like the petals of a flower opening to summer rain, they yielded to him sweetly, drank him in, swallowed his breath as he did hers.

Pushing aside his open shirt, Leah's fingertips traced tiny circles amid the crisp, black hair that matted his broad chest, causing his dark copper flesh to tingle, his sex to grow hard and heavy with desire. With a low groan, Hawk deepened the kiss and drew her even nearer, his hands gliding down her back to her hips, crushing her against him so she could feel the evidence of his desire, would know how much he wanted her.

As she wanted him.

No matter what, that much he was sure of. She trembled in his arms with the strength of her tempestuous emotions, her passion rising as he stroked her silky black hair, deftly eased one strap of her sundress from her shoulder to plant tiny kisses there. His mouth found the swanlike curve of her neck, his tongue and teeth wreaking havoc on the sensitive spot where it joined her shoulder. She shuddered in his embrace, her breasts burgeoning against him.

Molten heat pooled at the core of Leah's being, then surged through her entire body as she felt Hawk's maleness thrust against her provocatively— bold, hard, and promising. His lips and hands roamed over her in ways that taunted and excited her, intensifying the passion he had aroused within her, and which now increased steadily with each savage kiss, each intoxicating caress, making her heart hammer in her breast, her blood sing in her ears.

Her breath came quickly, shallowly, as though she had run a very long way and had no air left in her lungs. Her bones seemed to be dissolving inside her, so she felt weak and helpless against his onslaught upon her senses, as fluid as quicksilver slipping through his fingers.

She had no conscious awareness of time passing. She did not know how long they lay there, locked in each other's arms, kissing and touching, breathing in each other's scents, tasting each other's flesh, exploring the curves and angles of each other's body. She knew only that she had never before felt so vibrantly alive, a mass of exquisite feeling, every sense almost painfully heightened and expanded.

Hawk seemed to know instinctively what would fan the flames of her burning desire. She didn't object when he slowly drew the straps of her sundress down her arms, baring her to the waist, for she wore no bra beneath. Her breasts, swollen and aching with passion, their nipples flushed and engorged, were fully exposed to him then, pushed eagerly against him, as though pleading to be fondled.

He inhaled sharply at the sight before one strong, slender hand snarled in her hair, gently but inexorably pulling her head back. His lips sought her throat again, scorching the length of the graceful column, while his other hand squeezed and kneaded her breasts, his palm rotating across the nipples, stimulating them even more. His mouth blazed a fiery trail down her throat to seize one ripe, rosy bud, sucking hotly, greedily, sending waves of pleasure radiating through her whole body.

In unwitting entreaty, Leah whimpered and moaned, ardent sounds that excited and inflamed him, goading him on. He tugged away her sundress, heedlessly tossing it onto the floor. Then his hand dipped inside her French-cut panties, cupping her feathery soft mound. His fingers twined in her damp curls, parted the delicate folds to caress the mellifluous seam of her—a swift, light stroke that was but a tantalizing prelude of what was to come.

Leah's breath came even faster now, tiny gasps for air that mingled with Hawk's own in the otherwise still and silent room. Sweat beaded her upper lip, trickled slowly down the valley between her breasts. Deliberately, he licked it away, then kissed her mouth hungrily once more, his tongue dancing with hers before he bent his head to her breasts again, teasing and laving her nipples.

As his lips and tongue and hands had their sweet, tormenting way with her, he drew her panties down her legs until at last she lay totally naked beneath him.

Her pearlescent skin was as white and pure as the snow upon the summits of the distant desert mountains, Hawk thought as his eyes devoured her avidly, taking in her disheveled hair, her tremulous mouth bruised and swollen from his hard kisses, her pouting breasts with their pebbled nipples, and her slack, quivering thighs.

With his eyes riveted on her face, he stroked her mound once more, a second quick, butterfly touch that caused another shudder of arousal to ripple through her. Unable to go on meeting his gaze, Leah averted her own eyes. Her throat worked with emotion. Her hands clenched into fists.

At the sight of her lying there, exposed and vulnerable to him, his for the taking, Hawk's groin tightened unbearably with desire. He wanted to make her come until she begged him for mercy, was drained to the dregs and had nothing left to give. Spreading her thighs even wider, he took her with his mouth, lapping the tiny, hidden nub that was the key to her delight, until Leah was poised on the brink of orgasm, longing fervently to be filled by him.

Sensing her desperate, aching need, Hawk drove his tongue deep inside her, again and again, before thrusting first one finger and then two fully into the wet, welcoming heat of her. Her body shook uncontrollably at his heady assault, her thighs opening even farther for him.

Leah's head thrashed; her nails dug into the sheets, and she cried out unrestrainedly as her release abruptly came. It was so powerful that Hawk, too, felt the explosion that rocked her, the tremors that quaked through her violently, leaving her gasping raggedly for breath, pulsating wildly in the aftermath.

"Now, *you* do that for *me,* Leah," he insisted after several long moments, his voice thick and hoarse with emotion.

"Yes...yes...I will," she murmured brokenly.

He cast away the rest of his clothes then, looking in the silvery moonlight like some barbaric Indian warrior of old, she thought, his tall, naked copper figure as supple and heavily muscled as that of the tiger he always reminded her of, his hair loose now, streaming over his shoulders.

When he settled back into bed beside her, his dark eyes gleamed with a predatory light as they lingeringly appraised her. His nostrils flared slightly at the rich, rose perfume she wore, which mingled with her own musky scent.

Ensnaring her tangled hair, he gently guided her head downward.

He was like no other man she had ever before known, she thought as she found him with her hands and mouth—beautiful, strong, and sensual. She reveled in the smoky, masculine scent of him, the salty musky flavor of him, as she began to stroke and then, finally, to taste him, her lips enveloping him, sucking him, taking him deep.

Hawk's sharply indrawn breath was a strangled, serrated rasp followed by a long, low groan of pleasure as her soft, wet mouth worked its sweet, torturous magic on him, her tongue licking and swirling, making him feel as though he had died and gone to heaven. He was a mass of pure sensation, incapable of coherent thought.

Involuntarily, his hands caught hold of her head again, tightened in her hair. Unable to restrain himself, he pushed between her lips again and again, until he knew that if he continued, he wouldn't be able to hold back any longer. With another anguished groan, he abruptly pulled her up on the bed, his breath coming hard and fast as he rolled her over.

The muscles bunched and rippled in his corded arms as he momentarily poised himself above her. Then, with a low growl, he plunged into her, swift and hard and deep, burying himself to the utmost inside her. Leah gasped and then cried out, a sound

Hawk smothered with his mouth as he kissed her fiercely once more, his tongue stabbing her with its heat, mimicking the movements of his body as he began to thrust in and out of her, quickening exigently against her, driven by blind, primitive need.

Her climax came within seconds, seizing her with such unexpected force that she bucked wildly against him, spurring him on. Gripping her hips tightly, Hawk rode her until his own release came just as rapidly and violently, racking the length of his body and leaving him collapsed and panting for air atop her, his heart thudding furiously against her own.

After a very long while, he kissed her lips tenderly, then slowly withdrew from her to turn over onto his back, his breathing still harsh and labored. Raggedly, he ran one hand through his long, glossy black hair, then wiped the sweat from his chest before drawing Leah into his arms, cradling her head gently against his shoulder.

Reaching for his chinos lying on the floor, taking a lighter and a half-crumpled pack of Marlboros from one pocket, he shook a cigarette from the pack and lit up, exhaling a cloud of smoke into the air.

"I love you," he told Leah quietly.

More than anything, she wanted desperately to hear those words. But now, as he spoke them, she was abruptly and cruelly reminded that she had no future with this man.

None at all.

Yet she was lying here beside him, envisioning such things with him. She must be totally mad, completely out of her head!

He was her mortal enemy.

That thought came, unbidden, into her mind, utterly dismaying her. How could she have forgotten that—even for just a little while? Leah didn't know. It seemed unfathomable to her, as though Hawk had worked upon her some Native American magic that he had learned from his Apache shaman grandfather.

She felt a sharp stab of guilt at that notion. As hard as it was for her to believe, she had tonight forgotten all about her *own* grandfather.

"I love you, too," she forced herself to reply softly—and knew with bitter despair that it was no lie she spoke, even if it *was* intended to deceive him.

Eventually, Hawk had her twice more before he at last fell into a thoroughly sated slumber. But despite her own exhaustion, Leah did not sleep. She was too keyed up. Even had she not been beset by emotional turmoil, there was still her plan to be enacted. She waited, lying there silently in the moonlit darkness, her head still resting upon Hawk's chest, listening intently to the steady beat of his heart, the quiet sound of his breathing.

And then, finally, when she felt certain that he would not awaken, she carefully rose from the bed and dressed.

Hurriedly, in the living room, she guiltily but determinedly searched the pockets of his jacket. From the inside one, she withdrew his wallet and riffled through it until she found his corporate key. She tucked it into her purse.

Then she stealthily let herself out of the house, into the night.

Twenty

A Thief in the Night

The day is for honest men,
The night for thieves.

Iphigenia in Tauris
—Euripides

The semiautomatic pistol held purposefully in Hawk's hand looked huge and lethal—and it was pointed straight at Leah's heart.

He's going to kill me, she thought with a strange, cool detachment that utterly bewildered and amazed her.

It was as though, somehow, she were no longer a whole person, but had been split in two. Half of her was sitting behind the steering wheel of her automobile in the parking lot of Marlowe Micronics, Incorporated, completely frozen with fear as she stared, stunned and disbelieving, at the man with whom she had made love only a short while ago. The other half of her seemed not to be a part of the unfolding scenario at all, but merely watching it from a distance, perversely calm and accepting, recognizing the fact that she was surely about to die and there was absolutely nothing she could do about it.

"Start the car, Leah," Hawk ordered, his voice low and steely with intent, the muscle flexing in his taut jaw, as she had learned it always did when he was wholly furious.

For a moment, still petrified and incredulous at his entirely unexpected appearance, she didn't move. But instead of shooting her, as she had fully believed he would, her boss waited patiently for her to gather her wits and composure as best as she was able under the circumstances.

Her hands trembled violently as she at last turned the key in the ignition—once, twice, without the proper result, seemingly incapable of making the vehicle respond.

"Take a very deep breath, Leah," Hawk directed coolly, although she didn't make the mistake of assuming that this apparent act of understanding and compassion augured well for her. "Count to ten, then try it again—and get it right this time. It will be messy for us both if I have to shoot you right here in MMI's parking lot.''

She swallowed hard, nodding wordlessly in reply, her heart beating as horribly as though it were a drum being madly pounded during some frenzied Native American ceremony.

What were the first two vital rules of survival? Know your enemy, and always expect the unexpected? She had failed miserably on both counts, Leah realized, and that was an error likely to cost her her life.

She had simply never dreamed that Hawk would awaken from the slumber he had fallen into following their lovemaking—much less that he would not only discover that she had taken his corporate key, but pursue her here to the MMI complex. She had intended to have rescued her grandfather and be safely at a police station by the time her boss became aware that she had even left the house.

So much for the best-laid plans of mice and men.... Leah sighed heavily. She simply *had* to get a grip on herself and her emotions! Panicking was *not* going to help! And that's the state she'd been in ever since Hawk had, without warning, wrenched open the passenger door of her automobile and slid in beside her, gun in hand.

She had never known such fear as she had felt in that instant. Surely, he was aware of her true identity, that she had stolen his corporate key and the prototype for the new code breaker, and that she had planned to use both to free her grandfather. No doubt her boss had been under orders from Winston Pryce from the very beginning to watch her every move.

Leah felt violently ill at the idea, and it was all she could do to choke down the gorge that rose in her throat. That Hawk had slept with her, whispered words of love to her, knowing he would eventually murder her, sickened and revolted her. Her own betrayal seemed paltry in comparison; at least her ends had been justified!

Compelling herself to take the deep breath that her boss had suggested, she turned the key in the ignition once more, not knowing whether to be relieved or terrified when the engine finally started.

"What now?" she managed to ask, trying not to think about the weapon still aimed at her threateningly, her mouth tasting as dry as cotton.

"Just drive. I'll tell you where as we go along."

Her hammering heart sank even lower at this terse, uninformative answer. She felt quite certain that Hawk intended for them to travel out to some isolated spot in the desert, where he would then murder her and make sure her body disappeared without a trace.

In light of this horrifying prospect, Leah didn't know what action to take. If she didn't do what he had demanded, if she attempted to scream for help or to make a break for it, he would undoubtedly kill her immediately. At least if she obeyed his dictates, she would remain alive for the time being.

That was better than nothing.

So in the end, Leah did as her boss had instructed, using the time as she drove to try to get herself under control.

She had to think. There must be some way out of this situation, if only she could concentrate on saving herself. But no matter how hard she tried to focus on that goal, she couldn't seem to formulate any kind of coherent plan for escape.

Hawk was much bigger and stronger than she was. The odds of her being able to overpower him and wrest the pistol from his grasp seemed impossibly remote. If she could take him by surprise, she might stand a chance. But surely, he would be on his guard against her.

There appeared to be no other realistic alternative at the moment but simply to drive and hope that some opportunity for her to elude him would eventually present itself before it was too late.

So Leah followed her boss's directions, her palms sweating on the steering wheel as she anxiously guided the car along the brightly lit city streets that, even at this late hour, were busy with traffic.

It seemed impossible to her that no one in the other vehicles recognized her desperate situation—that she was in the process of being kidnapped—or did anything to help her. But of course, it must appear to passersby that she and Hawk were just two more locals or tourists, out on the town for a night of drinking and gambling.

Presently, even the dubious chance that she might somehow, without her boss becoming aware of it, make her perilous predicament known to anyone was lost as they swept past the city limits and onto the two-lane highway that led into the desert.

As the flashing neon lights and the incessant, raucous noise of the city were left behind, Leah's fear began once more to escalate wildly. Being alone with Hawk in the darkness and silence was somehow even worse than having been so suddenly and alarmingly confronted by him in MMI's parking lot.

Crazy notions chased through her mind…things like abruptly swerving the automobile, hoping to throw him into the windshield and knock him out cold. But the part of her that was sensible knew how reckless such a maneuver would be, that she was likely to lose control of the car and wind up accidentally killing them both.

"Slow down, Leah." Hawk spoke without warning, breaking the stillness that lay heavily between them. "There's an old dirt road up ahead, and it's easy to miss if you're going too fast, especially in the dark. When you see it, turn onto it."

"But…isn't that the road that leads to the Apache

reservation?'' she asked slowly, puzzled, not understanding why he would take her there.

"That's right," he confirmed taciturnly. "You seem confused by that. What did you think I intended? To drive you out into the boonies somewhere and kill you?"

"Well…yes, quite frankly. After all, you *did* threaten to shoot me in MMI's parking lot, didn't you?"

"Only so you'd do what I told you. That wasn't the time or the place to conduct an interrogation, and I couldn't take the chance that you'd scream or put up a fight, attracting security's attention. Not that I don't mean to turn you over to the proper authorities myself once I'm finished with you, of course. After all, technological theft is an extremely serious crime indeed, as I'm sure you're aware. So make no mistake about it. I intend to see you prosecuted to the fullest extent of the law and sent away to prison for a very long time, Leah." His copper visage was grim in the moonlight that streamed in through the car windows. "But I *would* like some answers first."

"You're wasting your time," she forced herself to insist curtly. "Do you take me for a fool? Handing me over to the police is about the *last* thing you'd do under the circumstances!"

"Oh? And what makes you think that?"

She started to reply, then abruptly clamped her

mouth shut. Could it be that her boss truly *was* oblivious to her real identity? That he actually *did* think she was nothing more than a high-powered, white-collar thief, bent on selling the prototype of the new code breaker to the highest bidder?

If, by some miracle, that really *were* true, then she had a fighting chance—albeit a slim one—to save herself. Telling Hawk anything at all would be to throw that away.

"Silence isn't going to help you, Leah, I assure you," he declared when she mulishly refused to respond. "One way or another, I'll get what I want. I promise you."

Her pulse leaped erratically at that, all kinds of wild, horrible images filling her mind.

"You'll hardly be in a position to turn me over to the proper authorities if you've tortured me." She pointed out that fact with a false bravado meant to mask her trepidation. "And I don't think they're going to look lightly on your having kidnapped me at gunpoint, either."

"I'm not in the least worried about that. It'll be your word against mine in that regard, and who do you think the police are going to believe? Me or a woman who took my corporate key and used it to steal a highly sensitive technological device from MMI?"

"How do you know that I took anything at all?"

she countered, determined now to brazen it out with him.

"Oh, for God's sake, Leah! Don't continue to play games with me!" Hawk snapped, exasperated. "While I'll admit that I fell for your act hook, line, and sinker before, that doesn't mean I'm fool enough to let you reel me into shore now that I know what you're up to. When I awoke and realized you'd not only left the house, but also taken my corporate key with you, I didn't just follow you to MMI. I sat and watched your entire little escapade on the department's security monitors in my office. Quite a videotape I have here," he said, patting his suit jacket.

"Jesus! I couldn't believe it!" Hawk continued harshly. He laughed shortly, mockingly, his eyes filled with a queer, hurt light before he abruptly hooded them against her. "Of everybody in the entire department, you were the very *last* one I would have suspected of being a traitor and a thief, Leah! Was it your intention all along to steal the prototype for the new code breaker—or did that only occur to you the day I brought it over to your house?"

Hawk motioned toward her attaché case with its false bottom, which sat on the floor of the automobile. "You came well prepared, at least. Did you order that briefcase specially, or is it just one of the tools of your trade? I can certainly see that I'm going to have to remind security about the ways and means technological secrets and equipment can be smuggled out of the MMI complex. Do you already have a buyer lined up...some Third World government or, worse, some international terrorist organization?''

More than anything, Leah wanted to tell him that it had never been her intention to sell the code breaker. However, she knew that not only would he *not* believe her, but her life would be jeopardized if he learned what she really *had* meant to do with the device. So she remained determinedly mute, refusing to answer his questions.

Hawk sighed heavily at her silence. ''You're *not* doing yourself any favors, Leah. Turn here.''

Obediently, she wheeled the automobile onto the rough, serpentine dirt track he had indicated, which wound its way deep into the desert bluffs. She followed it for some distance before it abruptly came to a dead end at a crude wooden cabin.

''What is this place?'' she inquired, her heart beating far too fast.

''A shack I built for myself some years back. It's not much, just a couple of rooms. But it's where I come when I want to get away from the city and back to my roots. Right now, it's main advantage, however, is that it's someplace for you and me to talk privately for as long as it takes me to get the answers I want. Now, shut off the ignition and hand me your car keys. Do it, Leah—and don't try anything foolish while you're at it. As you can see, we're miles from nowhere, and there's nobody around to help you, or even to hear you scream.''

Since she knew this was the truth, Leah did what he had told her.

"Now, get out of the car," Hawk directed.

Slowly, she opened her door, the wheels in her mind churning frantically. Now was probably the best opportunity she would have to escape from him. If he got her inside the cabin, there was no telling what he would do to her or how long he would keep her there. No one knew where she was, and even though her parents would eventually contact the police about her disappearance, the odds of anybody finding her here seemed practically nil.

Her boss could invent any kind of cover story, saying that she had quit without notice and he had no clue as to her whereabouts. Hardly anyone at MMI knew they had been dating, so it was unlikely that the authorities would suspect him of having had anything to do with her vanishing. And what if everything he had said to her had been a lie? What if he really *did* know her true identity and had merely been attempting to allay her misgivings?

All those thoughts spurring her on, Leah abruptly bolted.

"Goddamn it!" Swearing furiously under his breath, Hawk violently flung open his own door and gave chase.

As she raced desperately across the hard-baked desert, Leah could hear him behind her, the thudding of his boots sounding ominously nearer and nearer. In an effort to outrun him, she drew on every last ounce of speed she possessed. But it was no use. He was much faster than she, and in an instant, he was on her, knocking her to the ground and momentarily leaving her breathless.

Gasping for air, her fists flailing blindly, she struggled against him wildly, seeking to free herself, but to no avail. Still cursing, he easily pinioned her arms behind her back, roughly yanking her to her feet.

"You try anything like that again, and you'll regret it," he growled, giving her a savage little shake. Then, resolutely, he frog-marched her toward the cabin, pausing only to close the car doors and retrieve her attaché case.

Once inside the shack, Hawk flicked a switch that caused an overhead light fixture to flare to life, softly illuminating the interior so Leah could assess her surroundings. She stood in a single room that was living quarters and kitchen combined, attractively outfitted with comfortable, rustic, bent-twig furniture and Native American accoutrements. The light fixture was a chandelier fashioned from deer antlers, with a small metal shade over each bulb. A huge adobe fireplace dominated one wall; on the others hung Indian paintings and dream catchers. Brightly colored woven rugs lay upon the floor. Two open doors gave her a glimpse of the bedroom and bathroom beyond.

Dragging Leah into the kitchen, Hawk removed some soft leather strips from a drawer. Then, despite her renewed attempts to wrest herself from his grasp, he pushed her into one of the chairs at the kitchen table, tying her arms behind her back and binding her legs, so she was effectively imprisoned in her seat.

"Now, Leah, you and I are going to have that little chat I promised," he said, shrugging off his suit jacket and neatly hanging it over the back of a chair. From the waistband of his trousers, where he had tucked it earlier before pursuing her, he withdrew his pistol and laid it on the table. Then he deliberately, deftly, rolled up his shirtsleeves, revealing his copper arms corded with muscle.

Reaching for her briefcase, Hawk set it on the table and unsnapped the locks. Flipping open the lid, he scrutinized it carefully, sliding his fingers along the interior until he discovered how to release the false bottom. Freeing it at last, he lifted out the prototype for the new code breaker, which Leah had concealed there in order to sneak it past the security desk after she had stolen it.

"Why did you take it, Leah?" her boss asked as he examined the device for signs of tampering. "I can't believe it was only to sell it to the highest bidder. I mean, you don't appear to be in dire need of money. You earn a good salary at MMI, and if I'm not mistaken, you just spent several thousand dollars to have your house remodeled. During which time, I might add, you stayed in an expensive suite at the Sand Castle. But perhaps that's why you needed the cash, to pay for all that?" One thick black eyebrow quirked upward inquiringly.

"You won't get anywhere with this, Hawk," Leah asserted defiantly. "So you may as well go ahead and turn me over the proper authorities, if that's *really* what you intend."

He shook his head. "Not until I know why you stole the code breaker."

"What difference does it make *why* I took it? You know I did, so call the police."

"Well, you see, that's the other thing that's bothering me...the fact that you seem to *want* the law dragged in on this. And that just doesn't make any sense to me, either. Do you actually want me to report this, Leah? Do you want to be prosecuted by MMI and sent to prison?"

When she didn't answer, her boss sighed heavily. "You're right. This is getting us nowhere," he declared. "So here's what's going to happen if you don't start talking to me, Leah. I'm going to keep you here until I'm satisfied that I've learned the truth behind your behavior tonight. Virtually no one at MMI knows we've been seeing each other on a personal basis, and I can easily explain away any off-hours contact as being work related, besides. I can also account for your absence on the job by saying you quit without notice and gave your mother's recent illness as your excuse. Since nobody saw us leave the MMI parking lot together, there will be no reason for your disappearance to be connected to me, which means that no one will come looking for you at my cabin. So...do you begin to grasp the untenable position you are in, Leah...that I *can* and *will* keep you here as long as need be?''

She blanched as he outlined these same facts she had already gone over in her own mind. ''I don't understand why you are so determined on this course of action, why you just don't call the police!'' she wailed softly.

''Don't you?'' Hawk rasped, his black eyes smoldering. ''I—and I alone—am ultimately responsible for every single thing that takes place in the research-and-development department at MMI. As a result, I am now placed in a very difficult situation myself, in that I will have to answer to my own superiors as to how I allowed something like this to happen in the first place. You used me and betrayed me, Leah. And to think I was in love with you!'' He laughed tersely, bitterly. ''Christ! Of all the women in the world I could have had, I don't know why in the hell it had to be *you* I fell for! Did you ever care for me, Leah? Or was I just the means to an end for you all along?"

"I cared." Much to her dismay, at that admission—which she had never intended to make, which just seemed to slip out of its own accord—Leah abruptly began to cry.

"Oh, hell." Taking a clean handkerchief from his trouser pocket, Hawk knelt before her and tenderly began to wipe the tears from her ashen cheeks. It was the first kind gesture he had made toward her since he had surprised her in MMI's parking lot, and its effect upon Leah was not what he had intended, since she only wept all the harder. "Goddamn it! Sweetheart, can't you please trust me, and tell me what this is all about?"

"No," Leah sobbed quietly, shaking her head vehemently. "If I do, you'll kill me."

"After all we've shared, I can't believe that's what you really think of me, that I would actually murder you in cold blood. As I've already explained, I only threatened to shoot you earlier in order to scare you into obeying me, that's all. I had no idea what I was up against, why you stole the code breaker, whether or not you were a dangerous professional thief or just driven to it by something desperate, which I have yet to discover. And I *do* want very much to know the truth about all this, so that perhaps we can straighten it out on our own."

Hawk paused for a moment. Then, exasperated

when Leah didn't respond but only continued to cry, he growled, "Oh, for heaven's sake, baby! Don't you think that if I'd *really* wanted to harm you, I could and would have done so by now? That if I'd *truly* wanted the law involved, I could and would have marched you back into the MMI complex and instructed security to notify the police? So...won't you please tell me what's wrong, what drove you to this tonight? Is it your mother, honey? Is she so sick that she needs an operation or long-term care that you can't afford?"

"No, it's nothing like that. She's not even ill. I only told you that because...because..."

"Because why? Leah, you've just *got* to trust me!"

"I can't."

"Can you at least tell me why not?"

"No, you'll kill me," she reiterated, choking on her sobs.

At that, without warning, her boss adroitly untied her and carefully handed her the gun. Then, calmly, he sat down in the chair opposite her own. "There. Perhaps now you can tell me what's the matter," he said.

Leah was so stunned and confused by his actions that she didn't know what to do. "Aren't you— aren't you afraid *I'll* shoot *you?*" she asked, one hand dashing away her tears, the other leveling the weapon at him, just in case this was all only a trick.

"No. I've seen and heard enough at least to be convinced that you're not some lethal underworld thief out for monetary profit, and I don't believe you're connected with any international terrorist organization, either. No, whatever goaded you into taking the code breaker was personal."

"You can't be sure of that," Leah insisted, still not trusting him.

"Well, then, shoot me."

"I'd rather call the police myself. Now, try to take your pistol back. I'm certain that's what you have in mind."

"Would you like to tie *me* up? I give you my word of honor that I'll sit still for that, if that's what you want."

"If I really thought you would, I'd do just that. I know, Hawk. I know you're one of them."

"One of whom?"

"The consortium, the cadre, the clique...whatever you call yourselves at MMI. The group of powerful, unscrupulous men who, many years ago, ruthlessly incapacitated and imprisoned Merritt Marlowe, secretly seized control of his entire global enterprise, and brutally murdered his son and daughter-in-law. You didn't think anybody knew about that, Hawk, did you? But *I* know," Leah asserted fiercely.

Her boss's eyes narrowed speculatively, and he was suddenly as visibly alert as a tiger poised to leap upon its prey, filling her with fear once more. "I suppose the obvious question is *how* do you know, Leah?"

"You mean—you mean, you're not denying it?"

"No. Under the circumstances, that seems rather pointless. You're clearly aware of the truth—although *how* still remains to be determined, as does the reason why you believe me to be a part of the conspiracy and cover-up."

"I *saw* you! I saw you taking one of the two private elevators up to the top floor of the hotel wing, and I know that's where Merritt Marlowe's being held captive. And you told me that you'd never even met him—when all the while, you were serving as one of his jailers!" Leah accused, clutching the pistol tightly, preparing for Hawk to spring at her at any moment.

"My love, I would remind you that, as trite and clichéd as it might sound, appearances still often *are* deceiving. Yes, I lied about my relationship with Merritt Marlowe. But if you are willing to listen, I can, I believe, explain everything to your satisfaction."

"I'm listening."

"Good. Now, do you remember when I told you about picking up that crazy old man out on the highway who claimed to be Merritt Marlowe?" At Leah's nod, Hawk went on. "Well, the truth is that the more I thought about him, the more curious I became. So I actually *did* go back to Our Lady of Mercy Hospital and check on him. There was no trace of him, however. Whoever he belonged to had evidently come and retrieved him. Still, the incident stayed in the back of my mind.

"As you know, I became employed at MMI shortly afterward, and because I was smart, ambitious, dedicated to my job, and hard-working, I made my way up the corporate ladder relatively swiftly. Nevertheless, I figured I still had several more years to go before I would achieve my short-term goal, which was to be named head of the research-and-development department. Long-term, of course, I hoped eventually to sit on the board of directors.

"But then, three years ago, I was approached by Winston Pryce and some of the other important corporate heads. Basically, they told me what you just did—that they had effectively done away with Merritt Marlowe and were running the company themselves. Now, this wasn't as big a shock to me as you might expect, because over the years, I had come to realize there was *something* strange going on at MMI. I just wasn't sure what. But I *had* noticed that, too frequently for it to be mere coincidence, in my opinion, people who seemed poised on the brink of being promoted to department heads suffered some kind of fatal mishap instead.

"So when Pryce and the rest talked to me, I immediately recognized that if I didn't agree to play their game, they would find some means of getting rid of me permanently to ensure my silence. But even as I made it appear as though I were working hand-in-glove with them, I was, in reality, attempting to gather evidence against them. Merritt Marlowe, were you able to speak with him, would confirm this. He *was*, in fact, the man I'd picked up that night out on the blacktop, by the way. He'd outwitted his attendants and escaped, only to be recaptured later because I wrote him off as a lunatic—something for which I've never forgiven myself and for which I've attempted to make amends ever since.

"He's quite elderly now, of course, so the consortium, as you call them, doesn't worry too much about him these days. They figure he's been doped up long enough to be completely docile and that he's senile, besides. Neither is true. Ever since I've been one of his 'jailers,' as you termed it, and he's known there was the chance that I might secure his release, he's managed to avoid taking most of the medication his attendants regularly administer to him. As a result, his mind's gradually returned to a fairly coherent state—one that's as normal as can be for him, I expect, given how reclusive and eccentric he's always been."

"But...if you know all this, why haven't you done anything about it?" Leah queried slowly, puzzled but, for the first time, filled with hope, too.

Her boss shrugged. "Without proof, who would believe me? Would you, if you didn't have reasons about which I am *still* unaware?"

"No."

"There you go, then. Oh, I've accumulated *some* evidence, of course. But not nearly enough that without some kind of corroboration, Pryce and the others can't claim they fired me and that I'm now a bitter former employee bent on some kind of demented revenge against them. And, too, there's the need to get Merritt Marlowe safely out of their clutches."

"That's why I stole your corporate key and the code breaker. I needed them, to rescue Merritt Marlowe," Leah confessed at last, lowering the gun she held. "I'm going to take a very great risk and trust you, Hawk. If you've lied to me, I'm dead, and I know it. But I need help, and if you've told me the truth, you can provide it."

"Indeed? Then do you want to tell me, now, how you came to know all this, why on earth you got it into your head to attempt to spring Merritt Marlowe, Leah?"

"My name's not Leah. Leah Tallcloud was the daughter of Jim and Faith Tallcloud, who used to be employed by Roland and Natalie Marlowe, Merritt's son and daughter-in-law. The latter were both killed—murdered—by Pryce and the others, in a fatal car crash that was made to look like an accident but that was, in reality, the result of a miniature explosive device cleverly concealed in their Mercedes-Benz. Also in the automobile that deadly night were the Tallclouds, their daughter, Leah, and the Marlowes' daughter, Angelina. The Tallclouds were lucky. They both escaped relatively unhurt. But their daughter, Leah, was crushed to death in the crash. Angelina Marlowe, however, survived.''

For a moment, not able to credit what Leah was saying to him, Hawk just stared at her. Then, as the full import of her last statement abruptly struck him, he inhaled sharply. ''My God! *You're* Angelina Marlowe! That's what you're telling me, isn't it? Jesus Christ! Can you prove it?''

''Oh, yes—beyond a shadow of a doubt. My father...my *real* father, Roland Marlowe, made sure of that. That's why I thought you'd kill me, Hawk.''

''Kill you? Baby, I want to *kiss* you!''

And then, before she realized what he intended, he did just that...deeply, lingeringly.

Then, for reasons she didn't quite understand, Leah began once more to cry.

''Shh. Hush, Leah...Angelina, I mean—although I guess I probably shouldn't call you that, should I?'' He smiled down at her gently as he embraced her closely.

''No, it's too dangerous for now. Oh, Hawk, what are we going to do? I simply *have* to free my grandfather and see that Pryce and the rest are exposed and brought to justice!'' Leah bit her lower lip worriedly.

"I know, sweetheart. But thank God I awoke and followed you tonight. Merritt has two armed attendants with him at all times. Had you managed to get up to his hotel penthouse, they would have killed you, baby. Didn't you ever think about that?''

"Yes, but don't you see? It was a chance I had to take, the only one I had. Besides, I have a pistol of my own, in my handbag—although I *was* hoping I wouldn't have to use it on anybody.''

"Nevertheless, you leave rescuing Merritt to me,'' Hawk ordered quietly, his voice grim. "I love you, honey, and I don't want anything to happen to you. I've got a couple of friends in the police department. Tomorrow, I'll call them. We'll compile all our evidence, everything that you have and what I've got, as well. That way, we ought to be able to build a credible case...one for which a judge will at least issue a search warrant for the entire MMI complex. But at the moment, it's late, so I suggest that we turn in. We'll stay here tonight. I'm way too tired to drive back into the city, and no doubt, you are, too.''

"Yes, I am,'' Leah confessed, feeling suddenly so exhausted that she could barely keep her feet and was glad of his strong arms around her. "It's been a very long, eventful night.''

"It has indeed. But at least we know where we both stand now, and neither of us is alone in this fight anymore. If you ask me, that's half the battle right there.''

''I couldn't agree more. Oh, Hawk, you just can't imagine what a strain I've lived under all these years, ever since my parents revealed the truth to me about my real identity. And I've wanted so badly to tell you. But I was so afraid....''

''Shh. Hush, my love. You don't have to explain anything else to me. I understand, and I deeply regret having given you such a terrible fright tonight. But at least it was good for something—it's cleared the air between us. And even if you don't yet wholly trust me, you will in time, once we've freed your grandfather and you've had a chance to speak to him. It's enough, for now, that we've come this far.''

Gathering her in his arms then, Hawk swept her up and carried her into the bedroom, where he sat her gently on the bed. After switching on the lamp on the night table, so its soft glow filled the room, he began to undress her. Once he had finished, he turned down the covers so she could slip into bed.

Moments later, he joined her, pulling her close and cradling her snugly against him. In the warmth of his embrace, Leah determinedly banished the last of her niggling doubts. Hawk loved her, and she loved him. She had done the right thing in trusting him.

With that knowledge tucked securely in her heart, she fell at last into a deep and peaceful slumber.

Twenty-one

The Gamble

If Hercules and Lichas play at dice
Which is the better man, the greater throw
May turn by fortune from the weaker hand.

The Merchant of Venice
—William Shakespeare

They decided on the weekend for their raid on Marlowe Micronics, Incorporated. At that time there would be the fewest employees on the premises and the most traffic in the Sand Castle—all of which would make it more difficult for Pryce and his cohorts to attempt to spirit Merritt Marlowe away before he could be rescued.

Leah was so nervous and keyed up that she could hardly sit still as Hawk and his two detective friends from the police force went over their plan. The assault on the MMI complex was to be conducted as quietly as possible, in the hope of minimizing to some extent the corporate shock waves that were inevitably bound to result when what had befallen MMI was learned publicly.

There was no chance of covering it up completely, of course. What had occurred was far too big for that, so the media were sure to get wind of it somehow. But Leah had thought of a way to control the damage. They would present a cleaned-up version of the truth, making it appear as though there had been an ongoing power struggle within the worldwide company, between her grandfather and his faction and Pryce and his confederates, culminating in the discovery of the crimes of the latter.

The police operation had to be timed and coordinated very carefully. Otherwise, it would be doomed to failure. On the roof of the hotel's wing was a helipad, and if the consortium got wind of the scheme to free Merritt Marlowe, they would simply whisk him away, and Leah and Hawk would be left with no effective means of proving that her grandfather was a prisoner.

So, for the moment, the authorities were more or less treating the matter as a hostage situation. That meant that her boss alone had to be the one to get Merritt Marlowe out, since, as Hawk had explained, security cameras monitored both private elevators, and kept an eagle eye on her grandfather's penthouse, as well. If anyone but Hawk were seen approaching, Merritt Marlowe's attendants would immediately radio for the MMI helicopter, and in minutes, he would be gone.

The job of the police was to keep the MMI complex under surveillance to ensure that Hawk had a fighting chance to bring her grandfather out safely. Once Merritt Marlowe was free, the members of the cadre would be rounded up and arrested, charged with everything from bribery to murder. Hawk felt certain that more than one would cut a deal to sell out his cohorts and turn state's evidence.

Leah—who *still* had difficulty thinking of herself as Angelina Marlowe, even though her secret was now out in the open—compelled herself from her reverie as she heard Hawk saying, "In the meanwhile, I want Leah...Angelina...to have around-the-clock protection. She believes that Pryce suspects, if he doesn't already know for sure, her true identity. If that's so—and I have no good reason to think it isn't—there's a strong possibility that he will move against her in some fashion...perhaps even try to kill her."

"Don't worry." Philip Richardson, one of the two detectives, spoke. "We'll make sure nothing happens to her."

"You'd better," Hawk growled to his friend. "Because if anything *does,* I'm going to hold you

and Yates both personally responsible." He gave
Jared Yates, the other detective, an equally hard
stare. "I don't care if Leah...Angelina...is Merritt
Marlowe's granddaughter or not. She's the woman
I love, and I'm not having her wind up at Pryce's
mercy because the two of you couldn't do your jobs
properly!"

"Hawk!" Leah—no, she simply *must* start thinking of herself as Angelina—chided gently, smiling.
"I'm certain that both your friends are extremely
capable detectives. Otherwise, you wouldn't have
called them in the first place."

"That's right, ma'am," Jared Yates confirmed,
grinning at her. "So don't mind him. Phil and I
don't. Even if he himself hadn't told us as much,
we can see that old Hawk's a man in love. We always *did* say that once he finally fell for a woman,
it'd be as hard as a ton of bricks!"

"Yeah, well, it isn't every day that a woman like
Angelina comes along," Hawk insisted, hugging her
close. "Not to mention the fact that her real parents
were murdered, robbing her not only of them, but
also of her birthright. As a result, she had a relatively poor, furtive childhood growing up, and has
spent most of her adult life preparing to take on
Pryce and his cohorts all by herself. Anything else
is more than she should have to endure."

"We understand," Phil said soberly. "And I
promise you, Hawk. We're going to do everything

in our power not only to protect your Angelina, but also to see that the men responsible for all her troubles are brought to justice.''

In order to conceal what Angelina had done, Hawk returned the code breaker to its vault at MMI and substituted a doctored videotape cassette for the one that showed her stealing the device.

All week, the two of them continued to work as though nothing had occurred and they weren't about to raid the MMI complex in conjunction with the police. On the job, neither of them discussed anything of a sensitive nature, not knowing who might be listening. And her boss was careful to call her ''Leah,'' even though, privately, he had taken to calling her ''Angel.''

Now that he knew her true identity, he had accompanied her to supper one evening at her parents' house. Angelina had been delighted when both Jim and Faith Tallcloud had expressed their approval of Hawk. Despite their continued fears for her, they were glad that she was no longer alone in her quest.

Still, everyone was on edge when the night of the raid finally arrived. In theory, the operation was relatively simple. In practice, they all knew there were a million things that could go wrong.

''Oh, Hawk, you *will* be careful, won't you?'' Angelina glanced up at him anxiously as they stood together in the parking lot of MMI.

"Of course. You don't have to worry about me, baby. I know what I'm up against, and I've got the element of surprise on my side, besides." Gently, he cupped her face with his hands, gazing down at her lovingly. "Everything will be all right, Angel. You'll see."

"I wish I were going with you!"

"I know. But you can't. I have to do this alone, and you have to wait here for me. But I'll be back before you know it, and then your grandfather will be free, and all this will finally be over."

Bending his head, he kissed her deeply, lingeringly, reluctant to let her go. And Angelina clung to him fiercely, feeling as though perhaps he would not come back to her, after all. But at last, he released her, turning to Philip Richardson and Jared Yates, who stood nearby, waiting in respectful, if impatient, silence.

"Okay, let's do it," Hawk said.

It was quiet, as usual, when he stepped into the private elevator that led to the uppermost story of the Sand Castle's hotel wing. His dark, copper visage impassive, Hawk reached into the inside pocket of his suit jacket, drew forth his corporate key, and ran the magnetic strip down the slot of the keypad mounted on the front wall of the elevator. Then he punched in this week's code.

In response, the doors whooshed softly closed,

and the car began its swift, almost noiseless ascent up through the long shaft. As it reached the top, it braked slowly to a halt. The doors slid open to admit Hawk into the elegant landing beyond.

Just in case anyone who wasn't supposed to ever made it this far, the landing was designed to be everything expected of someone possessing Merritt Marlowe's riches and status. A Venetian chandelier hung from the ceiling. Yards of exquisite, expensive French fabric covered the walls. The floor was a checkerboard of black and white squares of marble. A single ornate table upon which reposed a huge vase of flowers dominated the center of the room. The front door was flanked by hand-painted bombé chests over which hung gilt-framed mirrors.

For the benefit of the security cameras mounted in the four corners, Hawk made a show of straightening his tie and smoothing his suit jacket, knowing he had only three things in his favor.

The first of these was, as he had told Angelina earlier, the element of surprise. Hawk was a regular, approved visitor to the penthouse, so Merritt Marlowe's attendants wouldn't be expecting him to pull anything like the kind of stunt he was about to carry out.

The second of these advantages was the fact that, like all long-time jailers, Merritt Marlowe's attendants had got bored with their baby-sitting job, and careless as a result. The last several times Hawk had visited Merritt, they had performed only the most cursory of searches before admitting him into the penthouse.

The third thing he had going for him was that the hand-held metal detector the attendants used for scanning visitors wasn't designed to find the kind of weapon he was carrying tonight. Indeed, the tranquilizer gun he had concealed at his back might have been conceived for just such a mission as this one. It was fashioned almost entirely of the lightweight but strong polymer material that had gained notoriety when Glock had first begun using it in the manufacture of semiautomatic pistols.

Feeling himself ready at last, Hawk pressed the buzzer at the front door, and after a minute, the two attendants appeared.

"Evening, Mr. Bladehunter." Kevin, the senior of the two attendants, greeted him affably, smacking gum. "How's it going tonight?"

"Pretty much as usual." Unbuttoning his suit jacket, Hawk spread it wide to show that he wasn't packing a gun in a shoulder holster, while Stevie, the junior attendant, scanned him carelessly with the hand-held metal detector. "How're things with the two of you?"

"Oh, about as slow as always. What's that saying somebody made popular some years back? 'I'd quit this job, but it's the only place I can get any sleep'?" Kevin laughed at his own joke. "You know how it is. Ain't much to do up here besides watch TV, play cards, and look after the old coot."

"And how is Mr. Marlowe tonight?" Hawk inquired.

"Docile as a lamb." Finished with his scanning, Stevie stepped back and nodded to Kevin. "He's clean."

"So...what else is new?" Kevin asked, a note of boredom and sarcasm in his voice. "What'd you think, Stevie? That Mr. Bladehunter here was going to shoot us both?"

He was still laughing at the very idea when Hawk did exactly that.

Clutching their chests, from which the tranquilizer darts protruded, the two attendants went down like poleaxed steers. Their faces were incredulous, their mouths hanging open, Kevin's wad of gum falling out onto the floor as he slowly crumpled to his knees, then toppled over.

Certain that they were both out cold, Hawk moved rapidly, knowing there was no time to waste, that whoever was monitoring the security cameras tonight would have witnessed what he had done and even now be alerting the higher-ups of the cadre, taking action against him. A call was doubtless going out to the MMI helicopter even as he raced through the penthouse to the bedroom that was Merritt Marlowe's.

"It's time," Hawk announced as he barged into

the room, startling Merritt and causing him to sit bolt upright in bed. "I promised I'd find some way to help you, and now I have. I've incapacitated your two attendants, so you're free, Mr. Marlowe. But you must get up and out of bed! Quickly! We have only a matter of minutes, at most, to make our getaway from here. Do you understand?"

After a moment, in which Hawk feared that Merritt was hopelessly drugged again, the older man nodded his quivering head in comprehension.

"Give me your hand, young Mr. Bladehunter," he directed tremulously in his aged voice. "For while the spirit is more than willing, the flesh, I'm afraid, is old and weak."

Understanding at once, Hawk assisted Merritt to his feet, hastily grabbing a nearby robe and wrapping it around the pajama-clad, elderly man, brutally cutting off his sudden, querulous protests.

"I'm sorry. We have to hurry. There's no time for you to get dressed. But you don't have to worry or be afraid. If we're lucky, we'll be long gone by the time the media gets wind of any of this. Besides which, we'll be leaving the MMI complex by one of the back fire exits, so no one will see you, and it won't matter even if anyone does. An ambulance is waiting to take you straight to the hos...a place of safety," Hawk amended, realizing abruptly that Merritt might connect a hospital with him and their first meeting, and balk. "You've been ill. That's what we intend to tell the media, and there's no shame in that.''

The older man didn't answer. But much to Hawk's relief, neither did he continue to put up a fuss. He let himself be led from the bedroom into the living area, his arm slung over Hawk's shoulder and the younger man's around his waist, supporting him.

''Are they dead? Did you kill them?'' Merritt indicated the two attendants lying passed out on the floor.

''No. I used a tranquilizer gun on them. They'll be out for a while, but they'll live.''

''Good. I rather liked them, you know. They weren't vicious like some of the others—only young and stupid and greedy.''

''Well, pretty soon they're going to be prisoners themselves, instead of jailers,'' Hawk observed. ''And if they're lucky, their guards won't be vicious, either—only as young and stupid and greedy as they were.''

Out in the marble-floored foyer, where they paused for an instant in order for Merritt to catch his breath, Hawk swore as he heard, from above them, the unmistakable sounds of a helicopter approaching.

''Come on,'' he urged the older man. ''We've got to go. There's a police chopper that's supposed to prevent the MMI copter from landing on the roof.

But it's entirely possible that the men in the MMI chopper will prove desperate enough to make the attempt, anyway."

He half dragged, half carried Merritt into the elevator, continuing to curse, since he needed to run the magnetic strip of his corporate key down the slot in the keypad once more, and to punch in a second, different code to cause the car to begin its descent.

Presently, however, they were under way. When they reached the second floor of the hotel, the elevator came to a stop, and its doors glided open. The older man croaked in fear and shrank back against the rear of the car. But Hawk spoke to him soothingly.

"There's no need to be frightened. These men are friends of mine." He was greatly relieved to see Phil Richardson and Jared Yates standing there, pistols and walkie-talkies in hand. "They're here to help us."

Paramedics were on the scene, also, and swiftly took charge of Merritt. After coaxing him onto the gurney they had waiting, they took his vital signs and, as a precaution, hooked him up to an IV for dehydration until they could get him to the hospital for a more extensive examination. Then the entire group moved down the corridor, preparing to be intercepted at any moment by the hired guns of the conspirators at MMI.

They didn't have long to wait before they were indeed ambushed and fired upon.

"We're under attack. I repeat, we're under attack. All units move in."

Angelina's heart lurched to her throat as she heard the words that emanated from the radio in the unmarked police car in which she sat in the back seat, waiting with trepidation.

And then all hell seemed to break loose as, in response to Phil Richardson's broadcast, law-enforcement officers came running from every direction to converge on the MMI complex.

What was happening? Angelina wondered frantically. Were Hawk and her grandfather all right? She fumbled with the door handle, intending to get out and race into the MMI complex herself. But one of the two policemen who had been assigned to guard her spoke nervously.

"Please don't leave the security of the car, Ms. Marlowe. There's nothing you can do to be of assistance in this matter at the moment, and you'll only be endangering yourself if you attempt to intervene. You shouldn't even be here in the first place, but down at the station, where we could be certain of your safety."

"But...you heard the radio!" Angelina insisted. "Something's gone wrong! They've been set upon by Pryce and his cohorts!"

"Yes, ma'am," the officer agreed calmly. "However, under the circumstances, that wasn't unexpected, and so they were prepared for it. Believe me, the police will handle it, ma'am. We've an experienced SWAT team that knows how to deal with this kind of a situation, I assure you."

"Maybe so," she conceded reluctantly. "But still, I'd like to know what's going on, whether or not Hawk and my grandfather are all right. Couldn't at least one of you go and find out what's occurring inside?"

"No, ma'am. Our orders are to remain right here in the car with you, and to accompany the ambulance once it's en route to the hospital with your grandfather."

"Please," Angelina entreated earnestly. "I'll be all right with just one of you here on duty, and I've simply *got* to know what's happening inside!"

The two officers looked at each other questioningly for a long minute. Then, finally, sighing ruefully, one of them declared he guessed it wouldn't hurt for him to get out of the automobile and try to discover what she wanted to know.

"I won't go far...not actually into the MMI complex, you understand," he told her. "Just close enough to talk with some of the others on the scene to try to get a feel for the situation and whether or not anybody's hurt. Although the truth is, we'd know that from the radio, Ms. Marlowe."

"I know, but still..." Angelina's voice trailed away. She bit her lower lip anxiously, on the verge of tears at the thought that, even now, Hawk or her grandfather or both might be wounded or dead, and she didn't even know about it.

"Yes, ma'am. We understand. You just sit tight now, and I'll be back in a jiffy."

But much to Angelina's subsequent shock and horror, the officer never did return.

Everything had gone smoothly enough up until the point of the ambush, when the raid abruptly turned into a free-for-all, filling the hotel corridors with mayhem and gunfire.

Hawk's primary aim was to protect Merritt Marlowe from the flying and ricocheting bullets, because without him, the police had only Hawk and Angelina's word that her grandfather had been held captive. So Hawk used his own body to shield Merritt's prone one, while continuing determinedly to push the gurney along the hallway toward the back fire exit on the hotel's second floor, depending on Phil and Jared to cover them in the barrage.

Eventually, with the arrival of the SWAT team upon the scene, the attackers were compelled to fall back, leaving their wounded and dead behind, and Hawk and the rest gained the fire exit.

Now, collapsing the wheels of the gurney, they quickly carried it down the stairs and out into the parking lot of the MMI complex. There, the ambulance was waiting, surrounded by several officers now on the scene to guard against further assault. The paramedics loaded the gurney into the vehicle, ensuring that Merritt's vital signs were still stable and radioing ahead to Our Lady of Mercy Hospital.

"Where's Leah...Angelina...Ms. Marlowe?" Hawk asked one of the milling policemen anxiously. "She was to have been here, also, to accompany her grandfather to the hospital."

"I'm afraid I don't know anything about that, sir," the officer replied apologetically.

"Phil...Jared...have you notified Angelina that we've freed her grandfather?" Hawk turned to his two detective friends, who had been busy issuing orders to the uniformed police.

"We're trying to raise her now. There's no response yet from the two officers assigned to protect her," Phil explained, frowning. "However, there's a great deal of traffic on the radio right at the moment. So we may have too much interference to be getting through properly."

"I'll go after her." Hawk's heart had begun to pound fiercely at this news. "You take care of Mr. Marlowe, see that he gets safely to the hospital. We don't want any accidents en route."

"Hawk..." Jared began, to no avail. His friend was already running pell-mell across the parking lot, to the last-known place where Angelina had been seen.

Angelina was terrified.

The officer who had gone in search of information for her never returned. As a result, his fellow policeman had grown increasingly uneasy, and finally, he got on his walkie-talkie to radio his partner.

"Calhoun...talk to me. What's happening, buddy?" When there wasn't any response, the officer tried again. "Come on, Dave. This is no time to be playing games. Where are you, pal? What in hell's going on?"

But all that issued from the walkie-talkie was static. The policeman made several more attempts at various intervals to raise his partner, all unsuccessful.

"Something's wrong. He must be hurt or in trouble," Angelina declared worriedly at last. "Otherwise, he would surely have answered you by now."

"I'm beginning to think you're right, ma'am," the officer conceded reluctantly.

"Hadn't you better go and look for him, then? What if he's down and needs help?"

"Under the circumstances, there's nothing I can do about that right now, Ms. Marlowe. I was assigned to protect you, and I can't just go off and leave you sitting here in the car all by yourself. I'd be derelict in my duty. Like I said before, it would be better for all of us, ma'am, if you were down at the precinct.''

"Well, I'm not, and there's nothing I can do about that now. I have responsibilities and concerns, too, Officer. And two of those are the man I love and my grandfather. Their very lives are at stake tonight, and for all I know, they may be wounded or dead, even as we speak.''

"I understand that, and I'm sorry, Ms. Marlowe. But still, in my opinion, your being here on the scene has only complicated the situation. Now Dave's gone missing, and I don't even have any way to go and look for him.''

"Well, can't you radio somebody else to do that for you?" Angelina suggested.

"Yeah, I could. But the thing is, ma'am, Dave wasn't supposed to leave your side, either, so if I call in to report that he's disappeared, then we'll both be in one hell of a lot of trouble later. And naturally, I'd like to avoid that if I can, especially if it turns out that Dave's only temporarily unable to respond, for whatever unknown reasons.''

Ironically, the reason Officer Dave Calhoun had vanished became suddenly and horribly clear to both Angelina and the remaining policeman just moments later, when Winston Pryce appeared without warning at the unmarked car. In one hand, he held a semiautomatic pistol, and before the startled officer could even react, Pryce shot him at point-blank range right between the eyes.

Blood spattered all over the vehicle's interior, spraying warm and wet and sticky upon Angelina's flesh. She was stunned out of her mind, horrified by the cold-blooded murder to which she was witness. It seemed incredible to her that only moments before, the policeman had been alive and well, and that now he was dead, his head a pulpy mass of blood and brains.

Such was her state of shock that she didn't realize the hysterical screams reverberating through the parking lot were emanating from her own throat.

Before she grasped what he intended, Pryce ripped open the driver's door of the unmarked car and coldly, pitilessly, yanked the officer's corpse out onto the asphalt. Then he slid into the vehicle and, reaching into the back seat, brutally grabbed hold of Angelina by the hair of her head, savagely hauling her up into the front seat beside him.

After that, viciously twisting the key in the ignition, Pryce started the automobile with a roar. Loudly gunning the engine, he tore off, burning rubber and leaving skid marks yards long on the pavement.

By that time, Angelina had gathered her wits enough to recognize the peril she was in, and she tried frantically to wrench open the car door and jump out. But Pryce forestalled her, stretching out one hand to seize hold of her again by the hair, jerking her back and violently slamming her head more than once against the dashboard.

"Don't even think about trying to escape, bitch!" he snarled threateningly. "I know who you are, so you're a great deal more useful to me alive, as a hostage. But the police aren't going to know for sure whether you're dead or not, are they?"

As a result, she cowered in abject terror in the vehicle's front seat as Pryce drove like a madman along the brightly lit streets, dangerously running red lights and once or twice sideswiping other automobiles, sending them careening onto sidewalks and crashing into buildings.

Angelina was so petrified and her head throbbed so agonizingly that it was some time before she realized she ought to fasten her seat belt. Her hands shook so badly that she finally managed to get buckled up only after several futile attempts to do so.

In some obscure corner of her mind, she thought dully that Pryce must surely be insane. Strangely enough, he did not look in the least crazy to her as he continued to speed recklessly along the city streets. Instead, he appeared utterly icy and ruthless, in control of himself and his emotions. His gray eyes gleamed like steely twin gun barrels, and his jaw was set with grim, purposeful determination.

"You'll never get away with this, Pryce," Angelina warned him desperately.

But much to her distress, he only smiled wolfishly, a supercilious smirk. "Oh, I think I will. I'm extremely daring and intelligent, and most people, including the police, are extremely timid and stupid. So I've 'got away'—as you put it—with a very great deal for an unbelievably long time. Further, unlike most men in my position, I never permitted myself to grow so hubristic that I considered myself invincible. I knew there was always the chance, indeed the inevitability, that one day this highly profitable little enterprise would abruptly come to a screeching halt.

"So I planned well ahead, you see. I've got millions stashed in bank accounts all over the world, and more than one Third World country lined up where I can seek refuge. Men with my brains, talent, and money are a desirable commodity all over the globe, especially when they are willing to do anything for anybody, including murder—for the right price, of course. And I *am* the 'right Pryce.'" He chuckled mirthlessly at his own little joke.

"I knew who you were the very first moment I ever saw you and heard your last name…Tallcloud. With Natalie Marlowe's turquoise eyes and that surname, you just couldn't be anybody else but baby Angelina, Merritt Marlowe's granddaughter and heiress to the Marlowe billions. Naturally, I'd thought you long dead and buried. It was quite clever of Jim and Faith to pretend that it *was* you who died in the car crash that night, and to raise you as their own daughter. My compliments to them on that.

"In the beginning, I considered it a real pity that you had turned up very much alive after all these long years. But now that we've come to this pass, I don't think I'll mind settling for the compensations. I'm rich beyond measure, and you...well, you are, after all, very beautiful." Pryce's eyes raked Angelina in a way that left her no doubt as to his meaning and sent a horrifyingly chilling shiver down her spine.

"I'd rather die!" she cried softly.

"Yes, well, that, too, can be arranged, my dear."

"You're quite mad!"

"No, merely ambitious and unscrupulous. So wise up, Angelina. You could do much worse. Your grandfather's old and ill. He won't last too much longer. And then you'll be worth billions. MMI has profited under my direction, as it will again—although *you* will appear to be the head of the company, of course. You see, I haven't done so badly by you, my dear."

"You murdered my birth parents!"

"I did you a favor," Pryce sneered. "Roland Marlowe was weak and a fool, and Natalie was silly and vain. MMI would have gone completely down the tubes under their management."

"Lies...all venomous lies born of your spite. My

father was brilliant and honorable, and that's why you feared him. And my mother was beautiful and adoring. Jim and Faith have told me the truth about them—and nothing you say will ever make me believe otherwise."

"We'll see." Pryce shot her another arrogant, contemptuous smile.

"Where are you taking me?" Angelina abruptly demanded as they swept from the city and out onto the highway.

"I've got a place out in the desert. It's not much, but then, it doesn't need to be, since its primary advantage is that it has a barn in which I've got a small plane housed. There's also a landing strip. I told you I was well prepared for this day. Before morning, we'll be across the border into Mexico, my dear, and, shortly after that, en route to South America. Unlike the rest of my cohorts, I intend to enjoy all the fruits of my labors, not spend the rest of my life rotting in prison."

Angelina's heart sank even further at this revelation, at the realization that it was possible Pryce would actually succeed in spiriting her out of the country.

Then, without warning, he began to swear viciously as he glanced into the rearview and side mirrors of the automobile. As Angelina looked around to determine the cause of Pryce's sudden upset, hope flooded her being.

They were being pursued!

Despite how Pryce depressed the accelerator in an attempt to force the unmarked car to an even greater speed, the vehicle so clearly giving chase was faster still. It was coming up behind them at an incredible pace, its headlights on high beam, blinding Pryce so he had difficulty seeing the blacktop stretching away in front of them.

Still, he drove on recklessly—to no avail. Veering out into the second lane, the other automobile pulled up alongside of them. It was Hawk's Thunderbird. In the bright silver moonlight, Angelina could see that his dark, copper visage was grim with concern and resolution.

He motioned curtly for Pryce to pull over. But Pryce ignored him, instead abruptly wrenching the steering wheel of the unmarked car hard to the left and bashing viciously into the convertible.

The two vehicles slammed together like a pair of freight trains colliding, jarring Angelina to the bone and flinging her violently forward. Had she not been wearing her seat belt, she might have gone through the windshield. The hideous screech of metal scraping metal reverberated in the night air as the automobiles collided again and yet again, with Pryce rashly but determinedly attempting to compel Hawk off the road.

Now, from overhead, the whirring of a helicopter sounded, and a powerful beam of light shone down upon the highway, illuminating the speeding cars. An anonymous voice from the police chopper spoke through its onboard PA system, warning Pryce to pull over.

He paid no heed, however, instead smashing into the Thunderbird once more. This time, the impact of the two vehicles caused the unmarked car to careen wildly off the road, onto the verge, where it fishtailed crazily on the loose sand.

Driven now by desperation at how his carefully laid plans had suddenly gone so awry, Pryce kept the pedal to the metal, sending the automobile ripping across the uneven terrain, steering wheel spinning as the tires slipped and slid. Without warning, the front wheels left solid ground, falling into a small dry gulch that seemed to appear from nowhere.

The unmarked car lurched horribly, pitching Angelina savagely forward again. At that, the passenger-side airbag abruptly deployed, bursting into her face.

Darkness swirled up to engulf her, and she knew nothing more.

Epilogue

Power Regained

While with an eye made quiet by the power
Of harmony, and the deep power of joy,
We see into the life of things.

Lines Composed a Few Miles
Above Tintern Abbey
—William Wordsworth

Beyond the Boardroom

Yet beauty, though injurious, hath strange power,
After offense returning, to regain
Love once possessed.

Paradise Regained
—John Milton

A Desert Cabin, The Southwest, Six Months Later

"It was called, among other things, the wedding of the century.

"Angelina Marlowe, granddaughter of reclusive billionaire Merritt Marlowe, today married the newly elected president of Marlowe Micronics, Incorporated, Hawk Bladehunter, in a private ceremony held at an undisclosed location.

"Bladehunter rose to prominence during a fierce internal corporate struggle six months ago, when the then president of the company, Winston Pryce, and several other high-ranking executives, attempted to force out Merritt Marlowe, MMI's founder and chairman of the board. The culmination of the power struggle came when the ailing Marlowe suffered a stroke, and Bladehunter, his principal champion within the organization, stepped in, succeeding in exposing the fact that Pryce and his cohorts had been using their powerful positions to engage in numerous illegal activities, including the sale of extremely sensitive technology to black-market buyers.

"Pryce was subsequently killed during a high-speed chase while attempting to elude police, when he lost control of the stolen car he was driving and his airbag failed to deploy. Pryce, who wasn't wearing a seat belt at the time of the crash, was crushed to death as a result of being thrown through the windshield and rolling beneath the vehicle. His colleagues in the conspiracy at MMI are currently on trial in what has been dubbed the Southwest's 'Neon City,' home to MMI headquarters.

"Until the power struggle at MMI was made public, it was not known that Marlowe's granddaughter and sole heiress to his fortune, Angelina, was still alive. She was believed to have been killed during the same tragic automobile accident that had claimed the lives of her parents, Roland and Natalie Marlowe, many years ago. In a rare interview granted to the media, Marlowe, since recovered from his stroke, explained that he had kept the fact that his granddaughter survived a secret in order to shield her from the media while she was growing up. She was raised by loyal friends of the Marlowe family, Jim and Faith Tallcloud.

"Bladehunter and Ms. Marlowe had apparently grown close during the power struggle at MMI, and they announced their engagement shortly afterward. It is not known where the happy couple is honeymooning—"

"And thank God for that!" Hawk growled as he abruptly pushed the Power button on the remote control, switching off the television set and thereby effectively silencing the CNN broadcast that he and Angelina had been watching. "Otherwise, we would have been hounded at every single turn by the media and never had even a moment's privacy!"

"And *that* just wouldn't have done at all, would it, darling?" Angelina inquired, her voice bubbling with laughter as, tossing aside the remote control, her husband rolled over on the bed they shared, pressing her down into the mattress.

"No, it wouldn't!" he staunchly confirmed. "I intend to spend several days alone with my beautiful bride, a great deal of which time will be employed in making love to her at every opportunity—and I *don't* mean to do it wondering if some paparazzi's camera lens is focused on our bedroom window!"

"Ah, the perils of being rich and famous..." Angelina said with a sigh.

"Indeed. I myself much prefer the perks of being hitched and shameless, sweetheart." Hawk grinned at his bride wickedly before deftly dispensing with her gossamer negligee and passionately claiming her as his own.

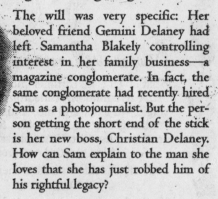

New York Times bestselling author

ELIZABETH GAGE

brings readers an unforgettable novel about the destructive forces of love and obsesssion.

Rebecca Lowell is the perfect wife and mother—on the surface. But underneath she's living a life of polite, well-bred, never-to-be-mentioned desperation.

Then her daughter, Dusty, brings home her young fiancé. He's everything Rebecca could wish for her daughter. For herself…

An unstoppable chain of events starts with one bold act, one sin committed in an otherwise blameless life.

Confession

Gage's writing is "…utterly captivating." —*Kirkus Reviews*

On sale mid-January 1999 wherever paperbacks are sold!

MIRA